MISTER
MAX

NEWBERY MEDALIST

CYNTHIA VOIGT

MISTER MAX

The BOOK of SECRETS

Illustrated by IACOPO BRUNO

A YEARLING BOOK

 Published in the United States by Yearling, an imprint of Random House Children's Books, a division of Random House LLC, a Penguin Random House Company, New York.
Originally published in hardcover in the United States by Alfred A. Knopf, an imprint of Random House Children's Books, New York, in 2014.

Yearling and the jumping horse design are registered trademarks of Random House LLC.

Visit us on the Web! randomhousekids.com

Educators and librarians, for a variety of teaching tools, visit us at RHTeachersLibrarians.com

The Library of Congress has cataloged the hardcover edition of this work as follows:
Voigt, Cynthia.
The book of secrets / by Newbery Medalist Cynthia Voigt ;
illustrated by Iacopo Bruno. — First Edition.
p. cm. — (Mister Max ; 2)
Summary: Self-reliant Max Starling, a twelve-year-old detective and problem solver, struggles to keep his identity a secret as he investigates a case of arson, while cryptic messages from his still missing parents indicate that they need rescuing.
ISBN 978-0-307-97684-0 (trade) — ISBN 978-0-375-97124-2 (lib. bdg.) —
ISBN 978-0-307-97686-4 (ebook)
[1. Mystery and detective stories. 2. Problem solving—Fiction. 3. Self-reliance—Fiction. 4. Missing persons—Fiction. 5. Parents—Fiction.]
I. Bruno, Iacopo, illustrator. II. Title.
PZ7.V874Bq 2014
[Fic]—dc23
2013050301

ISBN 978-0-307-97685-7 (pbk.)

Printed in the United States of America

10 9 8 7 6 5 4 3 2 1

First Yearling Edition 2015

Random House Children's Books supports the First Amendment and celebrates the right to read.

For Grammie and Grampy,
who do not have minor roles

CONTENTS

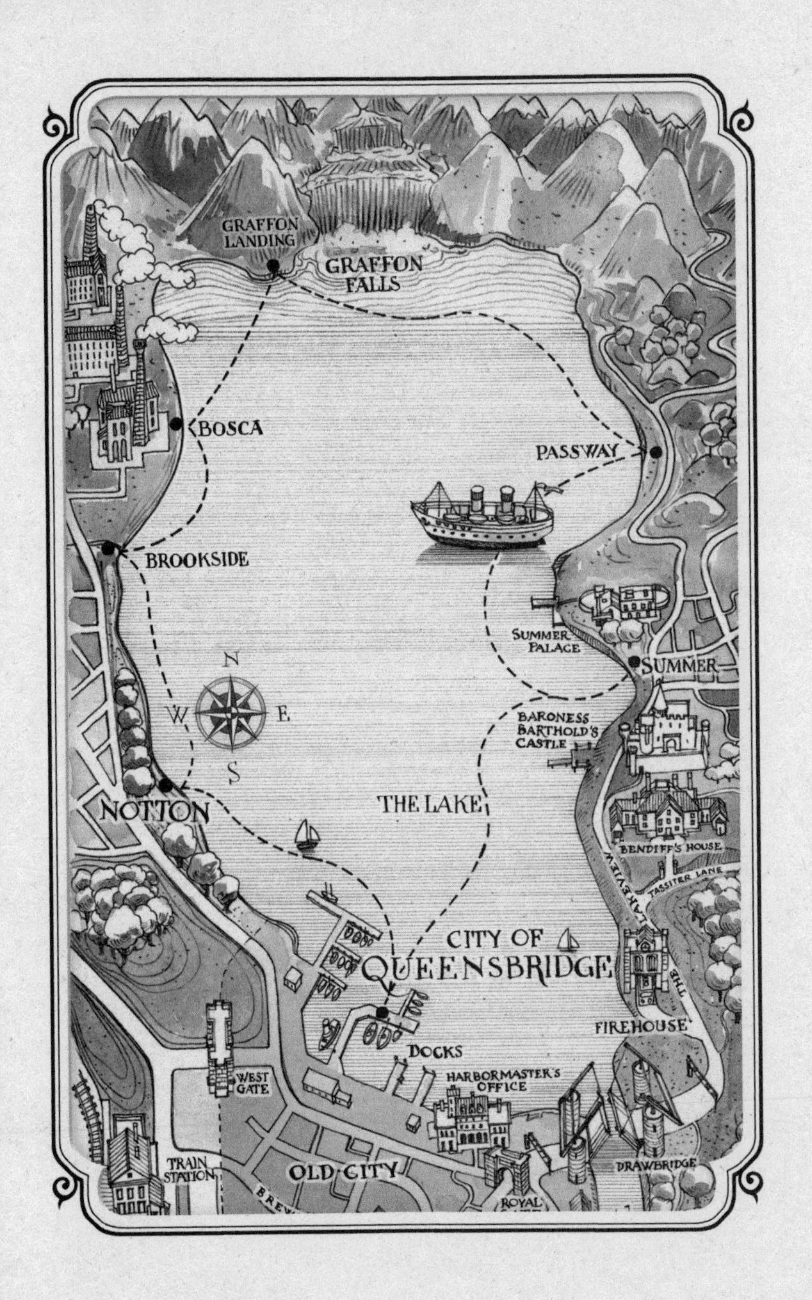

GRAFFON LANDING
GRAFFON FALLS
BOSCA
PASSWAY
BROOKSIDE
SUMMER PALACE
SUMMER
N
W
E
S
BARONESS BARTHOLD'S CASTLE
NOTTON
THE LAKE
BENDIFF'S HOUSE
TASSITER LANE
THE LAKEVIEW
CITY OF QUEENSBRIDGE
FIREHOUSE
DOCKS
HARBORMASTER'S OFFICE
WEST GATE
TRAIN STATION
OLD CITY
DRAWBRIDGE
ROYAL

"I am not that I play."
—William Shakespeare, *Twelfth Night*

PROLOGUE

In the early years of the last century, on a Sunday, to be precise—Sunday, May 20, in fact—Max Starling sat down with a sheet of writing paper at the dining room table. The walls of the dining room were lined with the posters of the Starling Theatrical Company, and images of his parents in their various roles surrounded him. His father as Banker Hermann in *The Worldly Way* looked across at his mother in her finest role as the much-wooed Adorable Arabella. Arabella's smile looked particularly sly—but perhaps that was because Max had discovered her secret, that is, that her frame was filled with gold coins. Max smiled right back at her. He could be sly, too. He began to write in large, fat letters that were wobbly at the curves:

Dear King,

My name is Aurora. I am seven years old. I go to the Hilliard School in Queensbridge. I do not have any brothers and sisters, but I have a cat named Henry. I live right next door to Banker Hermann, who is rich, and his new bride, Arabella, and she showed me your picture in the newspaper. She says you were just crowned. Did you always know you were a king? Or was it a surprise?

For his holidays, my da likes to have adventures. He likes to sail and climb mountains. He likes to eat new things. Can we come visit you? In the picture, your Queen is as beautiful as Arabella, and if you have a little girl, she could be my friend.

Yours truly,
Aurora Nives

That was Max's grandmother's name and it was her address he put on the envelope, which he then addressed to *King William, City of Apapa, Country of Andesia, Continent of South America.* He put five stamps on the envelope, which was many too many, and took it to the nearest postbox.

In which the true story of the *Miss Koala* comes out and there is work for the Solutioneer

Max Starling, the third principal member of the Starling Theatrical Company, was—as far as most people knew—off with his parents on tour, perhaps in America performing for cowboys, perhaps in India riding elephants, or in Russia, where they would surely be kidnapped by anarchists after a performance, but in any case, acting.

Only the acting part was true. For almost six weeks, Max had been acting the role of Mister Max, Solutioneer, as played by Max Starling, twelve-year-old boy. He had been living independently and supporting himself so well that he did not need a single coin of the fortune his father had hidden away. He had been living independently despite the closeness of his grandmother and her insistence that he have dinner with her every evening. For that he was, in fact, grateful—Grammie was a good cook. Also, they could comfort one another.

There had been a lot of cooking and comforting since April 18, the day William and Mary Starling had boarded an ocean liner and sailed off, unexpectedly leaving their son behind. They had been invited by a maharajah to tour India and been given first-class tickets on the *Flower of Kashmir.* Max now knew that there was no such ship and no such maharajah . . . but nevertheless he had no parents. Max *had* received two strange messages from his father before his parents had unexpectedly reappeared in a newspaper photograph as the newly crowned King and Queen of Andesia, half a world away. That made no sense, either, but at least he now knew where they were, even if he didn't know why they were there.

And so, late on a Monday afternoon at the end of May, Max Starling was seated on the back steps of his grandmother's small house, looking across the shared lawn and vegetable garden to his own equally small house, thinking about his lost parents while Grammie read the newspaper.

"I wrote him a letter," he said.

"You know that boat that sank?" she asked. "The *Miss Koala,*" she reminded him.

Of course Max remembered. Two weeks earlier a Sunday Extra Edition of the *Queensbridge Gazette* ("News for the people, of the people, and by the people") had broken the story that the great ocean liner, which set off the same morning that Max's parents had also sailed, had been lost, with all

435 of her passengers and all but three of her crew of 173 on board.

It was a sad and frightening story. After twelve tranquil days, the unlucky ship had crossed paths with an equally unlucky pod of migrating whales. Nobody knew what damage was done to the whales, although the water filled with blood, but both of *Miss Koala*'s great propellers were damaged. Captain Eustace Trevelyn set a new course, heading back toward Gibraltar, but it was not three days later that a fierce storm blew up. The crippled ship floundered, lost her bearings, and was tossed mercilessly about. Battered by winds, pounded by waves, blinded by darkness, she ran onto a rock, or a shoal, or a reef, and foundered. Water poured into her hold, to pull her down into the ocean's depths. Wind-driven waves slammed into her metal hull, to topple her over and drop the human creatures that clung to her decks deep into watery graves.

Miss Koala might have become yet another ship that vanished without a trace had there not been survivors. These were only three, men who endured perilous days on shark-infested seas before being picked up by a passing freighter and eventually set ashore at Lisbon. The Captain, a steward, and a cook were hailed as both lucky and heroic. "Rub-a-dub-dub, three men in a tub," the newspapers joked. The Captain's daughter, who had been awaiting *Miss Koala* in Cape Town in order to join her father for the final legs of the voyage, rushed northward to celebrate his survival. The steamship company released a list of passengers, and all over the world mourning clothes were purchased.

Max Starling and his grandmother had been as caught up in this drama as the rest of the world, even though they were pretty sure by then that his parents had not been on that ship. Now, not much more than two weeks later, the *Queensbridge Gazette* was trumpeting a new story, and this was what had captured Grammie's attention. "Look at this," she said, passing the paper to Max. "Honestly," and she sounded disgusted, "some people."

Max read the headline, TRUTH WILL OUT, and the headline in smaller print under that, THE CAPTAIN WHO DIDN'T. When he read on, he understood Grammie's disgust. The real truth of the "heroic" Captain and his two "stalwart" crew members was a shameful tale of three cowards who jumped into a lifeboat before anybody else had even been notified of the disaster. There was, however, heroism aplenty on the *Miss Koala* among the abandoned crew and passengers, though of a more ordinary and practical kind. Foremost among these quiet heroes was the First Mate, who as soon as he knew the ship was aground asked for volunteers from the crew—and there had been several—to lower one of the lifeboats into the stormy waters and assess the exact damage and danger to the ship. Discovering that their vessel was impaled on a rock and thinking that, thus anchored, she might ride out the storm, they returned to calm the passengers and give them hope. Those hopes were realized in a stormy dawn, when they sighted land, not too far distant. As soon as the seas and winds permitted, fishing boats came out to rescue all of the

605 people aboard the ship. Everything movable was then carried safely to shore.

It was because their good luck, as blind as the previous bad luck, brought them to shore at the most remote of the remote Canary Islands that it took so long for the survivors to reach the mainland and for their story to reach telegraph wires. The newspapers seized gleefully on this new, and for a change happy, development.

Max passed the paper back, and envied the children who had just discovered their relatives weren't lost after all, the families that would be joyfully reunited.

"Who'd have thought it?" Grammie murmured, then, "That poor motherless girl." She shook her head. "I don't blame her one bit."

"Are we absolutely positive that my father *isn't* of royal blood?" Max asked, his mind veering back to his own lost relations. "He wasn't born around here. You never met any of his family, did you? What do we actually know about him, except what he told us, which is almost nothing? He said he ran away from home when he was twelve, but he never said anything about where home was or who lived there. What if he really *is* the legal King of Andesia?" Max had glanced through the day's mail but there had not been a second postcard from his father. "What if he is? Like in *Whatever Happened to Princess Gloriana?*" Max reminded his grandmother. "Or if there was some nefarious plot when he was just a baby, like in *The Queen's Man*?"

Those were two plays Max always enjoyed putting on, for the elaborate costumes and for the many minor parts he got to play and especially for the sword fights. Those scenes were a display of his father's fencing skills, and included duels in which Max sometimes took part although, of course, he never prevailed.

Grammie looked at him over the top of the newspaper, because she had, in fact, been listening. "What did you say in the letter? Why would he only write nonsense to us if he *was* king?"

Max had been listening, too, and asked, "What poor motherless girl?"

Grammie shook the newspaper, as if it were the one behaving badly. "That Captain Trevelyn's daughter." There was a flash of anger in her eyes.

"What's happened to her? What's she done?"

"Never showed up, that's what. Never arrived in Gibraltar and it serves that man right, after the way he . . . The Captain," Grammie announced, outraged, "is supposed to go down with his ship."

"But he's her father," Max pointed out. He was rather acutely aware of how irreplaceable parents were. Personally, he would have preferred that his father *not* go down with the ship, if there was a choice. Max might be able to live just as independently as his father had so confidently claimed a twelve-year-old could, but he would prefer to have his parents home, and safe, and in charge. Would he feel the same, he

QUEENSBRIDGE GAZETTE
TRUTH WILL OUT
THE CAPTAIN DIDN'T WHO

wondered, if he was a grown-up and if his father had done something so . . . so *bad*?

Grammie snorted, "What would *you* do, with a father like that and no mother? No other family, either, it seems."

"I'd have to think about it," Max admitted.

"Probably, that's what she's doing," Grammie decided.

Max returned to the mail.

Grammie had two letters from libraries in other countries, one of them Brazil. She had written to the capital city librarians in each South American country—except Andesia, which had no library, either public or private—for information about the nation of which her daughter now seemed to be the Queen. There was also a water bill for Grammie, and something with the Mayor's official seal, perhaps a research request, perhaps notice of some meeting. For years, Grammie had been the City Librarian, in charge of the big stone building across the square from the bigger stone building that housed the municipal offices as well as the courts. She was often asked to supply information the Council needed to reach its decisions. Besides Max's own water bill, for his father of course, there was only one letter addressed to 5 Thieves Alley, but that was for Mister Max, Solutioneer.

Max passed Grammie her mail. Without hesitating, she set aside the envelope from the Mayor's office, as if it was too predictable to even look at. Her muffled "Hummph" made him look carefully at her, but all he could see was that she had erased all expression from her face. Max didn't let his grandmother distract him from his own anticipation. The Solutioneer had a letter, maybe a job.

Max Starling had become the Solutioneer out of necessity. It was necessary for him to earn a living, because his parents were gone. It was also necessary for Max Starling to be as invisible as possible. A visible Max Starling would be in danger of being carted off to an orphanage. Max couldn't go to school, and he couldn't take a job where anybody had the right to know anything about him, any little fact—such as who his parents were and where he lived.

In fact, Max was continuing to live in the little house he and his parents had occupied together for all of his twelve years. He even had a tenant, who taught him mathematics—Euclidean geometry, to be specific—in exchange for room and board, an arrangement that made it possible for Max to go on living in his own house. Ari knew the truth about Max's situation, and often joined him for dinner with Grammie. Besides those two, the only other person in whom Max had confided was Joachim, his art teacher.

Max's deeper secret about the hoard of gold coins, kept even from Grammie, raised troubling questions. The first was, Why hadn't his father told him they were so wealthy? And the second was, Did his mother know? Finally, there was the most disturbing question of all: Where would William Starling have gotten so many coins, and in gold? However, as long as nobody but Max knew that he had enough money for both him and Grammie to live comfortably on for years, he was free to have to work for a living, and the way Max saw things, unless you were self-supporting, you weren't really independent.

Thus, a letter for the Solutioneer was always welcome, even if he didn't take on all the jobs he was offered as satisfied clients spread the word about his services. Unfortunately, many letters came from students at the Hilliard School, where a dissatisfied client boasted about getting the best of the famous Mister Max. Most of these were silly requests, like "Can you make them give us bigger servings at lunch?" or unkind and unpleasant ones, like "Dear Mister Max, Can you get Pee-pee in so much trouble she gets expelled? She smells bad and she is so stupid she ruins classes with all her stupid questions." Max happened to know that Pee-pee, really Pia Bendiff, did not smell bad and was certainly not stupid. He suspected that anyone who wrote a letter like that probably wasn't overly concerned with the truth of things. He didn't even answer those requests.

Today's letter, however, troubled him. "Dear Mister Max," he read, on the kind of lined paper students use in the early grades, when they need help in keeping control over their pencils.

My da goes out after supper. He thinks I am asleep but I'm not. I don't know where Da goes. He never says. I think he is going to find my mother. She went away last winter. We are waiting for her to come back, Da says. But what if he doesn't come back too? I can't wait alone by myself, I am too little. Can you help me?

The letter was signed *Simon.* At the end the boy had added: *PS, I always save my allowance so I can pay you.*

There was no return address and the boy had not given his last name, but this was not a request Max wanted to ignore. "Hmmm," he said, thinking.

"I know what you mean," Grammie said.

How could she know that?

But Grammie's attention was still on the *Miss Koala.* "It's amazing, sometimes, what rotters people can be," she said. "It's discouraging."

Why was Grammie getting so worked up about this Captain and his dishonesty instead of being relieved that everybody was known to be safe? He suspected there was something else bothering her. He wondered suddenly if she had found out something more about his parents, or Andesia. Something bad. "Did you find out anything?" he asked.

He didn't need to say what he was asking about. Grammie knew. "No." She shook her head. "Nothing about them. Nothing new about the country, either, or General Balcor." She sighed. "Some days, everything is pretty discouraging."

Max thought then that he would distract her with a change of subject. "Aren't you going to read the Mayor's letter?" he asked.

"What's it to you?" Grammie answered quickly.

Quickly, Max noticed, and also quite crossly.

2

In which Max and Pia work together, sort of

When Max rode off on his bicycle the next morning to deliver a message to the Bendiff mansion, he was the Solutioneer, in disguise. He had dressed himself in the shabby brown suit of an unsuccessful suitor in *The Adorable Arabella* and stuffed a pillow under the bright blue waistcoat. With a round pork-pie hat set square on his head, he became Inspector Doddle, the unflappable, unassuming detective from *An Impossible Crime* who, although he moved unnoticed along the edges of the action, discovered the guilty party and brought him to justice.

Of course Max enjoyed playing the various roles his solutioneering work required, wearing the various costumes, trying to think and sound like various people, even, once—although it wasn't his most successful impersonation—a female. He enjoyed it and it was useful, too. He needed to be as unseen, unrecognizable, and most important, unknown in his work as in his life.

Later that day, Max wore a struggling university student's floppy gray trousers and frayed cotton shirt while he waited for Pia to arrive at their usual meeting place. In the little shop, nobody paid any attention to him where he sat, alone by the window, cap on his knees. The customers were interested in ice cream or whatever pastries Gabrielle Glompf had been inspired to bake that morning.

At this hour of a warm afternoon, when schools were getting out, business was brisk. Max had treated himself to a lemon tart and a bowl of chocolate ice cream, savoring the tangy sweetness of lemon and the buttery sweetness of the pastry, alternating these with spoonfuls of the rich, smooth sweetness of chocolate. Beyond the window, the street was busy and the sidewalk crowded. Inside the small shop, shiny clean pots hung on a wall over the ovens. Shiny clean pans were stacked on the shelf over a long worktable. Shiny clean bowls were nested beside them and on top of them, while two pottery jugs on the shiny clean worktable held mixing spoons and wire whisks and spatulas. Gabrielle moved efficiently, serving ice cream in bowls and cones, putting pastries into boxes, taking payments, and making change. Max recognized the red hair of the man behind her, who was bent over a deep sink, washing bowls and plates, forks and spoons, cups and saucers. The man's presence surprised Max, although, when he thought about it, he wasn't surprised at all. The man was his mathematics tutor and tenant, Ari, who happened as well to be the next Baron Barthold. More significantly, the man was courting Gabrielle, trying to show her how much he had changed, trying to earn her trust so that he could once again win her heart.

Six weeks ago, Max had known none of this, neither the people nor the place. Sometimes it dumbfounded him how much everything in his life had changed, in a mere six weeks. What with one thing and another, one thing after another—

Pia Bendiff, whom he had also never seen or heard of six weeks ago, charged through the shop door. She wore the uniform of a Hilliard girl—boring blue cotton blouse, boring blue pleated skirt, and high boring blue socks—but she had tied a rebellious red ribbon at the end of her long white-blond braid.

She plunked herself down in the chair facing him and demanded, "What's the case?" Then she popped up from her seat. "I'm going to get some ice cream. Wait here," she told him, as if she was the Solutioneer who had called this meeting and he was only the part-time assistant, instead of the other way around.

Max grinned to himself, watching her square, sturdy shape. Her face matched her shape, being square in jaw and forehead. She had dark blue eyes and dark eyebrows, despite her hair being so fair, and her personality was as square and contradictory as her face. Pia Bendiff kept things hopping.

When she returned to the table, she carried a bowl holding scoops of dark chocolate and bright pink raspberry ice cream, topped with a triangular sail of cookie, and she was laughing. "I asked Ari what he was doing and he said"—she picked up her spoon, preparing to dip into her treat—"he said he was showing Gabrielle that he isn't a useless slug. He's washing *dishes,*" she told Max.

"What's wrong with washing dishes?" asked Max, who had done his share of dishwashing.

"He's a University student, for one thing, and he's grown up, even older than you," Pia told him, between bites. "*And* he's the next Baron Barthold. He could *hire* somebody to wash Gabrielle's dishes."

"That wouldn't be the same," Max pointed out.

"That's what I'm saying." Having, as she felt, won that argument, Pia repeated her opening question. "What's the case you want me for?" Her eyes shone with eagerness.

"Not a case—a job," Max answered patiently. He had given up repeating that he was a Solutioneer, not a detective, but continued to insist that he had jobs, not cases. He told her about the boy's letter. "This Simon's got to go to Hilliard to have heard of me," he said, and was about to continue when Pia interrupted.

"Let me see it."

"Why would I bring somebody's personal letter with me?"

"If you expect me to help you—" she began.

"Nobody is making you," Max countered.

Pia went back to her ice cream, not giving in, but no longer actively arguing. So Max went on to tell her what the boy had written in his letter, about the missing mother and the wandering father. "But he didn't know to sign his last name, or give a return address. He must be very young."

"What do you expect me to do?" Pia asked, her attention on the ice cream in her bowl.

"Can you find out who he is? And where he lives?"

She shook her head. She pushed the bowl away. It was as if what he had said took away her appetite. All the eagerness left her face. "You know I can't do that. I can't find out things at school. You know that, you know nobody talks to me, they just want to call me names and . . . and . . . try to make me cry. Which," she announced fiercely, "they can't do. You should give me something else to do," she said, angry now. "Like when we went to scare off Madame Olenka."

"You could try," Max suggested.

She shook her head again. "You were only there for the one midday recess. You don't know what it's like. If nobody likes you. I mean, *really* doesn't like you and you have to go to school with them, every day."

"But I do know," Max said, and it was the truth.

Pia didn't believe him. "You're not the kind of person anybody would have disliked," she told him, as if it had been years, instead of weeks, since he had sat alone in a classroom being ignored by the other students, or sat alone on a playground, with nothing to do but memorize lines. Pia thought he was years older than he was, possibly because he had been acting a grown-up when he first met her, or maybe just because he was tall for his age. Max was happy to let her continue thinking that.

"You'd be surprised," he said, but didn't explain. Instead he said, "Well, if you can't, you can't," as if he had given up. "I'll find another way, don't worry."

"You should at least give me a chance," she complained.

He put a lot of doubt into his voice. "I don't know . . ."

"It's not fair if you don't even let me try," she told him. "I'm your assistant."

"All right," he agreed, with still more doubt, as if now he didn't think she *could* do it.

"It might take me a couple of days," she warned.

"All right," he repeated, and then asked, "How's the tutoring?"

Pia pulled her half-empty bowl back toward her and started eating again. "Slow," she admitted. "Nance isn't very smart and nobody ever sent her to any school, ever . . ."

"That's why you're helping her," Max pointed out. He had arranged for this, and he wanted it to go well.

"We're just at the beginning, with three-letter words," Pia said, "and that Baroness? She isn't exactly friendly, is she? But she said the cook should have lessons, too—but the cook is as simple-minded as Nance, so it's no problem, it's no extra work. But I haven't made my mind up about that Baroness. Have you? Is she as bad as everyone says? It's hard to believe she's related to Ari, isn't it? Like me and my mother, we're—" She stood up abruptly. "I'll meet you back here in two days," she announced, "same time," and almost ran out of the shop, with a banging of the door and a clanging of the shop bell.

As if she didn't want someone to know where she'd been, or with whom, Max thought, watching her through the window. A large black automobile with a familiar gold *B* painted on its door was pulling up to the sidewalk and Pia entered it quickly. Max wondered if Pia could succeed with her assignment, and, if she couldn't, how he might go about finding the information himself. Maybe Grammie would know?

Max didn't need to consult Grammie, because when he and Pia met two days later, at the ice cream shop where Ari was, once again, washing dishes and spoons and pots and pans and cooking trays, the girl plopped herself down in the chair opposite Max with the expression worn by those who have successfully completed a task they think you thought was too difficult for them. A *so there!* expression, half smirk, half smile, and all self-satisfaction. Of course, being Pia, she didn't simply tell him what she'd found out.

"My father says you should be paying me," she said.

What could Max say to that? He'd thought he was doing her a favor, giving her a sort of job, but maybe he *should* pay her. He just nodded and said nothing. He was the Solutioneer and she was only the Solutioneer's Sometime Assistant; he would make up his own mind in his own time about any payment. He waited. It was a rainy day and he had put on the stained oilcloth jacket worn by the signalman in *Trouble on the Tracks,* a man who knew his job and knew his worth and didn't need anybody's father telling him what he should or shouldn't do.

Pia hesitated, then chattered on. "He says his restaurant will open in July. He's found a chef he likes and a carpenter to put in the wood flooring, and my mother is helping him with the furnishings, and Gabrielle is definitely going to be his pastry chef, so after next month this shop won't be offering pastries." This was not good news, her voice said, but Max was going to have to take it like a man.

Max nodded, slow and thoughtful as any experienced signalman. If he were on the stage playing this role, he would pull out a pipe and load it with tobacco as he waited, for the midnight express to roar through or to hear whatever she had to tell him, whichever came first.

"I'm going to get myself some hot tea, and maybe something else, too," Pia announced then, and burst up from the table. She had left her umbrella by the door, and her shoulders and skirt were dry although her shoes were rain-spattered.

A rainy, chilly afternoon did not make people want ice cream, so the shop was empty. Ari came out from behind the counter, to say hello to his landlord and pupil. He wore an apron tucked into the waist of his trousers and a smile on his handsome face. His red hair was stuck to his temples from the steam of hot dishwater. "How are you?" he asked, standing beside the table.

It wouldn't do for the dishwasher, even if he was the next Baron Barthold, to sit down with a customer.

Max asked, "Has it been a slow day?"

Ari nodded. "Which is fine by me since it gives me more time to talk with her. I think she's starting to come around. I think she's starting to forgive me." He looked over his shoulder to the round little mouse of a woman who was talking to Pia, writing down the girl's order and laughing a little, with a look in her eyes that said that Pia was a person she positively enjoyed.

This was the way Gabrielle looked at everyone, and every look was sincere. Gabrielle was the kindest person Max had ever met, and the best pastry cook, too. "I don't think she ever didn't forgive you," he said to Ari.

"Then, maybe, starting to be able to think she might marry me," Ari said. He had not taken his eyes off the young woman, as if he feared that she would disappear from his sight and he'd have to spend another seven years in regret and searching. "However, there's a huge heap of mixing bowls . . . On a rainy afternoon, people will want pastries for their desserts, and cookies, not ice cream, for their treats, and she's been baking nonstop . . ." Still talking, he turned to take up his position at the sink, with a wave of his hand. As he passed by Pia, Ari stopped to say a word and she nodded, glancing over her shoulder at Max.

Out on the street, the rain continued to fall. Max looked at the heavy gray sky stretched above the buildings and the park opposite; even if you didn't see raindrops falling, you would know what that sky was doing. It was flat, with no visible clouds, and it crowded down close over the rooftops of the New Town. Max wondered how a watercolorist might go about making a picture of a rainy sky in May. He hoped Joachim could show him the technique at his next lesson, asking himself as he studied the low clouds if it was a matter of brushstrokes or if it was how you prepared your paper.

His thoughts were interrupted by the arrival of a crowd of school-age boys and girls, some with a parent in tow, some without, wanting cookies and turnovers. They formed into a chattering line and Pia returned to the table, carrying a plate and cup. "You can have half the chocolate cake," she announced, seating herself across from him, "but I don't want to share the almond croissant. What's the Pythagorean theorem anyway? Because Ari"—she held a second fork out to Max—"says he expects you to know it by tomorrow. What happens tomorrow?"

Max answered things in order. First, "Thank you," he said, taking the fork. Then, "It's Euclid, he's teaching me geometry," and at last he could ask, "Did you find out anything about that little boy?"

"It wasn't easy," she answered. "Do you know how many Simons there are at Hilliard?"

Max just raised his eyebrows.

"Eleven," Pia said. She took a big drink of her tea. She picked up her croissant, bit into it, and chewed slowly. She was enjoying herself. After a leisurely swallow, she told him, "Only three of them are young enough to write the kind of letter you described. Little kids don't mind me," she said then, with an expression he had never seen before on her face, part confusion, part amusement, and part surprise. "All I had to do was ask one of the little girls, out on the playground. It wasn't a bit hard," she admitted.

He nodded patiently.

"His name is Simon Melakrinos," she said. "Don't you want to write it down? I'll spell it for you."

Max took out the small notebook Inspector Doddle always carried, and the stubby pencil the inspector preferred.

"S, I," she started.

"I can spell Simon."

"How am I supposed to know that?" she asked, but at the expression on Max's face, she hastily spelled the boy's last name. "He lives on Tassiter Lane. It goes off The Lakeview, just inside the city limits. Do you know the road?"

"I can find it," Max told her.

"It's just past the firehouse, off to the right of course, since the lake is on the left. There are just houses on that road, no stores," she reported. "The houses aren't as small as yours but they're not big, and they all have gardens but they grow flowers, not food. Don't you want to know how I learned all this?"

"You want to tell me," he pointed out.

"What's wrong with that? I was only lucky, I know, but the little girl I just happened to pick to ask is in his class. She lives on the same street and she says his mother did go away. In the winter, she thinks. She said the mother just stopped being there and none of the other parents said anything. Even if you asked, they wouldn't tell you anything."

"What about the father?" Max asked. "What about Mr. Melakrinos?"

"He's like all the other fathers. He goes to work in the morning, he comes home for supper. He wears a suit and a hat, she told me, but you know little children. They never know anything about what fathers do."

Max folded the notebook closed and put it back in his pocket, with the pencil. "Thank you," he said again. "That's just what I needed to know."

The noise level in the little shop had gone up and up, in volume and in pitch, so they had to lean their heads close together to be able to talk.

"I did a good job," she told him.

"You did," he agreed, and she smiled, content. She picked up the last piece of croissant, and opened her mouth.

And then, out of nowhere it seemed, although actually it came out of the crowded confusion behind them, a large hand came to roost on Pia's shoulder.

Her head whipped around, and Max stared up at the big man who had loomed into sight behind her. Max was alarmed, alert for trouble. The man was both tall and broad. He wore a bright yellow slicker, with a yellow fisherman's rain hat on his square head, and he stared down at Max.

"You're early," Pia said crossly.

The man ignored her. Keeping one hand on Pia's shoulder, and thus keeping Pia pinned in her seat, he leaned over to hold out the other. "So you're the famous Mister Max," he said, eyebrows as inky dark as Pia's drawn together, not exactly in frowning suspicion but awfully close. His eyes, like Pia's, were small, and a dark, sapphire blue.

ICE CREAM

Max stood up to his full height, and took the offered hand. "You must be Mr. Bendiff."

Neither of them said, *Pleased to meet you.*

"You look young," Pia's father said, and his voice added that this was not a good thing.

"I am," Max agreed. He was Lorenzo Apiedi, youthful patriot and hero, so sure of the rightness of his cause that no man could abash him, not the great, not the powerful, and not the merely rich and successful, either. He might be doomed, but he was not going to bow down before his fate. He was untroubled by the man's size and authority. "Will you sit?" he asked.

And Pia's father laughed. "When I've gotten myself a cup, and maybe—was that a chocolate cake on that plate? I haven't yet tasted Gabrielle's chocolate cake and there's always someone with a taste for chocolate, after a good dinner. You two wait here," he told them. He dropped his wet hat onto the floor beside an empty chair and moved off.

They watched him go to the back of the line and loom there, over the children and their mothers. "He's like a bear," Max said.

"But smart," Pia said, keeping an eye on her father.

"Who says bears aren't smart?" Max asked, also watching the man. That was the effect Mr. Bendiff had: You waited for him to decide what was going to happen next.

Abruptly, Mr. Bendiff stepped out of line and returned to their table. "You get me what I want, will you, Pia? And I'll have a little conversation with your Mister Max."

Pia grinned at Max as she rose obediently.

"I can talk with Gabrielle later, or another time when it isn't so busy in here," Mr. Bendiff said, as if he was answering a question Max had just asked. He sat down in Pia's chair and went on to report, again as if Max had asked a question, "The restaurant's coming along pretty well. That was a good site you located—outside of that termites' nest of an old city is good, and there's been no vandalism either out there or not much. I'd like to see them try something with me. I'd show them, whoever they are."

Max didn't doubt it.

"And that's a good thing for Pia, tutoring that young woman." He nodded. "I didn't really mean you should pay her," he announced, and then he sat back in his chair, unfastening the clips on his raincoat, waiting to see Max's reaction to him.

Young Lorenzo Apiedi concerned himself only with justice for his people, so he did not speak, although his face was a portrait of readiness. He didn't know if he would end up at the end of a hangman's rope or in the seat of an elected delegate, but he wasn't afraid of either outcome. And he wasn't afraid of this man.

"It's not as if she needs money," Mr. Bendiff said after a while. "What she needs is something to do. But"—and now he leaned forward, his big, square-jawed face serious, earnest—"I don't want you putting my little girl in danger."

Little girl? Pia? "I wouldn't do that," Max said.

"I heard about the break-in at your house," Mr. Bendiff

warned him. "She told me. We have an understanding, Pia and I. I don't tell her not to do things, and she tells me everything she does."

Had she told him about discovering who Simon was and where he lived? Max wondered, and he wondered if Mr. Bendiff would be interested in such things and then he wondered how he might find out which house on Tassiter Lane belonged to the Melakrinos family. He could take his bicycle and wait at the head of the road at about the time the boy should arrive home from school— But how did Simon get home? What did he look like, other than six or seven years old?

"Listen up, you! I don't much care for not being listened to." But the growly voice sounded as much curious as cross.

"Sorry," Max said, and he was, sort of. He knew his mind had drifted. "I was thinking."

Mr. Bendiff studied Max again. There was nothing special, nothing out of the ordinary, about this fellow. But was he trustworthy? He'd found a good location for the restaurant, that was true, so he wasn't a fool. He'd gotten Pia interested in something besides picking fights at school, and also had her tutoring somebody, and in the kitchen of a Baroness for a wonder. His girl a guest in a Baroness's castle? Who'd have predicted *that*? So this Mister Max must be sharp enough to see the good in her. He had an honest expression, honest and also alert—but there were the eyes of him. Mr. Bendiff didn't know what to make of those eyes, the dark, variegated brown and black and gray color like the fur of some of the half-starved wolves that came down from the mountains in winter, and circled the isolated farmhouses. He said, "I know my girl, she's like me—and maybe that's hard luck on her—but she's not very good at being a child. It'll be better for her when she grows up. The bad news is, that's years away and . . ."

Max understood the man's concern. Now *he* leaned forward, the Caliph's doctor, assuring his master that the birth of his child was proceeding normally, emitting truthfulness and trustworthiness the way the sun emits warm rays of light, to tell Pia's father, "I'll do my best to keep her out of trouble."

"That's good enough for me," Mr. Bendiff decided. He sat back in the chair and told this strange fellow, "Pia will do what she wants, I know," with a fierce, not exactly friendly smile.

Max could have laughed out loud at how alike they were, this father and his daughter.

3

Simon's Job

• ACT I •

Max spent the next morning finishing his map of South America for Grammie, who was now focusing their tutoring work on that continent. She told him to include not only major cities but also geographical details such as rivers, lakes, mountains, and savannas. South America, he noted, was very large and Andesia not much more than a short, wormy squiggle alongside a long mountain range. After that, he studied the Pythagorean theorem for Ari. Then he dressed himself in overalls and a wide straw hat, tied a red bandanna around his neck, and set off on foot for the Starling Theater.

He wanted to assure himself that the empty theater had not been attacked by either fire or vandals. What he would do if it had been, Max had no idea, but certainly he ought to know. Almost every other day he dressed like Greek Jonny, whom Arabella had rejected particularly gently and which happened also to be his first and favorite disguise, and made his way through the twisting streets and alleys of the old city to see that the Starling Theater was still standing, undamaged. The theater had originally been a small warehouse for spices, a wooden building that faced out onto a little paved square with a fountain at its center in what had become a quiet, residential section of the old city. It was, William Starling declared, the perfect site for a theater. The shops and cafés clustered around larger squares were an easy walk from the theater but enough distant to give audiences a pleasant stroll to their suppers after a performance.

As usual, everything seemed in order. Max checked the stage door first, then strolled casually in front of the building, taking quick glances to see that the glass in the entrance had not been smashed, that the chains were still looped between the massive handles. He slipped around the corner of the building to be sure that the private entrance, a doorway at the rear of a narrow alley, was undisturbed. Something bright lay on the ground by the door, a coin? Had someone stood at this door? But no one except for the theatrical company, and Grammie of course, even knew about it. He picked the coin up, gave the door handle a quick turn and rattle to see that it was securely closed and locked, then returned to the street.

Max glanced at the coin in his hand, to see how much it was worth before slipping it into a pocket. But it wasn't a coin in his palm. Or at least, it wasn't any coin he'd ever seen before, and there was some thin hook on the back. . . . Had some foreigner been wandering around the old city, and hoped to see a play, and dropped a coin? Max wondered. He looked more carefully at it, to find out what country that foreigner had come from.

A familiar three-peaked design stamped onto the front of the coin took his breath away. He closed his hand around it—as if afraid to be seen with it in his possession. As if he had stolen it. Or—worse—as if someone, watching him find the coin and recognize it, would know whose son he was.

Max dropped it into his pocket and headed home. It couldn't be from Andesia. It was a simpler design than the one stamped on top of the writing paper from the nonexistent Maharajah of Kashmir. Also, it was not nearly so intricate as the brooch sent to his mother in the same packet with the letter and two first-class boat tickets. Also, too, and he felt in his pocket to be sure of this, the piece was much too thick for a coin. It was more like a button, an innocent lost button. Maybe it had fallen off the jacket of some servant or soldier charged with the duty of keeping a young nobleman safe as he completed his education with a world tour, which included a performance by the Starling Theatrical Company. Maybe it wasn't at all what Max was afraid it was.

As he walked, he pulled the piece out of his pocket and glanced down at it. It was definitely a button, with a delicate wire on the back for thread to pass through. It was also definitely gold. And those were definitely three mountain peaks stamped onto the front of it. Yes, there was the suggestion of a curve running across their base, which made the peaks look like a crown. . . . But Max knew he was fooling himself. The resemblance was too strong, the coincidence too great.

Max's heart shrank and he wanted to drop the button onto the ground, for someone else to find. But he couldn't, he knew; so he dropped it back into his pocket.

The button had to be a message from Andesia. But what *was* the message? And who was the messenger? Was the button dropped by an Andesian soldier who'd followed his father to this private door? Before the mysterious invitation was even sent? The button seemed too shiny to have lain in the alley for long. So, was there an Andesian soldier in Queensbridge even now, following Max? He resisted the urge to look behind him, but he did quicken his pace.

Or, and here was a happier thought, could the button be a message from his father? A bread crumb left for Max to follow? The notes his father had sent were certainly just as mysterious. But a button? To say . . . What? *Keep your mouth buttoned shut? Unbutton this secret so I can come home? Where are you* (if it was a *button-button, who's got the button?* message)? Or, it could even be one of his father's dramatic gestures, a wordless waving of the hand, while Max's mother looked on in approval and admiration, to say to their son, *Button your shirt, polish your boots, walk with straight shoulders while you are out there, being independent, the way I said you were.*

In fact, Max's shoulders slumped and his hand jerked

back out of his pocket as if some poisonous snake was in it. He hadn't done any of that, had he? He hadn't kept his mouth buttoned, or brought them back from Andesia, or even, really, been more than half independent. He doubled his pace again, to get to Thieves Alley more quickly. There, he ran up the stairs to bury the button in the back of a drawer crammed with underwear and socks, where he wouldn't have to see it and his grandmother wouldn't find it.

Because he didn't intend to tell her that there had been a message—in however strange a form—from Andesia. He felt bad enough about his failure, and maybe even ashamed, and her sympathy would only make him feel worse. Especially after that silly letter he'd written, thinking he was so clever, as if it was some child's game his parents were playing, and not real trouble. But they couldn't have gotten his letter yet, could they? In which case, they didn't even know he knew where they were. Which meant that the button must have been sent out—and how had it been delivered, anyway?—as some kind of clue to their location. His parents must be feeling so . . . lost.

Max hesitated, stopped in his tracks by a feeling so dark and shadowy he wasn't sure he had the energy even to pull out his dresser drawer. Then he shook his head, hard. It might be a clue, but it wasn't a very good one. He felt a flare of annoyance at a father who would send such ridiculous clues—and he dropped the button into his drawer and went back downstairs.

Simon's problem was something he could actually do

something about. Maybe. If he knew more. So he kept the overalls-bandanna-straw-hat costume on, mounted his bicycle, and headed out to make his way through the old city and over the wide drawbridge to The Lakeview and Tassiter Lane, where he might be able to find out the more he needed to know. He didn't bother eating any lunch. He didn't have any appetite.

The Lakeview ran along the eastern side of the lake, from the Royal Gate up past the gates of the summer palace to the little lakeside village of Summer. Wide meadows separated the roadway from the water. Closer to the city, small roads, lined with well-kept homes on broad lawns, led off into the low foothills, where they turned abruptly into mountain paths. Farther from the city and closer to the summer palace, great houses were announced by their stone or marble or wrought-iron gates, which were guarded by little gatehouses, but that afternoon, Max was going no farther than the lanes.

He slowed down when the long, one-story old firehouse came up on his left. The New Town had its own brick fire station, with big doors that opened only to let the two pump wagons in or out, but at the older lakeside firehouse the wide door stood open and the one pump wagon had been pulled out into the sunlight. Men sat around in chairs, enjoying the quiet of the afternoon, their sleeves rolled up. A few boys were occupied polishing the hubs and bells, the harnesses and hose ends. These were apprentices and those who hoped to be taken on as apprentices. More eager to be out working among men than sitting in kitchens with their mothers finishing homework papers, they made this their first stop every afternoon on their way home from school. Several bicycles and rucksacks lay in a jumble beside the wagons where they had been dropped.

Just as Pia had said, Tassiter Lane entered only a few yards past the firehouse, at a place where a high fence had been put up to keep private a wide section of meadow. The fence blocked the lake beyond from sight, and beside it grew undergrowth dense enough for Max to hide his bicycle among low bushes. He did not look back to see if anyone from the firehouse had observed this odd activity. If you do not wish to be noticed, one of the worst things you can do is look furtively around to see if anyone's suspicions have been aroused.

Bicycle safely stored, Max crossed The Lakeview and entered Tassiter Lane, his face shadowed by the broad straw brim of his hat. He walked down the road like a man on his way to work.

The houses on Tassiter Lane were painted cheerful pinks, yellows, and greens, with bright white shutters and flower-filled window boxes and wide grassy lawns all around, enclosed by low white picket fences. In front of some of the gates a woman waited, a young mother or a nursemaid, or an older mother or a housekeeper, and one might even have been a grandmother. They were all looking toward The Lakeview, and Max attracted no attention. Gardeners were a common sight on Tassiter Lane.

At the point where the lane began to curve up into the hills, Max stopped and turned around. It wasn't long before the children of Tassiter Lane came home from school, the older ones on bicycles, chattering with their friends, the younger in groups under the care of an older sister or brother. Max strolled slowly back down the lane, wishing he had asked Pia for a description of Simon Melakrinos. There were more than a dozen small children in the uniform of the Hilliard School being escorted home, and at least half of them were little boys. None of them wore convenient name tags.

He watched the homecomings. Some children ran up for a quick embrace, but a few just sauntered up to the waiting woman and those, he guessed, would include his Simon, whose mother was missing.

Max made his way slowly toward them, just a gardener on a June afternoon, looking lazily at these fine houses. Two of the boys seemed to him to be the right age. One of them was stocky while the other had long, skinny legs. One had pale brown hair, the other hair of a darker brown, in need of a trim. One, he saw as he walked past the house, took the woman's hand and carried his own rucksack inside, while the other handed his rucksack over to the woman and led the way into the house.

It could be either one of them, Max thought, making a mental note of the two houses, numbers 37 and 41; and then he heard the rucksack-carrying woman call, "If you go right to the kitchen, you'll see there's a nice piece of pie for you, Master Andrew."

This was a piece of luck. He knew now which boy was

probably his Simon and which was probably the house from which Simon's father disappeared in the evenings. If he was right, his Simon had dark brown hair and skinny legs, the knees like knobs, and lived in a pale yellow stucco house with an overgrown garden in the front, although the grass was in good trim. As he approached the house, Max tried to look like a man who had at last arrived at the address he had been looking for.

A worker who knew his place did not go to the front door, so Max followed a gravel path around to the rear of the house. This door had no polished brass knocker. He rapped on the wood with his knuckles and heard voices inside, then light footsteps. When the door was opened, the woman called back over her shoulder as she dried her hands on her apron, "You keep on with your milk and cookies, little fellow. I'll be right here where you can see me." She turned her plump, curious face to Max and smiled just a little. "Yes? What is it?"

Max removed his straw hat and held it clutched respectfully at his waist, as Greek Jonny did. "I see in front, Missus," he said, "I see"—and he gestured with his hand back toward the lane—"I see weeds. I garden, Missus, I garden good. You want me to garden you?"

She smiled sympathetically as she shook her head to say, "I'm sorry, I'm not the mistress here, only the housekeeper. I don't know if Mr. Melakrinos wants those gardens attended to or not. You'll have to ask him, and he doesn't arrive home until half after six. I'm sorry I can't help you."

She sounded as if she meant it. If Max had really been a gardener and looking for work, hers would be a kind response. "Maybe I come back," he said. "Thank you, Missus."

"You do that," she encouraged him. "It's a crime to let those gardens go, after all the planning, and work . . ."

Max listened hard, perhaps too hard, because she stopped speaking and took a breath, looked carefully at him, this man—a young man, clearly, with eyes the color of the undersides of overbaked cookies. Was he up to no good? Was he what he seemed? But those sad, neglected gardens decided her. She said, "They eat their supper by seven, and then he and the boy play ball, if the weather is fine, or he reads to him, so until the boy goes to bed—at eight I think it is—Simon?" she called over her shoulder. "What time do you go to bed?"

A high voice answered her. "Eight o'clock and I can read until half past. This is a good cookie, Mrs. Molly. Even better than yesterday."

The housekeeper gave Max the kind of glance exchanged between adults when they are amused by a child's innocence. "So it'll be late before he can talk to you," she advised.

"I can be late," Max assured her. "Thank you, Missus," he said again, and turned to walk back down the gravel path.

"He does need someone, to clear them out," she called after him. "If they go through the whole season neglected, it'll be that much more work getting them in order. So you be sure to come back."

Max turned to raise a hand to her as he put his hat on his

head. "I come back." He could promise her that. He walked down the lane, toward the lake.

He was careful to continue in his role as a gardener, shoulders and legs a little tired from a morning's labor. He even, as he pulled his bicycle out from its hiding place, took the bandanna from around his neck and wiped at his forehead as a man might who had spent hours in the sun. But he didn't remove his hat to do that. He sensed that the men and boys at the firehouse were watching him, so he carefully reknotted his bandanna and nodded twice, as a man might who had just found himself a job he was grateful to have. Then he mounted his bicycle and pedaled back toward the city.

"Max?" He heard a voice from behind him and ignored it. He heard running feet. "Max?"

He didn't even angle his head. He didn't shift his shoulders. He didn't increase his speed. It was someone else's name, after all.

The footsteps quickened. Max stood up on the pedals, to push down hard, but his rear wheel was jammed, suddenly, somehow, and he flew off. He smashed onto his left shoulder, and his chest slammed onto the hard roadway. If he hadn't been wearing the wide-brimmed straw gardening hat, his forehead would have cracked against the pavement, but luckily, the straw cushioned that impact. The Lakeview was the way to the Promontory, where the King had his summer palace, so of course it was kept in good repair, against the summer weeks when the royal family would grace the lake with their presences. It was a good road for fast travel, which made it a bad road to fall down on, hard. Max's brain was muddled and his reactions slowed, so that before he could gather his thoughts or even turn around to sit up, he found himself pinned down, face against asphalt.

"I don't think that's your bicycle you're riding," said a voice. A voice he recognized. Recognized from where? Whose voice . . . ?

The voice was bold and clear, not angry, just in the right. It was—Max remembered, as if from some time long ago—the voice of Tomi Brandt, who—as Max happened to know because they had been in the same class since level two—planned to be a policeman, or a fireman, or perhaps mayor, and see justice done. Max felt his head clearing now.

Tomi wanted to make the world a better place. His constant concern with what was right often drove his teachers and friends at school to the end of their patience. Worse, he was the kind of person who *did* something about injustice, or tried to. If you told Tomi a soccer call didn't matter, that he should just start playing again (or let the teacher get back to teaching, or give some smaller child his own pencil to replace the one that had been snatched away from him), Tomi would tell you the story of his grandfather and the cow that had been taken away to pay taxes after a year of drought, so that the family had no milk or cheese or butter to sell, so that the next year they could not pay taxes again and the sow was taken, and so on, year after year, chickens after corn crops, blackberry patches after basil seedlings, until the farm had been taken away, lost forever, and the four children had been sent to work in the city and send whatever they could back to the hills to their aging, broken parents. It was a long and dismal story and nobody wanted to have to listen to it more than twice. Tomi's father had gone for a soldier, so fighting was in his blood; also he was the oldest of six children, and his father often away, so he had early been allowed to run loose through the entire city. He knew people in all kinds of unexpected places. Max guessed he shouldn't have been surprised that Tomi was one of the boys doing odd jobs at the firehouse.

"Where'd you get that bicycle, Mister?" Tomi's voice demanded.

"Bicycle mine," Max muttered into the pavement, trying to think out how to play this scene. He definitely did not want word to get back to the school that he was still in the city. Once school let out, word would not spread, but until then the risk was high. Max lay on his stomach with the weight of the short, square, muscular Tomi on his back. Out of his right eye—the only eye with vision at the moment, the other being blocked by the brim of his hat—he saw only black macadam and a grassy verge beyond. Max thought fast and hard, every muscle tight to spring up should Tomi relax his grip. Then, thinking, he made himself relax. He loosened every muscle, starting with his clenched jaw, loosened his arms, back, and legs, loosened even his fingers, in surrender. If Tomi thought Max had given up, he'd allow him to get up onto his feet. It wouldn't be fair not to.

"Off?" Max grunted. He was Greek Jonny, the immigrant

day laborer. He was a nobody, at the mercy of everybody, like Tomi's grandfather. "Up?" he puffed.

Tomi climbed off his captive's back and tried to give the man a hand up, but it was refused. Tomi looked at his own hand as the tall fellow scrambled to his feet and pulled his hat angrily down on his head, and decided that if he had been accused of being a thief he wouldn't accept any helping hand from his accuser, either. This man was tall, but not muscular; he stood with his workman's hands jammed into his pockets and his head bent, as if he was used to being yelled at, like a troublesome student in a classroom. Tomi felt an unexpected confusion, and wondered if he was being unfair.

"Why you do that?" Max muttered, without looking up.

"I know this bicycle," Tomi answered, but all of the accusing, *I know I'm right* tone had left his voice.

"Is mine, this," Max said, which couldn't help but sound like the truth.

"There's only one bicycle I've ever seen with a basket like that," Tomi insisted, "and it belongs to . . . to a boy I know."

That, Max couldn't deny. His bicycle basket was, in fact, a discarded prop from *The Adorable Arabella.* He had claimed the deep wire container, too large for Arabella to carry her bouquets of flowers in, and attached it to the front of his bicycle to make a basket deep and strong enough to hold a large pad of watercolor paper, boxes of paints, and a pencil box. All Max could say was, "Is mine, this."

"Where did you get it?" Tomi insisted.

By then, Max had found his story. "On docks. Near big

boats. Was long time past, lots of weeks. Was—on ground, was—didn't nobody own it. Is mine now."

He could see that Tomi half believed him. "But I know who really owns that bicycle. He's—he goes to school with me." Tomi pulled at the short, wheat-colored hair just behind his ears as he thought it out. "It doesn't make sense for Eyes to just leave his bicycle out on some street, even if he *was* leaving the city for a long tour."

Max shrugged, a simple man who either didn't care about such fine points or, maybe, didn't understand everything that was said to him. Whatever else, Max didn't want to raise suspicions. He was going to have to do something about his bicycle basket—another problem for the Solutioneer to deal with. In the meantime, he could only wait for whatever Tomi would say next, or do.

Max thought he might just have time to grab the bicycle and leap onto it and ride off, and he would do that if Tomi decided to call back to the firehouse for help. Really, however, he wanted Tomi to decide that this gardener person was telling the truth. He bowed his head a little more, to look downtrodden and weak. To look like somebody who would never in a hundred years dare to rip a bicycle out of the hands of a healthy twelve-year-old boy.

"I've never seen you," Tomi said. "You live around here, Mister?"

Max nodded. "Yes, live here."

"Then I can find you," Tomi warned him. "If I find out you're lying to me, I can find you. Do you understand me?"

"Understand," Max said. "Is mine, this," he said again, hoping to convince Tomi that he had not, in fact, understood but that he was telling the truth about the bicycle.

"Maybe it is," Tomi granted. He stood with his hands in his pockets, watching as Max bent—trying to move like a tired day laborer—to pick up the bicycle by its handlebars. Then Tomi thought of something else.

"What's your name, Mister?"

"Bartolomeo," Max said, and quickly mounted the bike, as awkwardly as might someone stiff from a long day's work in hot sunlight. He rode away before Tomi thought to ask for a surname, not going fast, but not going slow, either. At the first bend in the road, he risked a look back.

He shouldn't have done that, because Tomi was still standing right where he'd left him, staring after the fellow riding off on the bicycle that once belonged to someone in his class at school, wondering if an injustice hadn't occurred.

Max couldn't worry too much about Tomi, however. He had other problems to think about. He had the problem of how to ride off after supper to see if Mr. Melakrinos left the house tonight, after he had put Simon to bed, in order to follow the man to wherever he might go. Luckily for Max, these were the longest days of the year, but he also had the problem of how to convince Grammie that he wanted to paint the evening sky over the lake, which would certainly be better than trying to sneak off after supper. It wasn't as if he *had* to have permission, or as if Grammie loomed over him like some cliff. But he was, as she had said, the last of her family she could be sure was safe, and of course she wanted to keep him that way. And he felt pretty much the same way about her. Maybe that was why he was determined to help Simon Melakrinos—because he knew just about exactly how that little boy felt.

4

Simon's Job

• ACT II •

That evening, Grammie looked across the table at Max and decided, "I have my doubts about you roaming the streets at this hour." She turned to Ari for confirmation. "Don't you?"

"No," Ari said.

"You don't? With all that's been going on in the old city?"

"No," Ari said again. He had been eating his baked lake fish with full attention but now he set down his fork and knife and looked at Grammie. "In the first place, there's light until nine or half past at this time of year. In the second, the trouble's all in the old city and Max is heading to the lake. In the third, he'll have his bicycle, so he could make a run for it, if he had to, which he probably won't. Besides which, in two of those big houses out on The Lakeview, they know who he is." Ari turned to look at Max and add, "Insofar as anybody knows who he is."

Max grinned at his tutor-tenant. "I'll be fine," he promised his grandmother.

"Nobody can be sure of that," Grammie grumbled.

"You're getting as gloomy as Joachim," he said.

"Joachim is no fool," she answered.

"I don't know about gloomy," Ari interrupted, "but it seems to me that you're worrying more about Max than you used to."

"I'm not worrying at all, not about anything," Grammie maintained, and put a forkful of rice into her mouth so she couldn't possibly say anything more.

Ari looked at Max but Max shook his head: he had no idea. So, "You could fool me," Ari said. "You know, don't you, Mrs. Nives? I'll do anything I can if there's anything that needs doing."

Grammie swallowed. "I know, and I'm grateful, and I don't mean to be gloomy. It's just . . . And I do know you're old enough to decide things for yourself, Max," she said in apology. "You've certainly proved that. So go ahead and get that picture painted. I'm being foolish."

"I'm not painting, just looking, preparing," Max said. He didn't want to have to produce a painting of the evening sky at the end of the night.

As soon as Max had exited the old city through the Royal Gate, the lake breezes washed the air clean of the smells of dust and roasting meats and garbage set out in the summer heat to be carried away, unless the dogs got to it first, or the feral cats, or the vermin in which a waterside city can abound. Away from the dark, crowded streets, the air glimmered with the rosy gold light of a long June evening. Max had his sketch pad in the bicycle basket in front of him and his red beret on his head. He wore a pair of loose, paint-stained trousers and pedaled at a sedate pace up to the firehouse and toward the long fence opposite Tassiter Lane. Riding past the firehouse, he was reminded of Tomi and the problem of his all-too-recognizable bicycle basket.

It was the streaks of color on his trousers, moving up and down over his pumping knees, that gave him the idea, and he was so pleased to have it that he wasn't even curious about the odd thunking sounds that came from behind the fence, as if a housemaid was haphazardly beating dust out of a carpet. Neither did he wonder about the grunts and indecipherable cries that accompanied the thwacks, as if the housemaid every now and then just lost her temper at the puffs and clouds of dirt flying out of the rug. As he turned onto Tassiter Lane, his mind was on those streaks, in colors from the various theatrical flats he and his father had painted together. If he left the bottom of his basket black but painted the top half white, then the basket would *look* as if it was the normal depth and Tomi Brandt would probably not recognize it, in the unlikely event that he ran into Tomi again. Max was pleased with the cleverness of this solution to the problem, so pleased that he almost didn't see the man emerging from the Melakrinos house, gently pulling the door closed behind him. As Max rode by, the man looked anxiously up at a dark second-story window, then turned to scurry down the street toward The Lakeview. The man didn't even look at whoever-it-was, going down his street on a bicycle.

Max didn't stop until he had passed two more houses. Then he dismounted and turned around. You couldn't use a bicycle to follow a man on foot so when he had reversed direction, he went back down the street pushing his bicycle, not riding it. He glanced up at the dark upstairs windows of Simon's house and thought he saw a movement, as if a curtain had been pushed gently aside. He lifted one hand in greeting, in case Simon was watching his father walk away, and worrying, and wondering if Mister Max would answer his letter.

But what kind of father would leave his young son all alone? And who knew for how long? And at night?

Max followed.

Mr. Melakrinos crossed the wide road and walked alongside the tall fence, going quickly. In a hurry to get to the city, Max thought, and begin searching for his wife. There was something of the rag doll about Simon's father, something flappy and floppy. His hair flopped on his head and his pants flapped around his legs as he rushed along. On the opposite side of the street, Max followed.

Then Mr. Melakrinos turned at the corner of the fence

and headed for the lake, which took Max entirely by surprise. Just at that time, two carriages, one close behind the other, came along at a quick trot, and he had to wait. Each carriage was occupied by a well-dressed couple and driven by a groom in livery, and they were both traveling north, out of the city, carrying dinner guests at one of the big houses, Max guessed, or courting couples on a romantic ride to watch the sun set behind the distant hills across the lake before sitting down to supper at one of Summer's little cafés. By the time they had passed him, Mr. Melakrinos was out of sight.

Max ran across the road, hampered by his bicycle. As soon as he could, he dropped it onto the ground, grabbing his sketch pad from the basket. His mind was working so furiously that he didn't even hear the sounds from behind the fence. He needed an excuse, so he had to carry the pad, but he couldn't bother trying to hide the bicycle, not if he planned to keep his quarry close.

And he did plan to keep Simon's father close. Because what would a man rush to do at the edge of the deep lake, at this late hour?

About halfway across the grassy meadow, the fence ended. Max stopped, looking around for the long-legged figure. The thumps and thwaps and voices were louder there, and clearer. He turned, to see twenty or thirty men scattered around the grass, kicking at a ball and running after it in a disorganized pack. Then he recognized Simon's long-legged father standing at one side of the grassy field, talking to two men.

Quickly, Max sat down. He leaned back against the fence

and opened the sketch pad, bracing it against his knees, and studied Mr. Melakrinos.

The man wore glasses, the lenses round on a narrow, bony face. He was rubbing at his ear and he seemed uneasy, maybe even afraid. He looked back, in the direction of Tassiter Lane, as if expecting trouble from that direction. Then one of the two men clapped him on the shoulder and Simon's father ran out to join the pack of running men.

Now Max recognized it: a soccer game. Now he understood what was going on: Mr. Melakrinos was leaving home in the evenings to play soccer. But why wouldn't he just tell Simon what he was doing?

Max took a drawing pencil out of his pocket. Just because he was out solutioneering, that didn't mean he couldn't do a little drawing as well. He'd never tried to draw people, only skies. But if he concentrated on this sky, the thin clouds stretched along the horizon waiting for the sun to sink into them like a tired man sinking down into a good night's sleep, he wouldn't see what happened with Simon's father. He might miss something that would explain what was going on. So he looked at Mr. Melakrinos standing out in the field, leggy and awkward, a little apart from everyone. Mr. Melakrinos had fixed all of his attention on the movement of the ball.

There was no reason Max couldn't try drawing people, was there? And Simon's father *was* the best person to practice on, of all the figures out there. Not only did his legs make it easy to identify him, but he was standing still. Sometimes he would follow the pack down the field, at a loping trot, but then he would stop again and stand, hands held a little out in front of him as if ready to catch the ball.

But the rules said you were not allowed to use your hands unless you were tending the goal. Max might not be an athlete, but he knew *that.* You had to trap the ball with your feet. Soccer was a game for feet, and balls, and—Max watched this admiringly—running. The men were constantly running up and down the grassy field, back and forth across it, kicking and chasing the ball. *Thunk, thwap,* and someone might call out, "I'm free!" or "Over here!" or even, once, "You clumsy fool!"

That last remark was directed to Mr. Melakrinos, who had somehow managed to be hit on the shoulder by the ball so that he whipped around in surprise and tripped one of the other men, who grabbed at a third to keep his balance, and so all three lay tangled together on the ground. While somebody else took the ball up the field, away from them.

Mr. Melakrinos had been looking up and off, toward Tassiter Lane, when the ball came at him, and that was how the accident had occurred. Max could hear him apologizing while the other two men burst up off the ground, already running after the ball. Mr. Melakrinos stayed down, his knees bent, one hand wrapped around an ankle.

One of the two men who stood watching at the sidelines hurried up. "Andros? Something wrong?"

"I think I twisted it. It'll be fine in a minute. Maybe."

"Let me give you a hand up. Hurt much? It's not broken but . . . Listen, Andros, tell you what. You go sit with that fellow there, find out what he's up to. I've never seen him before and you'll be doing us a favor if you suss him out while you see how bad the ankle is. Would you do that?"

"Sure," Simon's father said. "It'll make a change to do something useful." He looked over at Max.

Caught out, Max raised the hand holding the drawing pencil. He became, in his own imagining mind, Joachim, a real artist, and at work.

"By the way," the man said, "it looked to me like you were moving with the play a little better today. Like you had a better understanding of where the ball would go next. You're coming along, Andros, slow and steady, just keep it up and you'll be fine." And then he ran away up along the side of the field, to get closer to the players, calling, "Peter! You're offsides!"

Max kept his eyes on his sketch pad, but he turned the page over and made some fresh marks that might, if you knew what they were supposed to be, look like players on a field. He looked up, as if studying the scene before him—just the way Joachim studied the particular angle from which a blossom or leaf stood out from its stem. Then he started, as if surprised to notice the long-legged man limping toward him.

Mr. Melakrinos loomed over him and Max had to crane his neck backward to look at the round glasses, and the eyes behind them. Neither of them spoke for a moment. Joachim never spoke unless he had something to say, and anything that Max had to say—such as, "Why don't you tell your little boy where you're going? Do you know how worried he is?"—would be out of character. So he stared up for a minute, nodded, then turned back to the sketch, to draw more lines. He drew the ball, a round dark thing, alone in the grassy field, waiting to be kicked.

"Mind if I sit?" Simon's father asked. He had a soft voice and he hesitated, as if he expected to be turned away.

Max shook his head. He didn't mind. The opposite, in fact.

Simon's father sat down beside him. He turned his face to the field so that he could watch the play and also, Max suspected, so that Max wouldn't feel he was being pried at. This seemed to be the kind of man who would think about other people's feelings.

Except his son's, it seemed.

Max told the man, "I'm drawing."

Mr. Melakrinos nodded. "I thought you were an artist, you have the look. The beret, I mean, the pad. Anyway. It must be hard. Getting all that movement," he said. "I mean, hard to draw a soccer game."

A man with imagination, too, Max thought. "You're right," he said. "I'm not sure I'm up to it. But it doesn't matter if I'm not," he added, as Joachim, who believed in *doing,* rather than *sitting around talking about.*

"Turns out—doesn't it?—there's not much that does matter," Simon's father said sadly. "Not that really matters, I mean. Problem is," he went on, "that the things that do really matter? They really, *really* matter." He leaned down then, unlaced his shoe, and pulled it off, with a little grunt of pain. He peeled down his sock and considered his ankle. He poked at it with a forefinger, where Max could see that it was starting to swell up.

"Can you move it?" Max asked.

"Yes," Mr. Melakrinos said, gently rotating his foot, just once and with another small grunt. "It's probably just a sprain. So. I guess I won't be playing for a few days, but what I'll tell—" He looked over to Max and said in a voice that was even sadder than before, "I *knew* something like this would happen."

"Something like what?"

"Getting injured. Injuring myself. I've always been clumsy, even as a boy. I was never good at games. Are you young enough to remember what happens to boys who aren't good at games?"

Max nodded. He remembered.

"If it happens also that they are good at numbers? Good at school, in fact? Just . . ." Simon's father fell silent, like a windup toy that had run down.

Max finished the thought for him. "Just not very good at being a boy." Max had always had the Starling Theatrical Company to make him look all right, or at least to make him envied, but he knew enough about being different to make him sympathetic.

Simon's father nodded. "I'll have to think of something to tell Simon." He laughed unhappily. "You don't happen to be a clever liar, do you?" Then, looking at Max's sketch, he laughed again. "Never mind."

Max laughed, too. He agreed, and it was, after all, pretty funny. There was nothing at all clever about this drawing.

They sat side by side, looking at the field while the sun moved down toward the hills across the lake. They were talking without turning to face one another, as if they were old friends. Max thought hard, to find a way to advise Mr. Melakrinos without giving himself away, or giving Simon away, either. This was the kind of problem the Caliph's Doctor faced all the time, trying to cure the Caliph's aches and pains and diseases without acknowledging that anything was wrong. The Caliph was Caliph and Caliphs never fall ill, they have no weaknesses, so he had to be tricked into a cure. But it was Max's father who always played the doctor, not Max, and Max wasn't sure he could fill his father's shoes. Then he had an idea, and said, with perfect honesty, "I *am* clever enough. Look," and he turned back a page.

Mr. Melakrinos looked. "That's me," he said. "Isn't it? Is that me? I didn't know I looked so . . . so awkward. It's the legs, isn't it? I am such a stork, no wonder I can't . . ."

Max tried to sound surprised, as if he had just realized something. "You want help in thinking about how to explain your twisted ankle?"

Mr. Melakrinos nodded.

"Who's Simon?" Max asked.

"Oh. Simon's my son."

Max waited, just a couple of seconds, to give the impression of taking in new information. Then he asked, "Why not tell him the truth?" His hand, holding the pencil, was stilled. He listened to hear the heart of the problem.

"Simon's only seven. He's a little boy."

Max shook his head, as if he were confused, as if he were a passing stranger and knew nothing about the Melakrinos family. "Little boys love soccer, don't they? I did." This was not exactly true. At seven, Max had loved fencing and wanted to become good enough to be in a sword fight with his father, but it was true enough about little boys and their love of one sport or another.

"Simon certainly does and I can't bear to disappoint him. He doesn't know that I can't—" The man waved a hand toward the field, and the men running around on it. "He doesn't know I'm—" He gestured toward the picture of him that Max had drawn. "A seven-year-old boy doesn't care if his father is chief bookkeeper for all the Bendiff companies and well thought of in his office. He wants a different kind of father. You see, I'm all Simon has left," he said, and his voice, to Max's surprise because he didn't think it could get any sadder, got sadder still.

Max thought, and his hand started to shade in the sky over the head of the long-legged man in the drawing. Then he asked, "You're all he has? What about his mother? What about brothers and sisters? What about the rest of the family, like a grandmother?"

"His mother died. Last winter."

"Oh," Max said. He hadn't thought of that possibility. Poor little Simon. And poor sad Mr. Melakrinos, too. This was— Max could imagine how bad they felt. "Oh," he said again. "I'm—"

Mr. Melakrinos interrupted. "Simon doesn't know she's dead. How could I tell him a thing like that?" He pushed his glasses up onto his forehead so he could bury his face in his hands. "I'm all he has," he said in a small, muffled voice. "And you see the kind of father I am, who can't even go out on a soccer field without getting himself injured."

Max didn't say anything. He thought, and his hand moved and he shaded in a sky with a slender crescent of white moon already hung in it. With the empty sky behind him, the figure in the picture became solitary, and brave in his solitude against the darkening sky, and strong.

"Look." Max turned the picture to the man, who uncovered his eyes, adjusted his glasses, and looked. "I think you should tell Simon the truth," Max said.

Simon's father stared at the picture. "Tell him I can't play any sports at all?" he asked.

"Tell him about his mother," Max said, although he suspected that the man knew perfectly well that was what he meant. "I think you should go home, and tell him right now."

"How can I?" Mr. Melakrinos asked. He had his excuses ready. "He's only seven. He's already sad enough just thinking that she's disappeared. He's asleep by now."

Max shook his head. "Keeping it secret isn't good for him, or for you, either, and you know what? I bet he's not asleep. I bet he's awake, lying in his bed, waiting for you to come home so he'll feel safe enough to go to sleep."

Simon's father stared at him for a long time, but Max didn't stare back. He signed his drawing *Mister Max,* wrote *For Simon* across the top of it, and then tore the page out of his sketch pad. He folded the paper carefully in half, making it easy to carry. He passed it to Simon's father and then he did look at him.

The man's face was serious and unhappy. But the eyes behind the round lenses had a glimmer of hope in them. "How could I not have thought of that?" he asked. "But who are you? Do you know Simon? Are you from Hilliard or something?"

Max smiled and stood up. "No, I never met him. I'm just—" But he couldn't think of how to end that sentence.

Luckily, Simon's father was standing up, too, impatient now, and reaching out to shake Max's hand with the hand that wasn't holding the folded drawing. He wasn't listening. He didn't care who Max was. "All right, then, I'll just do it." He laughed. "And I'll tell Simon this is a present from some would-be artist with funny eyes."

Max laughed with him. "I don't imagine he'll care about that."

He walked away then, making his exit at normal speed, not walking fast and not slowly. He raised a hand over his head in farewell but didn't turn around. It wasn't until he had picked up his bicycle, placed the pad in the basket, and reached the firehouse that he did turn and look back, to see a tall figure, long-legged as a stork, crossing The Lakeview at a swift limp.

The air had just darkened to purple when Max set his bicycle in its place up against the kitchen door of 5 Thieves Alley. The lights were on in his kitchen. He could see Ari at the table, a textbook open in front of him. Across the garden, in Grammie's house, kitchen lights also burned. He set his beret and sketch pad down on his own back steps, then went to show his grandmother that he was home safe.

Grammie had a plate waiting for him, with a slab of peach and blackberry crumble on it. "That looks good," he said, and "I planned for it to tempt you," she told him, pouring him a glass of milk from the jug in the icebox before she sat down to face him, across the table. "Was it a successful jaunt? Whatever it really was, I mean, because you don't think you fooled me for a minute, do you?"

Max's mouth was full, so he only nodded in answer to her first question and shrugged in answer to the second. When he had swallowed he admitted, "I wasn't sure you'd let me go out at night, for work."

Grammie sighed, as if she were tired or as if she were too worn out to fight on. "Well, you might be right about that," she admitted. "I do want to hear about it. I *am* interested in your cases, and how you solve them. What were you up to?" she asked. "Can you tell me?"

And so Max explained about the father and son who needed to talk.

5

The Mayor's Job

• ACT I •

SCENE 1 ~ QUESTIONS

Then came several days during which the Solutioneer had no work. Long day followed long day with neither postcard from Andesia nor letter for Mister Max; dinner followed dinner with little to say and nothing to report. Max waited. What else could he do but wait? He studied his Spanish verbs and vocabulary; he studied the history of all the South American countries and waited. He studied Euclid and waited. He painted June morning skies and waited.

He didn't really have to worry about money, he knew, but since his earnings equaled his independence, he did worry, day after jobless day. So that when a letter finally arrived for Mister Max, it felt like a Christmas present, and Max, like anybody who has been hoping for weeks for a gift to be presented, was suddenly unwilling to open it and end the anticipation.

Seated on Grammie's kitchen steps in the warm afternoon, Max turned the letter over and over in his hands. It was Grammie who noticed who the letter came from, and sucked in her breath. "Whatever does the Mayor want with you?" she wondered, her voice casual but her eyes fixed on the envelope.

"No idea," said Max. It was addressed to MISTER MAX, 5 THIEVES ALLEY.

"Aren't you going to open it?"

It wasn't like Grammie to hurry him. "Are you worried about what it says?" Max asked.

"Why should I be worried?"

"Or do you already know what it says?" Max held up the envelope. He remembered that all surprises aren't happy ones. "Is it something I won't want to hear?"

"What would there be for me to worry about at the Mayor's office?"

"That's what I'm asking," Max said. He'd rather hear bad news from Grammie than from somebody official who didn't know anything about him, or care about him, either.

"Why don't you just open it?" she demanded.

Also, it wasn't like Grammie to get so easily cross, and at him, and over nothing. However, she obviously wasn't going to tell Max anything, so he shrugged and opened the letter. Its message had been typed under the city seal on heavy stationery.

Dear Mister Max,

Your name was given to me by one of our prominent lawyers, Fredric Henderson, who offered as reference also the Baroness Barthold. Both parties spoke of your perspicacity and your discretion. Those are qualities I am in need of. I will be aboard The Water Rat *Sunday morning when it leaves the city docks for its nine o'clock circuit of the lake. I will be standing at the bow, regardless of wind and weather. I ask you to meet me there, where we can talk privately on a matter of importance to the city, and to the welfare of the country, too, quite possibly. Thanking you in advance, I remain yours sincerely,*

Richard P. Valoury

Richard P. Valoury, Mayor, was typed underneath a signature so scribbled that among all the letters, only the *V* was recognizable.

Grammie was reading over his shoulder. "Why do people have such terrible handwriting?" she demanded. "Maybe I should go back into the classroom and improve things."

Max was surprised. "Do you want to teach school again? I thought you really liked the Library, with all the books and magazines and newspapers, with all the different tasks the job needs you to be able to do."

"Things don't always go the way we want them to," Grammie told him gloomily. "You should know that by now, Max."

~෴~

What the Mayor of Queensbridge saw that windy Sunday morning was not what he expected. He had been told by Fredric Henderson—but, he reminded himself, Fredric Henderson had only been repeating what his wife said and the Mayor had met Henderson's wife, a birdbrain if ever there was one. So she was likely to have gotten it all wrong when she told her husband that this Mister Max was a poor student, a brilliant poor student perhaps but nonetheless threadbare and a little underfed. He'd probably be glad of any kind of work, Fredric Henderson had advised the Mayor. Since this, at least, was just what the Mayor hoped, he was happy to believe it.

He also discounted the Baroness Barthold's report that Mister Max was a round little fellow, comical really, dressed in a nasty bright blue waistcoat that might be his Sunday best, but did nothing for his pumpkin-shaped figure. Was he clever? Or merely lucky? The Baroness couldn't swear to one or the other, but the detective seemed to care about the downtrodden, if the young woman he had brought into her employ was any example, and he *had* persuaded the Bendiff girl to do some tutoring in her kitchens, and in the Baroness's opinion that looked like a difficult child to persuade to do anything. So perhaps he was clever. Yes, he *had* done the Baroness good service but, really, she couldn't swear that that hadn't just been luck. Also, he wore this ridiculous pork-pie hat . . . Noting the Baroness's advanced age, the Mayor had decided that her eyes must be bad and that her memory, also, could not be relied on.

So, on balance, he was expecting an impoverished student, although perhaps not quite so thin as Mrs. Fredric Henderson had reported.

What he saw, however, was a dark-coated figure, slender as a rapier, striding toward him. The man had draped a long white aviator's scarf around his neck. The wide-brimmed black fedora gave him the look of some kind of artist, some poet probably, some bohemian free spirit. His back turned to the bow of *The Water Rat,* the Mayor faced the approaching figure. If he hadn't known that Captain Francis was watching, he might have feared for his own safety, although he couldn't have said why. There was something dangerous about this man, this Mister Max, this Solutioneer. When the figure came nearer, the Mayor was made even more anxious by the man's eyes. They were a strange, indefinable color, like the charred timbers of one of the wooden buildings burned in the recent fires of the old city.

That thought, however, reminded him of his urgent need for Mister Max, and his hope that the man—of whom he'd never heard until just recently—might be able to do what neither the police nor the various powerful citizens he had consulted had been able to. Even Hamish Bendiff couldn't help, and something that Hamish Bendiff couldn't do anything about was a serious problem indeed.

The Mayor stood up straighter and held his hand out

importantly. He might be in need of help, but he was still the elected mayor of Queensbridge, the man chosen by a large majority of the people. He cast a quick look up at Captain Francis standing at the bridge, took a deep breath to steady his voice against the wind, and said, "Thank you for agreeing to meet with me."

What Max saw was an ordinary gray-haired man, dressed in an ordinary gray pin-striped suit, stiff white collar and cuffs showing, a homburg on his head, a narrow briefcase at his feet. He saw the Mayor of Queensbridge, an important man who did not look like such an important person.

Max had chosen the hat and coat worn by the spy in *The Queen's Man,* in part because it seemed to him that was the best role for this morning's private meeting, and in part because the only other time the Solutioneer had boarded *The Water Rat,* this was what he'd worn. It would not do to underestimate Captain Francis's curiosity about his passengers, especially those who were not familiar to him. He strode boldly up to take the offered hand and shake it firmly, asking, "What is it I can do for you, Mayor Valoury?"

He might be dressed as a subtle and slippery spy, but he was Mister Max, the Solutioneer, on a job.

"You don't waste time," the Mayor said with an approving nod. "I like that, and this trouble is certainly serious enough. Let's sit." And he led Max over to a set of benches built up against the curving prow of the boat, freshly painted a bright white. The wind that morning was brisk, so the other passengers kept to the cabin, but even if it had been a calm, hot day, the two would have been able to speak privately. These benches, in fact the entire bow, were reserved during the summer months for the exclusive use of any royal party that boarded the little ferry to go from one lakeside village to another, and sometimes even on an outing into Queensbridge. If no royal party was on board, the benches remained empty unless—as happened that morning—Captain Francis awarded their use to someone. "Sit here," the Mayor said, indicating the space beside him.

They sat so close together that, were the wind to carry sound back to the main deck or the passenger cabin or even the bridge, their words would be confusingly mixed together and thus indecipherable. Max grew even more curious. Whatever could the Mayor want of the Solutioneer? That required such secrecy.

The Mayor took an envelope from his briefcase. It was a plain envelope, addressed in square capital letters to THE MAYOR. He put the letter on his knees and set the briefcase on the deck, between his feet. Max studied his potential employer.

The Mayor had a thick, graying brown mustache and lively brown eyes, with bags beneath them. Deep lines ran along his forehead and down from his nose to the sides of his mouth. He was a heavyset, well-fed man, and everything about him was self-assured as he turned to face Max, one hand holding the envelope firmly down so it wouldn't blow away. He was a serious man on serious business, and a worried man, too. He asked, "You've heard about the recent vandalism?"

Max nodded. "There have been fires as well."

The Mayor nodded. "I suspect—I strongly suspect—that something is going on. For one thing, it's always some small shop that gets broken into, or where a fire breaks out. Greengrocer, cobbler, newsagent . . ." He looked out over the water, recalling. "A bakery, a milliner, a fishmonger. Is that eight?"

"Six," said Max, who had been counting.

"There are two more." The Mayor thought. "A butcher and—there was one that surprised me, you'd think that would be the easiest to remember . . . Yes, it was a florist."

"What was surprising about the florist?"

"The shop was outside the gates, not in the old city. Granted, it's only four steps beyond the West Gate, but still . . . All the other victims are in the old city."

Max understood the significance of this, the difference between the rabbit warren of streets and lanes and alleys that was the old city and the wider avenues and boulevards of the New Town. "What do the police say?" he asked.

"That's the problem. The police don't have anything to say." The Mayor sighed and told Max, "They're suspicious, of course, but nobody will talk to them. Nobody has filed a complaint. Not one. The shopkeepers shrug, *bad luck,* they say, *faulty gas line, some dray horse must have thrown up stones.* This would be cobblestones from the streets. What hoof is ever going to throw cobblestones? Up from under flats filled with lettuces and peas and radishes—so they're all so tossed around and trampled that everything has to be thrown away? That's a whole day's earning lost. Lost by a man with five children to feed."

The Mayor waited, for Max to take in this information, to think about it.

After a minute, Max asked, "Where have the attacks—if they are attacks—taken place?"

"As I said, mostly in the old city, but they aren't limited to one street, or even to one district, any more than to one type of business. I have a list, names and addresses." He reached down for his briefcase but Max had a question.

"Are the shopkeepers all in one family, or joined in any way?"

"Not a one of them has anything in common with any other, except that each is in business alone and most of them have families."

Max considered all of this. The ferry's motor rumbled steadily as he thought, and the boat made its way through little waves up to the town dock at Summer. The Mayor waited patiently, as if he understood the value of thinking. Both of them ignored the business of landing—Carlo, the Captain's son, leaping onto a dock and making the vessel fast before unlatching the low gate to let passengers debark, off-loading whatever boxes or crates or animals the ferry was delivering, and then welcoming new passengers on board before untying the boat and leaping back aboard and fastening the gate behind him and calling up to his father, "She's set to go, Captain."

When on board, at work, Captain Francis and his son kept

things official. They might go home to the same little house in the evening, and eat supper together, and call one another Dad and My Boy, but once on board, they were Captain and crew and nothing more.

As *The Water Rat* chugged back out into deeper water, now moving around the base of the Promontory, from the top of which the summer palace overlooked the peaceful scene, Max broke his silence to ask the Mayor, "What about places that haven't been vandalized? Where there haven't been fires? Is there any pattern to those?"

His question apparently came as a surprise, but it didn't take long for the Mayor to realize, "None of the warehouses, no larger stores, not the theater—do you know the Starling Theater? It's empty, will be for weeks, I gather, maybe months, everybody knows. But nothing's happened there. You'd think, thieves? You'd think they'd at least take building supplies from that restaurant of Bendiff's. All the renovation he's doing. Although I hear he has dogs there, now. But they never went near it, even before the dogs, even with all that lumber and piping in piles, just asking to be stolen. You're right, Mister Max. It's curious. Why only small shops? What do you think?"

"Why are you so sure there's something going on?" Max asked now. He himself agreed. There had been too much vandalism and too many fires for it to be a coincidence. But he wondered why the Mayor seemed so certain.

The Mayor nodded, as if he had hoped for and expected this question. "When there had been—I can't remember, maybe four? or five? and not one complaint? I got curious. Worried, really. I called in one of our best young policemen and asked him to look into things, ask around, keep his ear to the ground. He knows the old city. He grew up in it, went to school there, lives there." The Mayor sat up a little straighter, to tell Max, "Just because his own home and his offices are in the New Town, that doesn't mean a mayor doesn't care about *all* of his citizens. Even the less important citizens—not that any one of us is more or less important than the other, you understand. I never think that."

Max smiled. The Mayor obviously thought of him as a voter.

"These are my people, these shopkeepers. Everyone is my people and it's my job to take care of my city. Also . . ." He hesitated, as if he didn't want to have to say it, but he made himself go on. "Not three days after I asked Officer Torson to look into things, I received this."

He held the envelope out to Max. Max took it, and removed the sheet of paper from it. The words had been cut out from the *Queensbridge Gazette* and pasted onto plain paper.

Mr. Mayor, You will do yourself and Queensbridge a favor if you forget about sending your policeman around asking questions. People don't want to hear those questions, in case you hadn't noticed. So call off your dog and you can tell him we know where he lives, we know his pretty wife and their three children. Things can get worse, Mr. Mayor.

Max looked up, across the sparkling water of the lake. They were approaching Graffon Landing, close enough now so that he could see the small waterfall that tumbled down the rocks into the center of the town, tossing tiny rainbows out into the air. The houses of Graffon Landing were painted in bright colors: whites and yellows, mossy greens and rusty reds. The houses gathered together, like friends around a campfire, between the steep cliffs and the blue lake, under a sky that shone with warm sunlight, and was home to a flock of soft little clouds.

It would have made a perfect watercolor sky for the month of June, for Max's imagined calendar of skyscapes, and for a moment Max was sorry he was on *The Water Rat* being the Solutioneer instead of being himself, a twelve-year-old boy who was learning from Joachim how to paint skies in watercolor.

The scene was lovely but the note he held in his hand was ugly, and he asked, "Has Officer Torson seen this?"

The Mayor shook his head. "How can I show it to him?"

This, Max was sure of, and he said it plain and clear, "You should." Saying it, he was Mister Max, the Solutioneer, who knew trouble's nasty face when it popped up in front of him. Even if he'd never before seen trouble like this.

The Mayor sighed again. "You're right. I'll tell him first thing tomorrow morning. Because if anything happened . . ." He couldn't finish that sentence. "*Will* you help? We'll pay anything you charge, there's no problem with paying you. *Can* you help us?"

"What do you want me to do?"

"Find out what's going on and who's behind it. Figure out a way to stop it." The Mayor had been ready for that question. He smiled a tired smile, removed another sheet of paper from his briefcase, and snapped it shut. Then he looked at Max, looked right into Max's eyes. "You're my last hope, Mister Max." He gave Max a list of the vandalized shops and their owners. "And we only have five weeks before the Royal Family arrives. I will *not* have my city in disarray, especially not while the King is here."

When he said that, he sounded quite fierce. "I don't want anybody in the entire royal party to even start to suspect. Think of the uproar." His eyes flashed as he imagined it. "Soldiers stationed all over the city. Or they'd pack up and leave and take all the coins they would have spent here away with them. We don't want that," the Mayor announced.

Max sat and thought. He didn't agree to take the job, and he didn't refuse it. He thought about it. Eventually, he asked, "Officer Torson couldn't find out anything?"

"Nothing. But he noticed that they got right to work rebuilding, repairing, mending, restocking their shops, as if—as if they knew it wouldn't happen again. He's a good policeman. Smart. Observant. I trust him."

So did Max. Grammie had taught Sven Torson in grade school and she thought well of him, but he didn't tell the Mayor that. Instead, he thought some more. "I don't know quite how I will go about finding anything out," he said.

"So you'll do it?" the Mayor asked. "You'll try? I'm a little

desperate," he added unnecessarily, and held out a purse. "Here's an advance of double what they said is your usual fee," he said.

Mister Max, the Solutioneer, costumed out as the Queen's chosen spy, a dangerous man who knew how to take care of himself in almost any situation, pocketed the purse. He smiled reassuringly. "I'll do my best."

The two shook hands, sealing the contract.

Captain Francis watched this from his position on the bridge, at the helm. He had known the Mayor was meeting with someone. Every now and then the Mayor had such private meetings on the foredeck of *The Water Rat.* Usually, Captain Francis knew the men with whom the Mayor wanted such private conversation, or who didn't want to be known to have an appointment with the Mayor. But this man he didn't know. Although he remembered seeing him once before, earlier in the spring, accompanying a lady up to Graffon Landing and then, later in the day and still in the same lady's company, making the return trip to Queensbridge. Captain Francis had already been curious about the man—artist? foreigner? confidence man? dancing master? He couldn't tell. Now he was even more curious. He looked down on the dark hat and dark-coated shoulders, and wondered. He couldn't remember the face. Possibly, he'd never really seen it.

When they docked at Queensbridge, Captain Francis called down to Carlo to make the boat fast and then make it ready for the afternoon passage around the lake. "I won't be long," he called, but said no more. "Put in a few extra stores. It's Sunday, there'll be the afternoon trippers. Can you manage?"

"Sure thing, Captain," Carlo called back. "I know what to do." Carlo didn't ask where his father might be going or what he might be doing. That wasn't their way. When parent and child lived so close together, and worked together as well, it was important that each should have his privacy. Carlo himself had slipped off alone several times recently, and Captain Francis had not questioned him about that. His son was a grown man, after all. Probably it had to do with a woman. Captain Francis hoped so. They had been living alone, the two of them, since the death of his wife, when Carlo was just a boy, just twelve years old. A woman would be a welcome addition to the family, and Carlo would confide in his father when he was ready, when there was something to confide. Captain Francis just wished he could be sure exactly what was going on, because Carlo had seemed low-spirited in the last two or three weeks, slow to laugh and quick to fall silent, maybe even anxious, which wasn't like him. Young men, Captain Francis knew, could get themselves into trouble, and they were often too proud, or kind, to ask their fathers for help.

For now, however, Captain Francis's attention was on the Mayor's mysterious companion, who had melted into the group of passengers crossing the ramp from the ferry down to the dock, well behind the Mayor, who had been the first off, in deference to his position in the city. The stranger crossed behind the large berthed vessels like someone who knew where he was going, but Captain Francis crossed behind him like someone just out to enjoy the warm midday sun.

In this way they wound their way through the streets of the old city, until the stranger turned into Thieves Alley and went through a gate and up the pathway to a small stone house. Captain Francis strolled on to the end of the street, a passerby, any wandering Sunday passerby. But he had read the sign that hung on the gate through which the man went: MISTER MAX, SOLUTIONEER.

Captain Francis returned to his boat, none the wiser, really, but knowing something he hadn't previously been aware of.

For his part, Max had no idea that he had been followed home. He was busy thinking about the problem the Mayor had asked him to work on, determining how to find out what he needed to know in order to solve it.

6

The Mayor's Job

• ACT I •

SCENE 2 ~ WHISPERS

Stewart McHenry, newsagent and stationer of Towpath Way, was a tidy and efficient man. Organization enabled him to support a large family with the income from a small business, without overburdening his wife or running into debt. His shop reflected his character: newspapers and magazines were set out in neat piles and no pile offered anything but the current issue; tissue paper and colored ribbons were kept on shelves against the rear wall; notebooks, pads, pencils, pens, and bottles of ink were displayed on one side wall; on the opposite side, where Stewart McHenry waited behind the counter to tally up his sales, the shelves were filled with brown paper and good twine, for wrapping parcels to be sent through the mail.

Behind the shop was the lean-to where spare stock was stored, as well as the outdated papers and magazines awaiting collection and pulping by printers. Nothing was neglected in Stewart McHenry's shop. Disorder was not tolerated. Even the shop's waste was kept carefully aside, in a galvanized tin trash bin set on the tiny gravel yard behind the storage shed.

In all of the old city, this shop was one of the least likely settings for a fire, which made it all the more surprising that early one morning Stewart McHenry had sent to the firehouse for help. The fire engine had arrived on the scene in time to restrict the damage to the storage shed's rear wall; the waste bin in the yard, where the blaze seemed to have originated; and the shed door, through which they had to hatchet their way. Within four days—four expensive and long working days—Stewart McHenry had repaired the damage, replaced the waste bin, and it was as if the fire had never happened.

On the other, slower, hand, it took almost two weeks for a building inspector from the city to come around. Not that Stewart minded the delay and not that the inspector's visit would make any difference, but a man would like his city government to be as well organized and energetic as he expected himself to be. Moreover, the inspector was a nondescript kind of man, neither young nor old, and his uniform was a little haphazard, as if the city had put it together out of leftover parts of other men's uniforms. Even his hat, which he wore so low on his forehead that it was hard to get a good look at him, seemed to have seen previous service, perhaps on the head of a conductor on one of the trains that ran daily from the New Town down to Porthaven.

But Stewart McHenry was relieved that this was the kind of man the city sent to examine his repairs and assess any permanent damage done by the fire. This was not the kind of man to ask the wrong questions and notice the wrong things. He didn't even have a clipboard with forms on it, just a little notebook he pulled out of his jacket pocket. He didn't even introduce himself, only said, "City Building and Works" as he held out his hand. "I've come to see what's been done."

The shopkeeper nodded and led the man through the shop without a word. He planned to say as little as possible.

Max, wearing the dogcatcher's uniform he had assembled for his first real job, followed. He'd given the trousers a good starch and press so that they would look like they belonged to a city official on the way up, and left behind the butterfly net the dogcatcher had carried. Wearing the wide-billed conductor's hat level on his head, his back held stiff, he was as wordless as the man he followed. He mimicked as best he could the important men who had appeared on the stage of the Starling Theater, rich Miser, wise Doctor, King, Banker, Caliph . . . the world of the theater was filled with such characters. Curious, Max thought, that the two most important actual men he'd met, Mr. Bendiff and the Mayor, were not so stiff and proud as those on the stage. But he didn't let himself wonder for long about that, because he had a job to do. Instead, he wondered just *why* this Stewart McHenry was being so silent. You'd think he'd have a lot to say about a fire that had been started on purpose right behind the storage shed where he stored his paper goods.

Unless he'd started it himself? But what business owner would destroy his own inventory?

In two steps they had crossed a small back office that had room for only a large desk tucked under a staircase, and exited out the rear door.

"What does that staircase lead to?" Max asked. He had his notebook open in his hand.

"I live upstairs," Stewart McHenry answered.

"Do you own the building?" Max asked.

"Rent."

The tiny graveled yard was fenced in on all sides. The storage shed leaned up against the rear of the building.

"Do you live alone?" Max asked.

"No" was all he was told.

Max stopped moving. The man turned to face him and he looked . . . What did he look? Angry? Afraid? As if he were defending himself against some enemy, Max decided. But how had Max—or, rather, the man from City Building and Works that he was playing in this scene—become an enemy?

They stood behind the shed, where unpainted boards marked the recent fire. Flames had eaten away most of the rear wall of the building, it seemed, and they had scorched some of the larger stones underfoot. Max stepped up close to the shed, studying it as if he understood what he was seeing. He made a few notes on his pad and turned the page over so that Stewart McHenry couldn't see that he had written only question marks. "I'll look inside now," he said.

There was no response, just a turning around and going up to a narrow door. The shopkeeper stepped back to allow Max entry into a narrow space.

The only light came through the open door, but it was enough to see by, if not enough to see clearly. Max took four steps and was at the rear wall, where new shelves had been built along the repaired section. Boxes and cartons were piled up on the floor, some empty, some unopened. The shelves were still only partly filled, with boxes of stationery paper and packets of shiny gift wrap. Once again, Max stepped close. He reached between two shelves to knock on the new wall. He pressed down on the shelves, testing their strength. He nodded, and made more question marks on his notebook, and turned another page.

Stewart McHenry said nothing. He lingered in the yard just beyond the door, waiting for the inspector to finish doing his job and go away.

Max stood in the dim light, thinking.

At last, the shopkeeper could keep silent no longer. "You're not going to find any fault with my repair work," he announced.

Max made a final note (two exclamation points) and folded his notebook closed. He stepped back out onto the gravel and considered the high fence, the narrow gate with a bright new wooden bolt across it. He said, "Everything looks good."

Stewart McHenry led Max back through the shop to see him gone.

"Funny that a fire started out there," Max remarked to the man's back. "You're obviously a very careful man."

Silence.

Max waited for a good while before he asked, "How'd you happen to catch it before it did much damage?"

They were at the street door by then, and the shopkeeper held it open so Max could make his exit. But this was a question he could look the City Building and Works inspector in the eye to answer. "I get up at half after four, every morning, when the papers are delivered. So I saw the smoke." When he looked right at the man for two or three long seconds, he noticed the odd eyes; but what was so strange about them?

"You were lucky," Max said.

Stewart McHenry looked over the inspector's shoulder, maybe at someone across the lane, maybe at nothing, and nodded without a word.

"Well, thank you," Max said. "For your time."

He was not surprised that there was no response. Stewart McHenry seemed to be a man of very few words, and none of them mere unnecessary pleasantries.

Max walked away from the newsagent's shop with the unhurried gait of a man going about his daily business, one task accomplished, moving on to the next on his list. He did in fact have a list, now down to seven names and addresses, but he couldn't feel that he had accomplished much. In fact, he felt uneasy, as if he had failed to see something that was right in front of him.

When Max felt uneasy, and if he had the time, he painted. Painting both soothed his spirit and loosened up his brain—setting out his easel, fixing the block of watercolor paper onto it, dipping his brush into the glass of water and then into a pot of sky color, setting to work. At lessons with Joachim he always felt alert and relaxed, ready. Joachim was a professional, a real artist, and Max was curious, so he had once asked his teacher, "Do you feel like that?"

"Sometimes," Joachim had answered, without taking his eyes off the canvas he was working on. "Good times," he added, still without looking up. "Not often enough," he concluded gloomily.

Joachim was never one to look on the bright side, look for the silver lining, wear rose-colored glasses, Max knew. The painter *had* cheered up with his new spectacles and his new dog, but these hadn't changed his essential nature. You could count on Joachim to look on the dark side and tell you what he saw, without sugaring anything over.

Max didn't know *what* his teacher would have to say about this interview with the newsagent. He didn't know, really, what he had to say about it himself, not yet. So instead of going straight on to the next name on his list, Flora Bunda the fishmonger, he went home to paint for an hour and let the back of his mind work on the problem of what there was to learn from the silence of Stewart McHenry.

That day, a blue sky was veiled by pale white clouds, so filmy and so still that it was almost like trying to look through a steam-fogged window. Max worked for almost an hour to try to reproduce the way a darker color shone behind the lighter one, but he couldn't do it. However, as he washed his brushes clean and set three disappointing attempts on the dining room table to dry so that he could study them and perhaps learn something from his failures, he *did* understand something about the vandalism/arson problem: He understood that he couldn't begin to even guess what was going on without more information. He needed to know more. So he took off the painter's shirt and red beret and got back into the City Building and Works costume, and rode on his bicycle down toward the docks.

Flora Bunda, fishmonger, did business just a block behind the long docks where the fishing boats came in to offer the day's catch to fishmongers and restaurants, as well as to the men and women who prepared meals in the homes of the wealthy. Hers was a very small shop, so small that she set two long ice-filled wagons out on the street in front of it, where she displayed the silvery fish and long black eels she had on offer. From just after dawn until midafternoon, her rangy, muscular figure could be seen either standing in the doorway awaiting custom or inside, bent over the sink and the long butcher-block table that took up almost all of the interior space. Flora Bunda could gut a fish and scale it and even bone it—after weighing it, of course—in ten seconds flat.

If there was anybody nearby, you could count on it that Flora Bunda would be talking. Her talk was like the final frantic flapping of a fish on a line, fast and furious and usually pointless. However, unlike a caught fish, Flora Bunda did not eventually fall still.

"Living alone like I do, what do you expect? Do you expect me to not want to talk when I'm out in the world?" she asked anyone who happened to suggest that perhaps she might like, just sometimes, to listen. "I'm an orphan child and no longer young and have no brother nor sister, not a one, and the only thing I know in this world is what my own mother taught me, how to know fish." Here, if she were talking to a customer, she might hold up one or two silvery choices. "Oh, and how to keep fish fresh, and where the narrow bones lie in their bodies, and how to hone a blade. And did you know I sharpen my own knives? None of your itinerant grinders for Flora Bunda: I can produce a blade so sharp all the butchers in the city would envy me, if they knew about it. But what do butchers know? Wanting people to eat meat," and she pronounced the word as if it were almost too heavy for her tongue to carry, "rather than sweet light fresh fish." And so on.

When the man approached in his uniform and long-billed hat, Flora Bunda welcomed this new pair of ears. Seeing her in her doorway, he held out a hand and she wiped her own right hand on the long white apron she wore and reached out. "City Buil—" was as far as he got.

"And you look to me like a young man who knows the

good taste of a fish stew," Flora Bunda told him, with a flirtatious smile that did not suit her stern features and the dark hair she kept severely contained within a white kerchief. "Fish is brain food, everybody knows, and anyone can see you're a young man with a brain. Although"—and she looked carefully into Max's face for a long minute—"I'm not sure about those eyes. They're like the skin on a monkfish, you've got monkfish eyes, young man, and now I notice them I don't find them at all pleasant. So what can I get you today?" she asked. "Not that I've seen many monkfish, not here upriver, but they have them in most of the seaport markets. Tasty they are, but you haven't said what you want."

"City Building and Works," Max managed to get out.

She nodded. "Are you married? You don't have the look, but you're too young for me and besides, I have my eye on someone suitable. Perfectly suited to me. A certain ferryboat captain who shall remain nameless. A man shouldn't stay a widower for too long, do you think? It's not healthy, and there's no need, when you have a grown son who'd probably like to marry someone himself but doesn't want to leave you all alone in an empty house. No need at all, when there's someone perfectly suited, with her own business, so she wouldn't be a drain on your purse."

"About your tables," Max said.

"My wagons, yes. They're wagons. Well, they're old, I can tell you that. They were built by my father when he just started out and my mother kept them after he died. Young, he died young, before he even knew me. Not as a person, I mean, a child was all he knew and what child can remember anything from so young an age? My mother kept the business going and—anyone can see—display wagons are needed with a shop this small. But wood rots, everybody knows, it's not stone, is it?" And here she smiled, with a sidelong glance at Max, who had crouched down as if inspecting the workmanship of the wagons, the fit of the spokes into the wooden wheels, the joints holding the corners together. All of the wood was bright and new except—he peered up underneath—the wide boards that formed the bed. Those were weathered gray, and stained by years of melting ice. Max rose to his feet and took out his notebook.

"Did you have trouble finding someone to replace the wooden wheels? After the vandalism," he said, scratching a row of question marks on a fresh page and then snapping the notebook shut.

"Vandalism? Is that what they call it in your fancy offices in the New Town? They're fine now, as you see. Nothing for me to worry about. It won't happen again."

"Who—?" Max tried to ask.

"You can't be in business without meeting a few people," Flora Bunda told him confidingly. "Carpenters, wheelwrights, everybody likes to eat fish, and a fish stew will feed a whole family without emptying anyone's purse. I don't think people appreciate fish enough, do you? What about you, do you prefer beef? Lamb? Pigs and chickens aren't even in the contest, if you ask me. You can't think highly of a chicken, nobody could, and pigs—well, pigs are pigs. I have a bit of nice fresh eel here, netted this morning in the river, if you like eel. Do you like eel?"

Maybe, Max thought, it was time for a direct question. She didn't seem to take time to think before she spoke. "Any idea who—?"

"Of course," she said. "It was Jacob, Jacob Fitz."

Max opened his notebook and wrote down the name, *Jacob Fitz.*

"He lives just inside the Royal Gate, it's a boardinghouse, he's never had his own house or even his own room, and you'd think he'd *want* a wife, wouldn't you?"

Max said nothing, just waited, notebook opened, pencil poised.

"He's been fishing the river all of his life, never wanted to go to sea, doesn't trust the lake, says it's too wide, too deep. He's the one I get all my eels from and they are always fresh, I can promise you that. All of my fish are always fresh," she announced triumphantly.

Flora Bunda was Max's height and she looked directly into his face when she said that, as if he had accused her of trying to sell him a fish that had turned bad.

Max closed his notebook and did not sigh, although he felt like it after all of that listening. "Yes, ma'am," he answered, as crisply as the young recruit in *A Soldier's Sweetheart.* He only just stopped himself from saluting her, before he turned on his heels and walked away. The docks were well behind him and he had entered Thieves Alley before it struck him: all of those words and absolutely no information.

7

The Mayor's Job

• ACT I •

SCENE 3 ~ HINTS

For dessert, Grammie had made a strawberry-rhubarb brown betty, and she had a creamy custard sauce ready to be poured over the succulent-tart-sugary treat. "Max knows how I find excuses to make custard sauce, and there's all this rhubarb in the garden," she said, in answer to their compliments about her cooking skills, "and I had the time." But she wasn't complaining about that. In fact, she looked entirely content and even pleased with herself, maybe even smug, which was a happy change from her recent mood, which in turn was something of a puzzle.

At that moment, however, Max had his own puzzling story to tell, and he hoped that by telling it, he could figure out what to do next. While they enjoyed the brown betty, he described the two interviews.

"They believed you were a city official?" Grammie asked.

"Yes," Max answered.

"Why did you start with those two?" Ari wondered.

"They were first on the list," Max explained. "They happened first." He took a bite and waited to hear what they thought. He had never before asked for advice in his solutioneering, and wasn't sure he'd done it the right way. Also, he wasn't sure he really wanted any help, because hadn't he done just fine so far on his own? On the other hand, serious damage had been done and also, as the Mayor said, it wasn't long before the royal family would arrive in Queensbridge. This job was more urgent than any other he'd had. There wasn't a lot of time to stand in front of an easel, painting the sky and waiting for a brainstorm to float by as naturally and easily as a cloud in the sky.

Max, too, had a weakness for custard sauce, especially custard sauce over a tart-and-sweet fruit dessert, and he was concentrating so hard on the flavors in his mouth that Grammie had to say his name twice. "Well, Max," she began, then sharply, "Max?"

He looked up.

"I'm glad to see you like the dessert, but isn't Pia your official assistant? Why not send her to one of the places? See what she can find out."

Ari agreed. "It could be that someone official makes

people nervous. You know, the way when you see a policeman, even if you know you haven't done anything wrong, you still feel guilty?"

"*I* don't," Grammie said.

"You're not like most people," Ari laughed. He turned to Max. "Pia could do it and she's about the opposite of a city official. She's just a girl, and a schoolgirl at that."

Max considered the idea, which wasn't a bad one except that Pia was already pushing her way into his solutioneering business and he didn't want to encourage her to push any harder. "Why couldn't I be a school*boy*?"

Grammie was quick to point out the risk of that. "Not if you want people to keep thinking you're off with your parents."

"I'll ask Pia," Max grumbled, because of course Grammie was right. "She's going to want to wear Adorable Arabella's dress," he predicted gloomily.

This prediction proved accurate, which gave Max no satisfaction. Being right meant he had another quarrel with Pia. "If I look like a grand lady, maybe even a countess, won't they pay more attention to me?" she asked.

"It's not attention I'm after. It's information," Max said. They had met, as usual, at Gabrielle's ice cream shop. On this warm June afternoon they were enjoying bowls of ice cream. Pia had three scoops of different flavors, strawberry, pistachio, and lemon; Max had three scoops of chocolate, covered with rich chocolate sauce. There was plenty of time for quarreling as they ate.

Pia reminded him, "I was perfect as a lady when we scared off Madame Olenka." She had loved the dress, its purple panels, the importance of its lace. Also, she had enjoyed playing the role of a woman of mystery.

"This is entirely different," Max told her.

"How different can it be?" she objected.

"What's wrong with you today?" he demanded. Then he asked, "Is something wrong?"

She shook her head and her pale pigtails slapped gently against her cheeks. She glared down at her ice cream. "Not one thing is wrong," she muttered.

Max couldn't help it. He laughed. "I can tell."

Pia glared at him, her blue eyes as fierce as her father's. Then she grinned and admitted, "I *liked* being Adorable Arabella."

"This time I need you to be yourself. Or, almost yourself," he specified. "Remember the first time we were in here and you talked with Gabrielle and she told you things about herself? Things she hadn't told me although I met her before you."

Pia took a satisfied spoonful of pistachio. She remembered.

"I'm hoping these people will talk to you like she did. Just you, just a girl, nobody at all worrisome or dangerous, just normal and not a bit important. I know," he said quickly, "you are important, everybody is, even children, but you know what I mean."

"I don't care about being important," she pointed out, but not crossly.

"These are the two shops I want you to visit. They're both in the old city. I don't know if your father's car . . ."

Pia agreed. "It's too fancy, too noticeable. I'll take my bike. I'll wear a summer dress, a cotton print, and sandals. But, Max? What would a girl be doing in these places?" She looked at the slip of paper he'd given her. "Why these two?"

"There was a fire at the bakery—"

"Bakery ovens are hot. And they're probably kept hot almost all night and day," Pia pointed out. "A fire would always be possible, wouldn't it?"

"It could be there's nothing in it. That's what I'm trying to find out," Max repeated patiently. "There's been a lot of this kind of trouble recently, a rash of fires, and vandalism."

Pia nodded. She read the newspapers.

"All in the old city, or once, right beyond a gate. Every single one involving a small shop. And," he concluded with the strongest argument, "there hasn't been one complaint made to the police."

"It's suspicious," Pia agreed. "My father has dogs on the restaurant site although nothing's ever happened there."

"That's suspicious, too, isn't it?" Pia opened her mouth to object, but Max continued. "Think about it. A big, empty building? People who break into places just to do damage? Arsonists who like to start fires? That would have been a perfect place for them, don't you think? All those piles of wood, and pipes, and window glass?"

"You're right," Pia said. "That is pretty curious." Her tone of voice told Max his assistant was now entirely on the job. "I see," she said, and then, "But how am I going to get them to talk to me? And exactly what do I ask?"

"I don't know. Mostly I want to find out if they're hiding something, some information. If they're keeping something back. If so, then"—Max stopped himself from saying *my* but he wasn't about to say *our*—"the next step is to find out what it is."

"It's *very* suspicious," Pia announced with satisfaction. She scraped at the edge of her bowl, to get the last of the ice cream. She licked at the back of her spoon, thoughtfully, and looked to the rear of the shop, where Gabrielle was filling a big glass platter with fruit tarts. She said, "I suppose a girl might have a mother who was particularly fond of pastries and she could be looking for something new to surprise her mother with, couldn't she? For a birthday treat, maybe."

Max's imagination kept pace with Pia's. "And she would have heard about all the troubles in the old city . . ."

"And she'd be curious . . ."

"And she would ask the baker about . . ."

"Exactly," Pia said. "But what would a girl, a schoolgirl I mean, be doing in a millinery shop?"

"Milliners sell hats, don't they?" Max asked.

Pia stared at him. "Do you see me wearing a hat? Did you ever?"

She was making Max cross again. "This is *serious,* Pia."

"A milliner makes fancy ladies' hats. My mother always

goes to R Zilla for her hats, because she likes having something different from everyone else. R Zilla makes only one of each of her designs. They're very expensive. Even my father notices the R Zilla bills. I don't like most of my mother's hats," Pia admitted, "but a couple look good on her. And all of them get noticed."

"Couldn't you be looking for a birthday present there, too?" Max suggested. "You could be a girl trying to find something special for her mother, couldn't you?"

"I could." Pia was doubtful. "But should I be the same thing twice in a row?"

"And"—Max did not let himself be distracted—"if you were someone whose mother might buy a lot of hats if she liked the one you found for her, then the shopkeeper would be happy to talk with you."

"That might work," Pia decided. "I can see how to do that. I think I'll wear my blue dress with flowers and just a band of lace on the collar, and a hair band. With my hair loose I look more like that kind of girl," she explained. "That would be the right way to look, don't you think? And I should be—not shy, just . . . modest. A well-brought-up girl, don't you think? You remember that blue dress, don't you?"

Of course Max didn't, but he wasn't foolish enough to tell Pia. "That sounds like just the right costume. I want you to write everything down after you leave each shop so nothing gets forgotten," he told her.

"You don't have to act like I don't know anything." Pia was impatient at his lack of faith in her intelligence, impatient about the way he kept ignoring her cleverness in dealing with Madame Olenka, impatient to be gone and begin her assignment.

"So we'll meet again tomorrow?" Max asked.

The spoon clicked sharply against the bowl as Pia set it down. "I'll let you know." She rose from the table. "I'll send a note," she announced, and before he could ask when, added, "Or I'll come by on my bike. I'll do it as soon as I can do it well," she said, as if he had been nagging at her for hours and days. "I *said* I'd do it, didn't I?"

Max shrugged. It wasn't as if he really was her boss. Pia was an unpaid, part-time assistant who was doing him a favor by helping him out. However, he wanted to be very sure she understood the assignment. "I need to find out if—"

"I told you, I *know.*" Pia huffed and puffed and left, snapping the shop door shut behind her.

Gabrielle came from behind the counter to collect their bowls. Her smile was friendly, and amused. "Pia looked happy."

"She could have fooled *me,*" Max said.

"Not Mister Max, she couldn't," Gabrielle answered.

Max had to laugh. She was right. "Where's Ari today?"

"Right now, he's in class but he'll be here later."

Max waited, but the young woman said no more, so, "I guess he's being a help around here," he hinted.

"A big help," Gabrielle agreed. "But I don't think he'll want to come with me when I switch to Mr. Bendiff's restaurant, do you? I don't blame him, either. How many dishes and pots can you expect the next Baron Barthold to clean?" There was no complaint in her voice and neither was it, really, a question.

Max treated it like a real question anyway. "For you? I guess, as many as you ask, as many as you need."

Gabrielle didn't say anything to that but as she turned away, Max saw that her cheeks were pink and a smile pulled at the corners of her mouth. She looked almost pretty then, like a little round brown mouse who had been given a big chunk of doughnut. She turned around briefly to tell Max, "Before anything else, Ari has his studies to finish. He's a good student, I think."

"He's a good tutor, I know," Max agreed, and her smile broadened.

Max intended to report this to Ari at supper that evening, but just when he was about to, and anticipating how happy this would make his tenant-tutor-friend, Grammie looked at him over a platter of roasted lake fish and roasted potatoes to ask, "Have you had any response to that letter you wrote? To your father."

Max had been trying not to remember about the letter. "Maybe he hasn't gotten it yet. If he's even going to get it."

"You wrote to him?" Ari asked. "But I thought . . . I thought you didn't want anybody—anybody at all, here *or* there—to know anything about you."

"I pretended to be a schoolgirl."

"Named Maxine?"

"Named Aurora Nives," Max said. "I used Grammie's name. And address. So," he told Grammie, "you'll know before me if he does answer."

"I hope it'll be soon," she said, almost as if she was warning him. But what would Grammie have to warn him about that she wouldn't just say outright?

At his painting lesson the next morning, Max painted a cloudless sky where four different shades of blue faded one into the other. He worked fast, concentrating on his picture. He was only half aware of Joachim, at an easel across the garden.

Joachim was working in the new style he had discovered when the dog, Sunny, in friendly excitement, had brushed her long golden retriever tail over the wet paint of a picture done in the old style. First, Joachim painted the branch of a flowering quince bush, as precisely as he could—and that was very precisely. Then he took a gray seagull feather to—tenderly, softly, gently—sweep up and down on the wet paint, which made the picture look misty, windblown, a little faded. That done, the painter stepped back from his easel to study the effect. "I don't know," he said, and took off his glasses. "I don't think," he said, and put them on again, remarking, "I'd do better to stick to the tried-and-true."

Max, his red painter's beret on his head and one of his father's old shirts hanging loosely down from his shoulders, did not look up from his own picture. Joachim talked like this whenever he came to the end of a painting.

"Max? What does this look like to you?"

Max put the three finishing streaks of the densest blue at the bottom of his paper before he put down his own brush, to see what Joachim had done. He looked at the painting, which the sweeps of the seagull feather had blurred so that neither flowers nor leaves had clear edges. He looked at it and looked at it and eventually decided, "It's as if I'm crying . . . as if . . . It looks like quince blossoms seen through tears."

"That's all right, then," Joachim said, and he signed the painting in small, dark letters, at the bottom right corner, ***joachim***, then took it inside to dry.

When his teacher came back out to the garden, Max had a question. "Can I ask a favor?"

Joachim answered without hesitation, "I'd rather you didn't," and Sunny trotted over to put her muzzle under his hand, as if to comfort him or maybe to stand beside him in this time of trouble.

"You can always say no," Max reminded him. Although he couldn't see why anyone would refuse a request as simple as the one he was about to make, and especially Joachim, when it was Max who was responsible for not only the company of the dog but also, indirectly, the new painting techniques the dog had shown Joachim, *and* the new glasses through which to see it.

"I guess that's true," Joachim admitted. "All right, what favor is it? I'm pretty busy these days."

"It won't take long, only—"

"With this dog you've foisted off on me."

Max didn't argue that point. Joachim was just grumbling,

and they both knew it. "It'll only take an hour, probably less. I want you to go to the flower stand just outside the West Gate—"

"Can't you buy your own flowers?"

"Of course, but—"

"Who are you buying flowers for anyway? Is it your grandmother's birthday?"

"No, nothing like that."

"Then why ever would you send me to a flower stall?"

"To talk with the owner, about vandalism. Her stand was smashed up, a couple of weeks ago, and—"

"Then it's probably closed down. *I* would, after something like that. Why are you interested in vandalism? And why ask *me*? Why not go yourself?"

"Because you paint flowers so you can talk naturally with her, and ask about what happened, while you're looking at her flowers. She probably even knows who you are."

"That would make it worse," Joachim said. He was silent for two long minutes, scratching Sunny behind her ears and studying the watercolor. Then he'd made up his mind. "I'm not going to do it, Max." He gave his student a sharp look. "Unless you can give me some urgent reason to."

But Max didn't think he was supposed to tell anyone what he had been hired to do, and he'd already told Grammie and Ari. Besides, Joachim didn't know that he was Mister Max, Solutioneer. He decided not to say. Joachim's refusal was an inconvenience, not a roadblock, and, in fact, he wasn't surprised by it. Not really. "It was just an idea," he said.

"I wouldn't put it past you to try to fix me up with some flower-shop-owning woman," Joachim grumbled. "Like you fixed me up with Sunny here."

"I never even thought of that," Max said. "Would you like to be fixed up?" He wondered how old Annarinka Friedle was and what kind of a personality she had. She already knew a lot about flowers, which would be a big plus with Joachim. But that was another idea for another day, sometime when the Solutioneer had no other problems to solve. For right now, Max needed to figure out who else he could ask to investigate the vandalism at the flower stall and find out what, if anything, the florist had to say about it.

Also, he hoped that Pia might have a report to make about the baker and the milliner, and he hoped, further, that she might have found out something useful. Pia might not get along well with people her own age—and Max could understand why that was—but she was the kind of young person older people enjoyed talking to. Adults would often tell things to young people like that, explain things. Max was a little bit like that but Pia was a lot.

However, when Pia summoned him to their usual meeting place the next afternoon, he found that she hadn't learned anything about the arson/vandalism. She told Max at length about her investigations, and in detail, but they both realized that she had been given no useful information. Karl Vantassel, the baker, was a short, wiry man, with a short, wiry wife who worked in the kitchen beside him, while two of their three wiry children served the customers and made change and the third washed the pots and baking pans and trays, then set them out to be used again. Nobody, not a one of them, had looked Pia in the eye. She had chosen, and tasted, breads and sweet rolls and coffee cakes. "I told them I was an assistant manager at the Hotel Iris, and that we were thinking of serving breakfast to our clients. I was looking for a good, reliable bakery to supply us with breakfast baked goods, I told them, so they didn't make me pay for anything," she announced proudly. "None of them spoke to me except for the father, and mostly he told me how good his products were and how bad everybody else's were."

Max interrupted with a question. "Including Gabrielle's?"

"Especially hers," Pia laughed, and took another bite of the tall slab of angel food cake on her plate. "I didn't contradict him. I was all business, all serious. I tasted and nodded and made notes. Then I asked him—and you have to say this was brilliant—if he could guarantee daily deliveries. *What do you mean by that question?* he asked, and he was suspicious, but I just told him I'd heard about some trouble in the old city and hadn't he had some trouble himself? A fire, a chimney fire? If that happened once, if his chimneys were old, I said to him, wasn't there danger that it could happen again? How long had he had to close down, after the fire? I asked. *I only missed two days,* that's what he said to me, and then, *It won't happen again.*"

"And the rest of the family didn't say anything? Not even to one another?"

"Not a word. They kept their eyes glued on Mr. Vantassel.

Even the children just waited to hear whatever he'd say. So I told him I'd let him know and thanked him for his time and left. He never even suspected that I wasn't an assistant manager," she reported proudly, and finished the last bite of cake before she announced, "Nobody bakes even half as well as Gabrielle. Certainly not Karl Vantassel."

"What about the milliner?" Max asked. "Tess Tardo, what did you find out there?"

"I found out she didn't mind me trying on a lot of hats, so she's patient; and I found out she's honest, when she said none of them flattered me at all."

Max sighed, loudly enough so Pia had to notice it. She smiled happily.

"*And* I found out it only took her half a day to get all the pieces of glass out of the hats in her window, and that the stones had dented but didn't really ruin any. She just had to shake them clean and then push them back into shape. She did have to take a little off the prices, she said."

"Did she tell you anything useful?" Max asked.

"Well, the attack took place during the lunch hour, but nobody saw who did it. She has no enemies, she says. She's only been open a few weeks. She used to work for R Zilla—remember? I told you about her. There was some kind of disagreement, I think. She's young."

"R Zilla?"

"No, Tess Tardo. R Zilla is old, she says, and stuck in her ways, and Tess Tardo says she can't imagine getting so proud and set in her ways that she'd charge that much for a hat.

Or so greedy. Do you think it's greedy to want to make as much profit as you can? Tess Tardo wants to make hats lots of people can afford. She sews little silk flowers to go on them and they are really nice. Not so noticeable as R Zilla's but do you think everyone wants to be noticed all the time? I don't. Except my mother and her so-called friends with their hats. I don't know why everybody wants to wear hats, anyway."

Max stuck to the point. "Did she say anything more about the vandalism? Did she have any idea why it happened?"

Pia shook her head. "And that *is* curious. I mean, here she is telling me all about how hard she has to work starting up the business, working alone, so she is the only one to do all the buying and designing and sewing and selling, too, but she didn't complain about somebody ruining three of her hats *or* costing her a half day's work. She told me personal things, about her mother's illness and how her aunt and mother never got along and how she'd like to find the right man to marry, and then how much she hoped I'd bring my mother into the shop just to see how good her work is, maybe tell some friends. But there was nothing about the vandalism, except to brush it aside as if it didn't matter. She says I have beautiful hair and she knows just the style of hat that would suit me. Nobody ever told me I had beautiful hair. Do you think I do?"

What Max thought was that Pia hadn't reported anything of use. "What do *you* think?" he asked.

"I think my hair is all right," she said, and at the expression on his face she broke out laughing. "All right, I know, you have no opinion about my hair. I know what you want to know and I can't help. Nobody was complaining, nobody seemed worried, there were no hints or winks or whispers . . . There wasn't anything anybody wanted me to learn."

Max nodded as if he entirely agreed, but—as so often happened when Pia chattered on—she had given him an idea. He felt its first faint stirrings, just a little breeze ruffling the hair at the back of his head, just one delicate wave licking at the lakeshore, just the hint of mint in a green salad. He sat motionless and speechless, so as not to dislodge it.

"What do you want me to do now?" Pia asked.

When he didn't answer, she went up to the counter to talk with Gabrielle and Ari, leaving Max alone at his table, wrapped up in his private silence.

8

In which we have an intermission

At dinner that night, Max asked Ari if he would be willing to go to a couple of the shops, the greengrocery, which had suffered vandalism involving smashed fruits and vegetables, and Boots Wallack's cobbler shop, where a fire had been set on the stoop of the entry, but succeeded only in scorching the door before it was put out by Boots and his wife, with the neighbors helping to form a bucket brigade. By the time the fire engine arrived on the scene, there was nothing for them to do except make a final check.

"Why set a fire there, where it would be sure to be detected, even at night, almost right away? Where's the fun for an arsonist in that?" Ari wondered.

"I don't want to even *try* to think like an arsonist," Grammie remarked without looking up from her bowl of vegetable soup.

"Do you think you could go as a reporter?" Max asked.

"Why not as a student?" Ari suggested. "I'm not much of an actor."

"A reporter has a reason to be asking questions," Max explained.

"How does a reporter act?" Ari asked.

Max thought about *The Lepidopterist's Revenge,* in which he had played a reporter sent to interview the Absentminded Professor about a time travel machine he claimed to have sent the missing lepidopterist off in, into another century. A reporter had no uniform, no identifying badge. All a reporter did was announce that he was a reporter and take out his notebook, ready to write down whatever anybody said. People liked appearing in newspapers. It was almost as good as being really famous. He asked, "Do you have a notebook you can use? If not, I do."

"But I don't *look* like a reporter. Do you think I look like a reporter, Mrs. Nives?" Ari asked, wanting to invite Grammie into their talk.

"What do I know about anything?" she answered, without looking up from the slab of bread she was spreading with butter.

Ari raised his eyebrows at Max, but Max shook his head. He had no idea.

"Could you try?" Max asked. "It is important for the city,"

he added, because as the next Baron Barthold, Ari had a more than usual interest in the city's welfare.

"The all-important city," Grammie muttered.

Ari and Max exchanged another puzzled look. Ari shrugged. "I guess I can try."

"Thank you," Max said. He'd thought he might ask Grammie to go to the flower shop and try to find out what Annarinka Friedle thought, but this was clearly a bad time to ask Grammie anything. Besides, he thought his grandmother might be— What if she was insulted? He was asking her to help, not as an experienced professional librarian but as a little old lady, a nobody special, an ordinary grandmother with nothing better to do with her free time than oblige grandchildren.

"It'll probably take me a couple of days," Ari told him.

"That's all right," Max said. In the meantime, he might think of something himself, some way to investigate his suspicion. He hadn't been able to think of anything yet, but that didn't mean that he wouldn't, any minute now, have an idea. Ideas, he knew from experience, arrived in their own good time, dressed exactly the way they wanted to be and saying only as much as they felt like.

"It has to be all right, doesn't it?" Grammie asked. "Since he's doing you a favor," she added unpleasantly. The look Max and Ari exchanged at this made her laugh, a humphing, sarcastic sound. "Don't pay any attention to me. I'll go up to bed now, I think." And she rose abruptly from the table, leaving them to do the dishes and the worrying.

Since the next evening was one of the nights Ari took Gabrielle to dinner with his great-aunt at the castle, Max and Grammie were on their own. That day, Grammie had gone from being uncharacteristically impatient and grumpy to being uncharacteristically silent and opinionless. As they sat on her back steps with the day's paper and the day's mail, Max tried to figure out a way to persuade her to tell him what was bothering her.

Because he was pretty sure there was something she wasn't telling him.

Their shared concern about his parents loomed over every day, like the mountains at the northern end of the lake, always waiting in the distance, varying with any day's weather but never going away. But this was more. Maybe, Max thought, Grammie was wondering about a response to the letter he'd written to the King of Andesia. Maybe *that* was what was disturbing her. It disturbed *him,* the waiting, the not knowing even if a response would arrive.

He held his own mail in his hand and waited until Grammie was turning the newspaper page to ask casually, "How long do you think it'll take to hear back?"

Grammie didn't even ask what he was talking about. She knew. "How long has it been now? You wrote just after that girl disappeared, didn't you?"

"What girl?"

"The Captain's daughter. From the *Miss Koala,* that . . ."

She couldn't find a word bad enough to describe him. "Skunk," she finally decided.

Max worked it out. "It was then, yes. So it probably has to be at least another week before I *could* hear from him."

"What if you never do?" Grammie asked.

Max had thought of that. "I don't know," he said. "I'm going to wait and see. And hope."

"Summer won't last forever. It'll be August before you know it and you'll have to think what you're going to do about school."

Max had his own ideas for school, but he didn't plan to share them with his grandmother. He could guess what she would think of them.

"It takes up a lot of my time, tutoring you. I might not always be able to help you out like this."

"I *am* grateful to you," Max said. "Haven't I said that? I really am and you're a good teacher, too."

"That's not what I was talking about. And don't go thinking I don't want to do it. It's just— Never mind," Grammie said, and turned another newspaper page.

Max looked at her profile. Her mouth was a straight line and the eyes behind her glasses were the distant blue of a pale December morning with snow on the way, not the lively warm April shade he was used to. He asked her, in the kindly, wise, sympathetic voice of the priest who sheltered an unknown wanderer in *The Stranger from Across the Sea,* "Grammie? Is something troubling you?"

"Whatever could be troubling me?" Grammie asked, with uncharacteristic sarcasm. "It couldn't be my daughter, who first disappears and then shows up in a newspaper photograph as the Queen of some tiny South American country, run by some crazed General, where revolution could break out any day. Why should I worry? Or there's my job, which I've been doing for so many years maybe I *am* getting old, but isn't experience an asset in this job? And oh yes, I've got a grandson who insists that he's old enough to live alone and has gone to work as a detective—whatever you call yourself, Max, that's what you are, and I'm no fool, I know it's dangerous. This project of the Mayor's worries me. And I worry whether you'll keep on with your schooling and go to university as your parents hoped. And that's without even mentioning the worry about supporting the two of us, or about being responsible—at my age—for an adolescent boy. What is there in that to trouble anybody? I should be as happy as a zucchini in a garden; I should just relax and lie around in the sunlight, getting greener and fatter. Until somebody picks me and eats me," she concluded sharply.

Like the old priest, Max nodded and murmured sympathetic humming noises as she spoke. When Grammie came to the end of her tirade, he murmured on for several seconds, "I see, yes; yes, I see," before he told her, "I can at least reassure you about me. I've already had lots of jobs and look"—he held up the two unopened envelopes, both addressed to MISTER MAX, SOLUTIONEER, 5 THIEVES ALLEY—"there are more coming in. I'm not worried about supporting myself. And you, too," he told her.

This was truer than Grammie could know, because there were the coins his father had secreted away in the frame of the poster for *The Adorable Arabella* that was hanging so innocently in Max's dining room, not a hundred yards away. But that was his own secret. "You don't have to worry about me."

"Yes, well, maybe it's not *you* I'm worried about," Grammie muttered, not looking up at him.

Max looked away, over the garden to his own little house and up over his rooftop to the cloud-choked sky. He admitted, "I try not to think too hard about them."

He felt Grammie's quick glance, as if he had just uttered a non sequitur.

Max made himself go on. "I mean, given how—bad—cruel—greedy—how nasty some of the people in the world can be." And then, it was as if once he had started giving voice to his fears, he didn't want to stop. "How cowardly, how selfish—like that Captain Trevelyn—how untrustworthy. He would have let all those people on the ship just drown, just—*die.* Even if that didn't happen, it could have. And his daughter—what can she do? She has to be his daughter and he— It could have been terrible what happened to all of those people in that storm, I know, and could be happening to her, wherever she is. Anything could be happening to anyone right now."

This was, of course, the thing he didn't want to remember, and worry about.

"Oh," Grammie said. She reached out to put a hand on his shoulder. "Oh, Max, I'm sorry. I didn't mean to bring that up. That isn't what I was— I'm pretty sure your parents are safe enough, for now. I'm as sure as I can be without knowing for really sure. I wasn't even thinking about them. I know how worried you must be, about them. No," she said, anxious to reassure him now, "I was worrying about me. It's selfish, I know, but I was . . . You didn't ask *me* to help you out. With the detecting. You asked Ari, but you didn't . . . Do you think I'm too old? Or unworldly?"

"Oh," Max said. It was his turn now to be surprised and apologize for misunderstanding. "I didn't think you had any time to help out, you've been so . . ." He decided he shouldn't say that. "You haven't been . . . ," he started, but that was wrong, too. He didn't know how to say it without it sounding like he was complaining to her, and really, he didn't have a single complaint about his grandmother.

"I've been feeling a little useless and unwanted," Grammie admitted.

"*Would* you want to help me out? Would you be willing to?" Max asked. "I thought you'd be insulted if I asked. I could pay you."

"It hasn't come to that," Grammie told him. "I don't need you to support me yet. But yes, I think I'd like to try a little detecting."

Max had a sudden suspicion. "What do you mean *yet*?"

"I'll tell you if I need to," Grammie said.

But Max persisted. "You know, you never told me what *your* letter from the Mayor said."

"I didn't, did I?" Grammie answered, adding immediately, "Where do you want me to ask questions? Which shop?"

If Grammie didn't want to talk about it, Max couldn't force her, so he answered her question. "The florist," he said. "She has a shop just outside—"

"I remember," Grammie said. "I read the newspapers," she reminded him, holding up the copy of the *Queensbridge Gazette* and shaking it, twice, gently.

Max could only smile and nod. She was looking at him now, looking straight at him with sparky blue eyes, in the amused way he was used to.

"Her name is Annarinka Friedle," Grammie said.

"I don't think you'll need a disguise," Max told his grandmother.

"But I'm not going to do this as the City Librarian," Grammie told him.

"No, no, that wouldn't be a good idea. Just be yourself. Your own self," Max said.

"A dotty little old lady." Grammie was grinning now.

"Not old." Max grinned back at her.

"I'll do my best," she told him, and opened the newspaper again, to take up her reading where she had left off. Her voice came to him from behind the thin wall of print. "This could be a whole new career for me." She rattled the pages, to straighten them.

Only then did Max look at his letters.

It was odd: Neither one had a return address but both seemed to be in an adult's handwriting, so the writers should have known to include one. He couldn't guess what they might say.

He opened the first, and read.

Dear Sir,

I know you spoke with the Mayor so I think you are the man for me. Meet me in front of the Harbormaster's Office on the docks. They do not come to work until half past eight so we can speak privately. I will be there from seven until seven-thirty from tomorrow (that is, Saturday) for four mornings (that is, through Tuesday), to talk with you. I have a family problem I hope you can help me with.

Yours sincerely,
Captain Francis Coyne

The signature was written in thick, straight letters.

Max stared at the piece of paper. He was of two minds about the job. On the one hand, work was work. On the other—maybe dangerous—hand, Captain Francis knew Max Starling, a boy who sometimes rode on the ferry, whose parents owned the theater in the old city. Max had gone out on *The Water Rat* only twice since mid-April, both times in disguise. Since the Captain stayed on the bridge, seeing his passengers from above, he had not recognized the man in the wide-brimmed black hat and long white scarf as Max Starling. Undecided about what to do, Max set this letter aside.

The second letter had been mailed the same day. When he opened it, he saw that it was written on the same kind of paper that Captain Francis had used. This, it turned out, was no accident. This second letter had been written by Carlo Coyne, the Captain's son.

Dear Mister Max,

I hope you can help me. Gabrielle from the ice cream shop said you were a finder of lost things.

I haven't lost anything but I have a friend—a very dear friend—who may be in trouble. It may be that she is not, but she acts as if she is. She acts afraid, but she will not talk to me about it. She will not let me help her. She says it is nothing, she says there is nothing bothering her, but I know, I know in my heart, that there is something. Until it is fixed, she cannot be happy I think. But if I do not know what it is, how can I fix it?

I hope you can help me. I earn a good living and have no expenses, so I can pay whatever it costs. Please write to me, in care of Flora Bunda, the fishmonger. She is a good friend of my father and me and will receive a private letter for me. Please answer quickly. I am worried sick about my friend.

Max was so deep in thought about both of these letters that Grammie had to ask him twice what they said, and who they were from. Because Max wasn't ready to talk about it, not knowing, really, whether he'd be giving away someone's private secrets, he answered only, "They're not from Andesia, not about Andesia."

Grammie waited.

"I'll tell you later, but it's nothing dangerous. You don't have to worry," Max said, and, as he had known she would, Grammie took his word for it.

9

Fire!

Black night was just melting to an ashy gray dawn when a clanging of bells and a thundering of hooves woke Max from a dream in which he was wandering through the dark engine room of an ocean liner, trying to find the bicycle he'd left there. Figures came after him, tall, cloaked, dangerous. To be yanked up out of a nightmare—heart already pounding—and then jerked awake, dragged along behind only half-recognized noises—all this before there is enough light to see just what is going on . . .

There was smoke in the air. Voices shouted from not very far off.

Max was out of bed and standing by the window, already half dressed, before he understood that the fire was on another street. Not Thieves Alley, and not Brewery Lane, either. How distant a street he could not be sure, as he fastened his overalls and grabbed his work boots to go down to find his bicycle. There was no sound from Ari's room.

He sat on the back steps to lace up the boots. No light shone in Grammie's house, so she, too, had slept through the commotion. In grabbing the nearest clothes, he had also, it seemed, picked up the straw hat that completed his gardener's outfit, but he didn't want to waste any time returning it to its hook by the door, so he jammed it onto his head and wheeled the bicycle through the gate to Thieves Alley. There, he mounted and rode off—cautiously, because the dark air was filled with darker shadows and he had only sounds to guide him.

They led him in the direction of the docks and into the heart of the old city. He could distinguish voices now, the clamoring bells and horses' hooves having been stilled, and he could see gray smoke, like a cloud against the darkness just ahead. When he turned onto Milk Lane he braked hard and jumped down, leaving his bicycle leaning up against a dark shop front.

Flames turned the air orangey red and Max tasted smoke—the firemen were getting the best of the battle. People clustered across the street from a narrow, three-story building, with a sign hanging down from the door frame advertising used books, old maps, letters written by famous people, and a collection of rare editions. On each side of the shop, the buildings were made of brick or stone, so the fire was not going to spread, but the shop itself was wood. Old, dry wood that burned hot. The pump wagon stood directly in front of the doorway, its hose fat with the water two boys pumped through it, stooping and rising—one down, the other up, the other down, the one up, never stopping to rest. Water gushed out of the nozzle of the hose, which firemen were now directing in an arc, up to the second floor, to discourage the fire from spreading. Men and women—children too—passed buckets of water from the corner fountain to pour onto the ashes at the ground level of the building.

Max joined the group of onlookers, an eye out to see if there was anything he could do to help. He couldn't recognize any of the firefighters in their helmets and heavy coats, but he thought that one of the boys busy at the pump might be Tomi Brandt, and he was glad for his straw hat. An older couple, gray-haired and plump and dazed, stood off to one side, alone. Both wore night-robes. Both were barefooted. The woman had paper curlers in her hair, and the man kept an arm around her shoulders. They leaned into one another, like two fishermen's shacks keeping one another upright. Tears ran down her cheeks. He looked grim. A woman wearing a night-robe and slippers, her hair neatly brushed, came up to give them mugs, probably full of tea.

"What happened?" Max asked, of nobody in particular.

"What's it look like?" a woman answered, and "The usual," a man said from behind him. "Those poor Nowells,"

BOOK
OSP SAMOCICE

a third voice said, "just when it looked like things were getting better for them, now this." An impatient voice responded to that remark, "He knew what he was getting into."

The crowd fell silent again, watching.

Despite all the smoke and the unnatural color of the air, it wasn't after all so big a fire. It was quickly brought under control and when the firelight faded, it left the air blue-gray with dawn. As a final preventive measure, the firefighters hosed the front room of the bookshop. Water poured over the shelves, soaking the books. They had broken through the display window on the street, so shards and splinters of glass lay all over the roadway, but the two boys had been set to sweeping it up. Close behind Max a woman's sympathetic voice said, "At least, the apartments upstairs will be untouched, and that's a relief because I don't know that any of us have anything left to give in aid. I surely don't, not a blanket nor flour—do you?"

Max did, and he stepped up toward the older couple to offer anything they might need, but he heard the man—who must be Mr. Nowell—answer an offer, "No, I thank you, Cecil, and we thank your good wife as well, it's very generous. But we'll be fine here. The stairway goes up at the back of the building, which is unharmed by fire or water. It's limited damage that's been done, even if—"

The friend, behind whose broad back Max stood, murmured something sympathetic.

"People who know nothing about books," Mr. Nowell said, anger in his voice. "Not even that they're made of paper if you want my—"

He fell suddenly silent and waited two or three seconds before continuing in a calmer voice, "We'll gladly dine with you tonight, however. Won't we, my dear?"

His wife had stopped weeping but was still wordless with distress. She only nodded and tried to smile.

Mr. Nowell went on, "It won't take long to repair—just—"

At that moment, Officer Sven Torson of the city police approached Mr. and Mrs. Nowell, and the friend slid back into the crowd. People began drifting away, disappearing into their own doorways. Max moved off, away from the bookshop owners. He didn't want to run the risk of being recognized by the policeman, who had seen this Mister Max once before, and not all that long ago. He moved a few steps toward the ashes, to admire the fire brigade as they stomped down the last of the flames and raked through the coals. He shook his head, as if wondering at this calamity, amazed by it—at the same time being careful to stay close enough to watch and listen to Officer Torson's conversation with Mr. Nowell.

Mrs. Nowell remained silent throughout, but she clutched at her husband's arm, kept close to his side, as if only there, with him, did she feel safe.

"Bad luck," Officer Torson said, and waited. He was holding his police cap in his hand, out of respect for the Nowells' loss.

"You could say that," Mr. Nowell answered, after a while.

"The rare books, though. Those you keep in the cellar, don't you?" the policeman asked.

"Where the walls are brick. They're how I'll be able to pay for repairs," Mr. Nowell said.

"It's a lucky thing they weren't harmed," the policeman said, and waited.

There was a long silence. The fire brigade began coiling up the long hose, talking to one another in ordinary tones, about how tired and hungry they were, about how they wished some of these fires would have the courtesy to start themselves up in daylight. Over the rooftops the rising sun silvered the sky.

Finally, Officer Torson asked, "Any idea what started it?" His voice was casual, as if he were a neighbor and not an arm of the law. His eyes were fixed on the firemen. He asked his question almost carelessly, as if he wasn't really interested.

Max took a step closer to hear the answer.

His movement drew the policeman's attention. The policeman glanced at Max, and then looked again, more sharply.

"I must have left a lamp burning," Mr. Nowell said. "Maybe the wiring. Or mice. I might have been hearing mice in the walls."

Max was stepping away, head bent.

"Excuse me? Sir?" Officer Torson reached out to put a hand on Max's shoulder. "Don't I know you?"

Max wanted to deny it but Grammie had a lot of respect for this policeman, whom she had taught in grade school, so Max thought it might be a mistake to try to put something over on the man. "Lady. Long ears," he said, to remind

Officer Torson of when they'd met. "Mrs. Nives, she is my friend. In her garden."

"Oh yes, now I remember. Are you still working there? In case it turns out I need to talk to you. Mister, wasn't it?"

"Yes." Max nodded as eagerly as if he really was glad to be recognized. "Mister."

That satisfied the policeman, but when Max turned away from the site of the fire, to reclaim his bicycle, he saw that Tomi Brandt was watching him from the edge of a group of firefighters. Tomi was too far away to have overheard, or so Max hoped. He pretended not to see his classmate and continued on his way, taking his bicycle by the handlebars, grateful that the new white top on its basket made it look like anybody's bicycle. But he could feel Tomi's eyes on his back. Before he could mount and ride off, footsteps sounded behind him, running footsteps, and a voice called, "Hey, Eyes! Eyes? Wait up!"

Max was Bartolomeo and the name meant nothing to him. He lifted a leg over the seat of his bicycle, ready to mount, but Tomi hadn't gone away. Max pulled the brim of his hat down lower.

Tomi Brandt stopped right in front of Max, making his square figure an obstacle no bicycle could ride over. "Bartolomeo, isn't it?" he asked in a friendly voice. His freckled face wore its usual smile, despite being grimy with smoke, and sweat had slicked his hair flat on his scalp. "You came to see the excitement?"

Max shrugged, staring down blankly at Tomi's rubber boots, as if he hadn't understood what the boy had asked him.

"You live around here?"

Max waved a hand in the general direction of Thieves Alley. "Live there. Near to here."

"My name's Tomi," Tomi said. He shifted his weight from one foot to the other. "We met at the fire station. You remember that, don't you?"

Max nodded.

"That's why *I'm* here, but what about you? You didn't start it, did you?" Tomi laughed.

But Max had already looked up, startled. The last thing he wanted was for a gardener named Bartolomeo, who might be riding Max Starling's bicycle, to be suspected of arson. "Came to help," he said, and looked down again.

"Hunh," Tomi said. He had a hand on the handlebars so Max couldn't leave. Max waited, straddling his bicycle.

Finally Max asked, "You fireman?"

"No, but I will be. For now I'm an apprentice."

"Work is good," Max commented, then realized that he shouldn't know that word, *apprentice.* "I work now. They want me. Soon," he said.

"Where are you working?" Tomi asked.

"Big house. Palace," Max told him.

"I don't believe that. The royal family has its own gardeners."

"Near big school," Max said. That was safe enough,

because the Hilliard School was on a street lined with homes of the wealthy or—in the case of the two sisters who had briefly sheltered Sunny—the formerly wealthy. "Old ladies," he said, and held up two fingers. "Three."

"You mean *mansion,*" Tomi said. At the blank expression on Max's face he smiled, but explained, "A really big house? That's a mansion, not a palace. A palace," he continued, "is much, much bigger than a mansion." Grinning, he spread his hands far apart.

"Mansion," Max repeated stupidly. He didn't like the way Tomi was looking at him and he also didn't like the teasing tone in Tomi's voice. Why would he block the path of a gardener who barely spoke the language? Tomi had never struck Max as a bullying type. He was rough-and-tumble but not unkind—the opposite, in fact. So what was the unspoken thing that was so amusing to Tomi?

Max was afraid he might know the answer to that question.

"Need to go," Max said. "I work," he said.

Tomi stepped back. "I know about work," he said.

Max mounted and pedaled away, more slowly than he wanted to and more awkwardly than he had to, as would someone who was new to bicycle riding.

"See you around," Tomi called after him, and added, as Max came to the corner, "Max."

Max didn't look back, but once around the corner and out of sight, he started to pedal furiously, which was all he could do with the burst of alarmed energy this new danger set off in him.

10

The Mayor's Job

• ACT I •

SCENE 4 ~ SUSPICIONS

Max went home by an indirect route, in case Tomi might be following, as much worried by Tomi's terrier-like concern for justice as by the danger of discovery. If Tomi suspected that something dishonest had happened, he wouldn't stop trying to find out the truth. Tomi was the kind of person who didn't sit back and wonder. He'd do something to confirm his suspicions. So, in case he was being followed, Max rode through the Bishop's Gate out into the New Town, across the park and in front of the Hilliard School to a decrepit mansion at the end of that road, where the bushes were overgrown and the two elderly ladies within seldom looked out the window. There he waited, hidden behind a large rhododendron, until he was sure no one suspicious—that is to say, Tomi Brandt—was coming along the road behind him.

Satisfied that he was unobserved, he returned to Thieves Alley, where he sat down to write to Carlo Coyne, asking the young ferryman to meet him Tuesday evening, in front of the Starling Theater. Then he waited for Ari to wake up.

As he explained it first to Ari and then later in the day to Grammie, at the city library, the problem was that Captain Francis knew who Max Starling was. "But you can always fool me," Ari said. "Starting from that crazy dogcatcher uniform you put on, I'm never sure it's you. Until . . ."

"Until what?"

"Until I get a look at your face. And see your eyes. I'd ask Pia. She's got a lot more imagination than I do," Ari advised.

Grammie's advice differed. "This one is too risky," she said. "You've been riding that ferry since you were first able to walk. I remember, I had to grab you when you tried to climb over the railing."

"I don't think I would have done *that,*" Max said in the lowered voice he always used in the library.

"I was there," Grammie told him. "I saw it. I'm an eyewitness. You better turn Captain Francis down, even if the money would, I admit, be welcome. It's just too risky." And that was that. She'd had her say. "Now scoot, Max. Who knows who's watching me waste my working time with chatter."

The note Max had left off at the Bendiff mansion on The Lakeview asked Pia to meet him after the midday meal, so he stopped to see Joachim, even though it wasn't a lesson day and even though he knew full well that Joachim preferred to think only about line and shape and color and shading. He didn't expect the painter to have any ideas for disguises, but Joachim was always glad to eat a lunch that Max would prepare for the two of them. Max brought bread and cheese and grapes out to the garden, where Sunny slept in a patch of sun-warmed grass. Joachim ate without speaking, staring at a half-finished painting of a long-tongued blue iris. He put his glasses on to see it clearly and then took them off to see it as only color and line. Max offered no opinion on the subject and left without himself saying more than four words, having washed the plates and replaced them on the kitchen shelves. "Hello" was one of the words, "Here's lunch" were two more, and the last was "Goodbye." Joachim just raised an inattentive hand and removed his glasses. The dog, at least, padded to the garden gate beside him for a final rub on her strong shoulders before Max left.

Pia was at the opposite end of the talkative yardstick. She gave him her complete attention and the benefit of all of her thinking, whether it had to do with his question or not.

"You have to try the gooseberry custard tart, I've always wondered what that would taste like," she told him while asking Gabrielle to give her one of the croissants with a thick filling of sweet dark chocolate.

Max would have preferred the croissant. He was about to point that out to her, but she asked, "How can I help you?"

and despite his irritation at her assumption that he needed help, he explained his difficulty.

"Well," Pia said, without any hesitation, "your eyes *are* . . . They're not weird, not exactly, it's just . . . I've never seen eyes that strange color, like . . . almost like the lead in pencils, not really human but . . . Not animal, though, that's not what's wrong with them and actually, they're nice eyes. Just . . . weird. How about a mask? Like a robber wears, the ones that look like raccoon faces? Or, we could cut holes out of a piece of cloth and hang it down over your face, from under a hat, maybe. You don't have a beard yet, or even any mustache, so that's no good. How old are men when they start to grow beards and mustaches anyway? I think my brother is starting one—the second brother, he's fifteen, not the oldest one, Sandor's still as smooth as an egg and it makes him furious. So do you like the tart? Can I have just one bite? My father wants Gabrielle to offer it on the first month's menu. They're going to change the desserts every month, to use what's in season. Do you know what he got?"

Max was thinking about masks. "No, what?"

"He got a letter from the King, well, one of Teodor's secretaries, asking when *B's* would be opening and if there will be a room where the King could dine privately. With his family, the letter said. He likes to go out among his people."

"How is it 'out among his people' if they're in a private dining room?" Max wondered. The kind of mask Pia suggested wouldn't hide his eyes; in fact, it might draw attention to them.

"It's because my father's businesses are so successful," Pia went on. "Everybody knows him. It's funny, everybody knows him and nobody knows you. Except maybe this ferry-boat captain. I remember him, from when we went to deal with Madame Olenka. He stared at me."

That thought did not displease Pia. She grinned at Max.

"Or a hat, could you keep the brim of that hat you wore pulled down low enough so he never sees your eyes?"

"He wants to meet in the morning, at half past seven. It'll be light by then."

"Do you have any other hats? Can you be a girl? Girls—or ladies—often wear veils and a veil would work. Tess Tardo is making me a hat. I'm going to pay her for it but she's not expensive. She's making me a summer hat, to show off my hair, she said." When she said this, Pia glared at him, daring Max to disagree with Tess Tardo's admiration.

"I'm no good at playing girls," Max admitted. "I tried once and even Zenobia was suspicious."

"Really? She trusts everybody. Do you think all cooks are trusting? Because Gabrielle is, too."

"Not really suspicious, she just . . . she looked confused by me."

"Did you wear a dress and all?" To explain what she meant by *and all* Pia waved her hand in the general area of her chest and waist.

"Of course not. I was— The Baroness thought I was plump so—"

Pia ignored him. "Anyway, I don't think you can talk to

anyone keeping your back to him all the time, so that won't work. But if all you have to do is hide your eyes, what if you were all bent over? A hunchback, so you could only look up sideways, or if you were really old and arthritic. Can you act old and arthritic? Do you have costumes for that? That could be a woman, because old men and old women aren't really very different to look at, do you think? Really old, I mean, not like your grandmother. And blind, can you act blind? An old, bent-over, blind woman would be a good disguise."

She stopped to take a breath, but no longer than that. "I went to your grandmother's library, did she tell you? She wanted me to and so I did, but she wasn't very friendly. Is she always unfriendly when she's working? Because she's been nice when I've seen her at home."

"Was she unfriendly or grumpy?" Max asked.

"Maybe grumpy."

"Do you have any idea why?"

That question, Pia stopped to think about before she answered.

After half a minute of consideration, during which Max finished the gooseberry tart, which was after all very good, and in a more interesting way than a chocolate croissant, Pia began again. "There could be lots of reasons, because she's not young anymore and sometimes people, my grandparents do this, get sad at, you know, the idea of dying. Unless she's sick. Do you think she's sick? Or maybe—she's your only family, isn't she? I know you're almost grown up but you're still her grandson, is she worried about you? Are you doing something that worries her? Or maybe she's remembering something terrible, because nobody ever says anything about the rest of your family. Unless she thinks that you're about to really grow up, leave home, leave her behind and alone. Or—"

"Pia!" Max cried, almost dizzy with trying to listen to her. "Stop yammering. Just . . . stop!"

"You *asked* me," she reminded him. "If you don't want to hear what I think, you don't have to ask me."

"But you're not thinking," Max pointed out, perfectly reasonably, he thought. "You don't think. You just open your mouth and let fly."

"Maybe." Pia was silent for about ten seconds; then she grinned. "But your grandmother told me you told her that my talking helped *you* to have ideas. You shouldn't tell her that if it's not what you mean. It's hard enough trying to get along with people—and be their unpaid assistant—if they don't mean what they say. I always mean what I say," she told him. "Always."

"Pia," Max protested, "you're doing it again."

"I have to go home anyway," she said, and rose abruptly from the table to leave without even calling a goodbye to Gabrielle.

Max was so cross at her he didn't call goodbye after her. *Some assistant,* he thought. *Some help.* He got up to pay his bill. "Did Pia pay for her croissant?" he asked Gabrielle.

Gabrielle, who never spoke ill of anyone and didn't like to even *think* badly of people, answered, "She will the next time she's in. She likes getting her own way."

"That's not news to me," Max said, but he couldn't help smiling at Pia's understanding of her importance to the Solutioneer.

"Don't you?" Gabrielle asked.

"But I know how to hold my temper," Max said.

"Also," Gabrielle went on, "she plans to make you wait for her to grow up and marry her. How old are you, anyway, Max?"

Max hesitated. He didn't know what Ari might have told her about him, and he didn't know what Gabrielle might have guessed, and he didn't know how not to say anything without seeming to avoid the question. Then he did know, because it was a line straight out of *The Adorable Arabella,* and Max spoke on cue. "Too young to think of marrying. Old enough to be flattered." The elderly suitor had reversed those two conditions, but the idea was the same. He smiled at Gabrielle, a man of mystery, he hoped. Or at least, almost a grown man, someone who wasn't a twelve-year-old boy.

Because Max wouldn't tell anybody more about himself than they absolutely had to know. The fewer people who knew Max Starling's true situation, the safer he was. And the safer his parents were, too, he thought.

Max rode his bicycle home slowly, his feet turning the pedals unhurriedly, his mind circling at the same slow pace. He laughed at Pia with her masks and veils and blind old ladies, and he smiled at Joachim with his art-absorbed life. Joachim could spend hour after hour putting on his new glasses, staring at a canvas, taking them off, squinting in the bright light, staring, thinking . . .

Max stopped.

He set his feet on the roadway, straddling his bicycle, and did not move. People and carts and horses and two dogs, as well, moved around him, the way a stream flows around a rock.

Then he remounted his bicycle and rode off, fast, into the twisting streets of the old city, rode home, ran inside to take coins out of a certain covered bean pot on a kitchen shelf before he ran back outside to mount his bicycle and ride fast to the spectacle-maker's shop.

It wasn't long before Max was admiring a reflection of himself in a pair of brown-tinted glasses. "How much?" he asked.

"Twenty," the man said, and before Max could protest at the price but assuming that he wanted to, added, "They're going to raise my rent. They haven't said but I know it. With all those people trying to move their shops out of the old city. Scared of what's going on there and I don't blame them. If my rent's going up, so are my prices," he announced.

Max took coins out of his pocket and asked casually, "What's going on in the old city?"

The spectacle-maker shook his head. "Who knows? It's a rat's nest in there and the kind of people who live on those alleys . . . ? They're not the best sort, I can tell you. Of course there's all kinds of trouble. *I* wouldn't want to have a business in the old city, either. You going to wear these or do you want me to pack them in a box for you?"

The reports came in on Sunday. Ari's was the first. He lingered at the kitchen table after his final tutorial lesson with Max, to relate what he had found out.

"Nothing," he said. "I didn't find out anything." It was a rainy day, so business at the ice cream shop would be slow and he could take a few extra minutes before riding William Starling's bicycle—he consistently refused his great-aunt's offers to buy him a motorcar—into the New Town to spend the afternoon working for Gabrielle. "They both saw through me. I did warn you, I can't act. I took out the notebook and everything, but neither one of them was fooled. I'm not a good liar, either. I'm sorry, Max."

"Maybe that's why you're such a good teacher?" Max suggested. Ari smiled and shrugged.

"I'm glad you think so."

"But the shopkeepers. Were they . . . were they polite to you?"

"Very nice, both of them. They seemed amused by me, mostly. They sort of teased me. *What is it you're really after, young man?* is what Mr. Bonelli asked me. *Are you hungry?* Which was kind of him. Although he did say I don't look underfed. He offered to give me the last of last year's potatoes, and an apple, too, because he doesn't like to see people going without, when there's food to be eaten. *Even if certain customers might turn up their noses at it.*" Ari studied the tabletop thoughtfully before he went on. "That was the perfect opening, don't you agree? So I asked him how he could have anything to give away after the vandalism, which must have cost him a pretty penny, and he said that he doesn't like to think about that, so did I honestly expect him to talk about it? He told me my wife could make a good soup from the potatoes, and I told him I had no wife, and he said I should get myself one. *A fellow like you needs a wife to steady him down, I know, because that's the kind of young man I used to be. Children, you need children, they settle you down.* He gave me the potatoes, anyway, and hoped at least I had a sweetheart who knew how to cook. I could tell him," Ari announced happily, "that I do."

Max was not to be distracted. "So he wasn't unfriendly?"

"Not a bit. He was nice."

"Not frightened, either?"

"Why should he be frightened of me? Neither was the cobbler. Boots Wallack? He didn't believe me for a minute when I told him I was a reporter. He said I should go back where I belonged and stop slumming around. He could tell by my shoes, he said. I was no reporter and I was nobody looking for work, unless I wanted to hire him to make me a pair of fine boots. So I did," Ari admitted.

Max had to laugh. He guessed Ari really couldn't act.

"Riding boots," Ari added. "The most expensive riding boots Great-Aunt's money can buy." And he laughed, too. Then he stopped. "But it *was* strange—even maybe suspicious? What neither of them would talk about. Boots Wallack, when I tried to ask, looked puzzled, the way you do when somebody doesn't seem to understand something everybody knows. Does that make sense to you?"

"It might," Max said. "I'm not really sure, not yet, but it might."

"What are you getting mixed up in, Max?" Ari asked.

"I'm just finding things out, for the Mayor. I'm not *doing* anything about anything. Do you think Gabrielle would be willing to talk to the butcher whose shop was—"

"No."

Ari spoke so sharply that Max fell silent.

"Not a chance. I don't want you to even mention it to her, Max. I don't like the smell of it and I don't want her put at risk in any way. I may have failed to protect her before, but never again," Ari announced—and at that moment he looked as formidable as any of his ancestors.

"I won't," Max assured him. "You have my word."

Ari relaxed. "That's all right, then. But you can let *me* know if there's anything else I can do? Because . . . something wrong is obviously going on. Don't you think?"

Max did think. And he thought, further, that he was beginning to get an idea of just what it was.

Grammie joined Max in the garden at midday that Sunday to tell him, "She's a good businesswoman, that Annarinka. She has done so much with just the one cart, plus a kind of tent behind it for the actual shop. It's all legal, she has the license. When her husband died, she took their savings to start up this little business. She's not young, but she's not old, either, and she manages well enough to be feeding, clothing, and housing two growing children. I have to admire her determination. Her enterprise. It's not easy being a widow with children."

The soil around the plants had been tamped down by the rain. Max loosened it and Grammie trailed behind him, pulling up weeds, tossing them onto a pile in the grass.

"It made me wonder," she said.

"Wonder what?"

Max was uncostumed and had no part to play; he was only himself, Max Starling, an ordinary twelve-year-old. After he finished in the garden he planned to set up his easel and try getting the particular blue of the June sky, which was friendlier, somehow, than the blue of other months. But even out of costume, he was still the Solutioneer, so he was listening closely to everything Grammie said.

"Wonder if I could have done something else when your grandfather died."

"Was there something else you wanted to do? I always thought—they always told me—that you liked being a teacher. I thought you said that, too. Wasn't it true?" Max couldn't imagine his grandmother *not* working with books, and reading. "Don't you want to be the City Librarian?"

For a long few minutes, Grammie weeded without answering. Then she gave a little soft laugh and said, "No, there was nothing and you're right, I did, I can't say I have regrets. But I may want to think of something else to do now. Like a little shop of my own, selling . . . I know a lot about books," she said. "Annarinka told me, and this might interest you, that this isn't the best time for anyone to open up a shop. She didn't say why, and when I asked her what exactly she meant, she began to babble, the way people will when they've said something they didn't mean to, telling me how summer is the best season for shops, with tourists coming to the lake, and especially when the royal family is in residence, was I going to watch the arrival? And the procession from the station out to The Lakeview, had I ever . . . ? Just babbling. I pretended I didn't notice."

"But you did notice," Max said.

Then Grammie looked up from her weeding and directly at her grandson, who looked so ordinary but—was it his unordinary childhood that made him this way?—understood more about human nature than many grown-ups. She wanted to make a report that would be useful to him, as if he were some library patron who had asked her for information, and not someone she had known since the first day of his life.

"I bought a nice little bouquet, then, and we had a long talk about flowers, and gardens, and growing vegetables, and raising children alone. It was as I was about to leave that I asked her if she took her cart into shelter in the evenings, took down the tent. *Why ever would I do that?* she asked. *The cart's heavy, the tent's clumsy, why would I want to move them every day?* I said I'd read about her misfortune in the newspaper, so I thought she might be nervous about leaving them up when she went home at night. She lives in the old city, just three blocks from the gate, with an unmarried sister," Grammie explained. "The shop is empty all night."

That was exactly what Max *was* interested in. "What did she say then?" he asked, and he thought he could guess at the answer.

"It won't happen again," Grammie reported. "Saying that got her babbling again and she told me all about police patrols of the area and how she has good neighbors who keep an eye on everything, so she didn't need to worry." She returned to her weeding. "Is that what you wanted me to find out? Does it help? What do you think of my detecting skills?" she laughed. "Although I don't see that I found out anything."

"Annarinka wasn't worried about talking with you?" Max asked.

"No, not a bit. Why should she be? I told her about the horticulture books we have in the library and she said she'd like to come look at them, so I expect to see her again," Grammie told him, but Max wasn't listening. He was now almost positive that he knew what was going on.

Max ran his final test the next morning, a drizzly June Monday, at the butcher shop belonging to Bert Cotton.

To begin, Max loitered in the street in front of the shop, as if admiring the shine of the new glass windows. Their wooden frames had not yet been painted the green of the doorway. He loitered, for everyone to notice, walking back and forth in front of the shop until the housewives had all gone off with their chosen cuts of beef and lamb and pork, their chickens and ducks and geese. When the shop was empty except for Bert Cotton himself, Max sauntered in. He was wearing gray trousers and a blue cotton jacket; he did not respectfully remove the cloth cap he had on his head. His boots needed a polish and he kept his hands in his pants pockets, jingling the few coins he carried. He was an unemployed youth, loitering.

The butcher was at his wooden table, cutting chops off the carcass of a pig. At the sight of Max, he fell still, the cleaver high in the air. Bert Cotton was a rangy man, who did not look strong enough to lift whole sides of beef onto the hooks in his storeroom, but he must have been because he had no sons to work with him, only daughters. His grip on the cleaver was relaxed, comfortable, familiar.

He said nothing. He did not lower the cleaver onto the chopping block. His eyes narrowed with dislike, and distaste, and fear.

Max smirked, the aristocratic suitor so sure Arabella would accept him that he did not even phrase his proposal with a *please.* He watched the butcher.

Bert Cotton lowered the cleaver, but he did not put it down. He straightened up to his full height. "Your kind of vermin is not welcome in the shop," he said, slow and clear. "Not you and none of your friends, neither. If you have something to say to me, you can go around to the back door like the rest of your kind."

Max smirked for a few more seconds, and then he turned

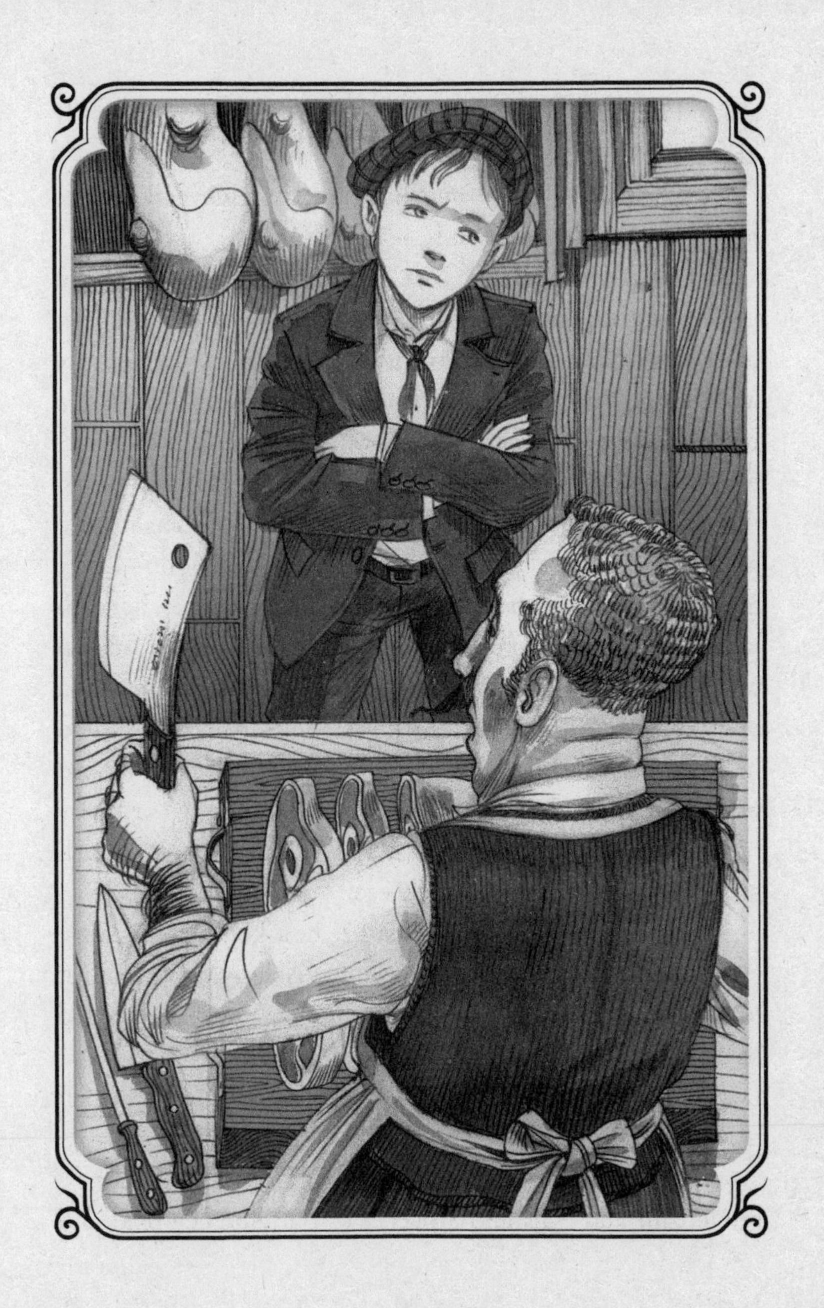

around abruptly and left. He stopped to scrape sawdust off his soles on the doorsill.

"I won't have you in my shop," the butcher called after him. "Nor your three friends, neither."

Suspicions confirmed, Max wound his way over to Eel Lane and then followed its curves until the alley came out onto River Way, not far downstream from the former city workhouse that Mr. Bendiff was transforming into *B's,* a restaurant where a king would want to dine. On that section of road, beyond the warehouses but before the farms, there were small houses with spacious yards used as market gardens and animal pens. There, he entered Willson's Dairy Shop and smiled at the young woman behind a table, beneath which large rounds of cheese were lined up on a shelf, and on which a scale waited. Pails and jugs for milk and cream stood behind her. Half a dozen thick rectangles of butter floated in a wide bowl where chunks of ice melted. The girl looked up. Max took off his cap and smiled, just a boy, any ordinary boy, with a few coins in his pocket and a thirst for good fresh milk, or maybe a hunger for cheese.

"May I have a taste of that, please?" he asked, all politeness.

She cut a thin sliver of pale yellow cheese and offered it to him, on the wide knife blade. He took it, ate it, and smiled again. "That, too?"

She gave him an equally thin slice of orange cheese, which he also ate.

The shop bell rang and two women entered together, to buy cream and eggs and a packet of butter. They paid and left. The girl, with a glance at Max, put the coins into her apron pocket, not into a money box.

No money box was in sight and he couldn't see where it had been hidden.

"I wonder if I can taste your milk?" he asked with the same pleasant smile.

She looked as if she was beginning to doubt this smiling, but three more housewives came in, each carrying an infant, one after the other, to fill their pails with milk and buy chunks of cheese. From the open door behind the girl came the lowing of cows.

When the shop was empty again, the coins once again added to her apron pocket, he asked, "The milk? Please?" And he smiled.

"I'm not sure," the girl said. Her brow was furrowed, now, with worry. She pushed the ends of her mouth up in what was supposed to be a friendly way and asked, "Shouldn't you be in school?"

"School? With summer so close? Why would I go there when the vacation is about to start? You do a good business here, don't you?" he went on. "Enough, I'm sure, to give me a taste of your milk and have the loss count nothing." He smiled.

The girl twisted her hands in her pocket, muffling any clanking of coins. "I have to ask my pa. I'll be just a minute."

"Don't hurry on my account. I'm happy to look around," Max assured her.

He was not surprised that the dairyman himself burst into

the shop almost immediately, wiping his hands on a cloth and not smiling. Like the girl, he had a short nose and very pink cheeks. "We don't give samples of milk," he said, before Max could utter a word. "We're not a café, or restaurant, with clean glasses and cups to hand."

"You look to be doing well, even without the cups and glasses," Max observed.

"Looks can be deceiving," the man answered sharply. "Can I sell you something? Or are you leaving?"

Max took a long, slow, last look around the small shop and out through the open doorway, where two cows and a calf were visible. "I think I'll be back," he said. "At a later time."

The dairyman's face grew wary and his mouth stiffened into a straight line. His fingers clutched at the cloth he held. But he did not say a word more and Max went out, back onto River Way.

He walked through long grass beside the river now. This was the river down which his parents had sailed, back in April, to their unforeseen destination. Max wondered if there would ever be a letter from Andesia, and at that unhappy thought he looked across the road, to distract himself from worry.

He had just come to a blacksmith's shop where Milk Lane entered River Way. On impulse, he crossed the street and sauntered toward the wide doorway, studying the fire pit with its anvil, and the row of mallets and horseshoes hanging from nails on the wall behind it. Two men who waited in the yard beside their horses saw him, and then the blacksmith—his face grimed with smoke—looked up. The blacksmith didn't set down the mallet with which he was pounding a curve of metal but he did stop hammering. He shifted his grip on the mallet handle. The boy at the bellows turned around when the hammering ceased. The horses stamped their feet. The only sound now was the stamping of hooves on the dirt yard and the soft hiss of flames. Everybody stared at Max.

"You'll be moving on," the burly blacksmith called out to Max, and there was no mistaking the threat in his voice. "And what're you gawping at?" he asked the boy at the bellows.

The boy looked down to say, "Nothing, Master," and then looked immediately back at the man's face, afraid he hadn't said the right thing. He began a vigorous pumping of the bellows at the same time the blacksmith said to Max, "I'm waiting, boy."

Max moved on.

That afternoon, when he was alone in the house, Max wrote to the Mayor. He rode his bicycle into the New Town to deliver his letter by hand, wearing no disguise, just a cap. He was any boy on his way home from school, earning a coin by delivering a letter. It asked that the Mayor be at the stage door of the Starling Theater at seven on Wednesday evening, at which time the Solutioneer would present his conclusions.

11

The Water Rat *Jobs*

• ACT I •

For Captain Francis, it was the last long morning of waiting and the fourth since he had written to this Solutioneer—Mister Max, whoever he was. The first morning, the Captain had turned eagerly at each sound of footsteps, and each time he'd been disappointed. The second, he'd waited confidently. By the third, he was beginning to wonder. What if the Solutioneer—and what did that mean, anyway?—what if the fellow was not interested in helping him?

Captain Francis was worrying what he would do next, without the Solutioneer's help, when the figure approached and stopped right in front of him. Captain Francis was so lost in his own thoughts that he was entirely surprised to see the man.

The stranger was no taller than Captain Francis, who was not a tall man, and he was slender compared to the muscular, compact ferryboat captain. He was younger than Captain Francis expected, closer to Carlo's age than his own, and he wore that dark overcoat despite the warm, overcast June morning. The white scarf hung loose around his neck, its long, tasseled ends dangling at his hips, and the same wide-brimmed black hat was set low on his forehead. He wore brown-tinted spectacles, even though at this hour and with the clouds covering the sky his eyes needed no protection from the sun's glare. Had he worn glasses when he met with the Mayor? Captain Francis couldn't be sure.

The man was so freshly shaven his skin looked as smooth as a boy's.

"You came," Captain Francis said—pretty stupidly, he thought. He smiled, foolishly he was sure, at his own clumsy greeting. You'd think *he* was the oddball, spooking around the city in a long black coat and aviator's scarf and tinted glasses. Why should *he* be feeling such a fool when he was the one with a normal job and normal life?

Why, Max wondered, should the ferryboat captain be so uncomfortable? Captain Francis flushed and jammed his hands in his jacket pockets, then jerked them out again. Just what *was* the problem he wanted help with? "You asked me to meet you," Max reminded Captain Francis, pitching his voice lower than its normal range. He was grateful, once again, for all his years with the Starling Theatrical Company, for all the roles he had been called on to play. Taking pity on the man, he added, "What can I do for you, Captain?"

"Let's walk along the docks, so we can talk in private," Captain Francis suggested, but immediately changed his mind. "No, let's go this way." And he turned into one of the alleys that ran away from the waterfront. "I don't want my son to see me."

"Whatever you prefer," said Max, in the voice of a man who could be patient.

They walked in silence for ten or twenty paces, until Captain Francis spoke, without slowing his pace or turning to look at Max. "It's my boy. It's Carlo. Do you know Carlo?"

"He's not a boy," Max pointed out.

"I'm a father, he's always a boy to me, and he's bothered by something. Or he's up to something. Or there's something he doesn't want me to know about, and that could be because he knows it's wrong, or he thinks it will worry me. Or something—somebody?—is worrying him, threatening him? Threatening me?"

"He's a grown man," Max said, because if a grown man wanted to keep a secret from another grown man, it seemed to Max that he should be able to. As long as nobody was going to be cheated, or hurt, or taken unfair advantage of, that is. Even children, he thought, should be able to have their own secrets.

"I know, but I know him, and he's not happy and that's not like him. Carlo has always been a happy person, boy and man, but these days . . . He doesn't laugh, he's not cheeky the way he usually is, he almost never smiles. Even in our saddest hours, when we had just lost his mother, he didn't seem to have lost hope, but now . . . He goes out at night, it's not like him. None of this is like my boy," Captain Francis said. "I'm worried about him."

"Have you asked *him*?" Max wondered.

"He says there's nothing wrong."

"What do you think it—?"

Captain Francis stopped in his tracks and grabbed on to Max's coat sleeve. "Can you find out what it is? So I can help him if he needs help."

"But what if—?"

"If it really is none of my business, you don't have to tell me. If it's just . . . something ordinary, some girl has broken his heart or . . . But it could be that he doesn't want to keep on working with me, working on *The Water Rat* with me, being a ferryman, don't you see? He wouldn't want to tell me that, but he should. I don't know what he does when he's gone, nights, probably he's up to something on his afternoon off, too, but I just don't— I'll pay you whatever it costs, Mister Max. All I want to do is see that Carlo is all right."

"I don't doubt that," Max said, but he had to go on. "I'm just not sure—"

"What do you charge?" the Captain asked, pulling a purse out of his pocket and opening it.

"Wait." Max held up his hand. Captain Francis fell still. He waited quietly and Max thought. He thought about what the Captain was asking, and about how Carlo had already written to him, so he already had some idea of what was troubling Carlo. He thought about how even without a meeting with Carlo he could probably answer the father's questions—and he wondered if, in that case, it was honest to take money for, really, not doing anything.

Captain Francis waited.

Max thought. If he refused to take on the job, Captain Francis would probably turn to somebody else and a thing that was a simple problem might turn into a great boiling pot of misunderstandings and unintended betrayals. You couldn't act in a lot of plays and not learn in how many different ways people could fall into misunderstandings, which led to unintended betrayals and general misery.

So he decided to quote the usual rates to Captain Francis. "It's twenty-five to start with and another twenty-five if I find a solution."

Captain Francis put the coins into his hand without hesitation. "You'll start right away?"

"I'll start as soon as I can. There's something else, another job . . . How will I let you know any results?"

"Do you know Flora Bunda? The fishmonger on Stink Alley? She'll bring any message to me; she's a good friend."

To this, Max only nodded, because what could he possibly say?

Captain Francis went on. "All I really want to know is, is there anything I can do? When there's only you and your boy in the family, you worry," he told Max.

Max nodded. That was how Grammie probably felt about him, right now.

"If you tell me I don't have to worry, I'll believe you," Captain Francis said.

That afternoon, a letter from Mister Max to Carlo Coyne was put into the ferryman's hands by a dirty-faced fellow in overalls, wearing a wide straw hat, who just said, "For the son," and walked away. The letter suggested a meeting, early that same evening, and asked Carlo to send a message if he couldn't be there. The meeting place was the alley by the stage door entrance to the Starling Theater, which, the letter said, "is closed indefinitely, and that will allow us to talk privately and without interruption." What the letter did not say was that in that place, at that hour, it would be difficult for Carlo to see the Solutioneer clearly.

Max changed into the blue waistcoat and gray suit Inspector Doddle wore, fixed the pillow firmly over his stomach, and settled the round pork-pie hat on his head. He scuttled out of his own front door and rode his bike quickly around the corner. Grammie was probably in her kitchen, making supper, but he wanted to take no chances of being stopped and questioned. He leaned his bicycle against the wall in the alley on the other side of the theater, arriving early to position himself in the deeper shadows beyond the stage door. He didn't have long to wait before Carlo Coyne arrived, a young man so distracted by his own worries that if Max had been disguised as himself, Carlo might well not have noticed.

Carlo was built for strength, like his father, and he moved with a sailor's agility. He rushed up to Max, taking off his cap and holding one hand out in greeting, and before Max—or Inspector Doddle—could say a word, the young ferryman was speaking.

"*Will* you help me?" he asked, an eager expression on his face, desperation in his voice. "I don't know what to do, I don't know what I *can* do and I'm so worried about—"

He stopped speaking and stared at Max so intently that Max was afraid he'd been recognized.

Carlo, however, only went on speaking. "She's friendless. There's only me. But she won't tell me anything."

Max shook the offered hand and waited to hear more, patient Inspector Doddle, not put out by the meaningless phrases the young man had spoken to him.

Carlo rubbed at his temple, as if to organize his thoughts, and ran his fingers through his thick, curly hair. "I know I'm not speaking sensibly. It's just that—I'd do anything, *anything*—to make her happy. But I don't know how."

Max took out the little notebook in which Inspector Doddle wrote down the things he wanted to remember, or—more accurately—pretended that was what he was doing. As he fished the small pencil from his pocket, he thought how alike Carlo and his father were, both of them wanting to help someone out. Captain Francis was doing it for love, but Max hadn't yet been told Carlo's motive.

He had a good guess, however, and Carlo's next words confirmed it. "I'm not asking her to give me anything in return; I've told her over and over. But I don't think she believes me. She knows how glad I'd be to marry her but not if she didn't want to marry me, I promise you. She says she'll never marry. She says she doesn't know how long she'll be in Queensbridge. She doesn't know where she'll go next. She has no home, no family, no hope or plan for any future. And she is such an extraordinary person, how could this be? What could have happened?" he asked, and then he put the question differently. "What could she have done? From which she wants to run away? Or who could she be hiding from?"

Max thought of what *his* first question should be, and chose two. "What is the lady's name? How did you meet her?"

That the answers to those simple questions were not simple did not surprise him. Carlo Coyne was obviously in an emotional state, not capable of organized thought. "It was a Friday, the midmorning run, she boarded *The Water Rat* at the docks. It was a round-trip ticket she had. Late May it was, and cool on the water, but she wore only a thin sweater and she was standing out on the deck. Alone. She got off at Summer—that village below the Promontory. It starts getting ready in May for the holiday season and maybe she has work there? She didn't come back on board until the last run of the day and she was waiting on the dock. I don't know how long she'd been waiting. Still with a carpetbag. Still alone. I didn't know how to approach her. Usually I'm easy with people but"—he ran his fingers through his hair again—"she isn't like anyone else, she's— Her name is Nissa. Just Nissa, she says, no other name, but what kind of a name is that? Have *you* ever heard it before? It's not a name, is it? She has fine manners. She speaks like an educated person. I'm a simpleton next to her. She's not highborn, I don't think, but she should be. Or maybe she's a lady or duchess in another country? She asked me if I knew of an inn where an unaccompanied female might sleep in safety, and I escorted her to The Dog's Tooth, where the innkeeper's wife was a friend of my mother's and . . ."

Max waited. Carlo seemed lost in thought, or in some memory, looking out into the fog. In the silence, Max thought he heard . . . What? Footsteps that suddenly stopped? In the little square across the street from the theater entrance? At this hour, however, on a weeknight, when the theater was dark and silent, everybody had arrived home to their dinners in their own warm, well-lighted rooms. Had Carlo been distracted by something in the park? Max stared out toward the street. Was that a moving shadow? Or moving figures? Suddenly he was reminded of a glittering gold button. Suddenly he was afraid. He wasn't used to feeling unsafe, not in the old city, not anywhere in Queensbridge. But these fires, and the vandalism, too, had made him just as uneasy as any of the shopkeepers he'd tried to talk with. He would be glad to hand over that problem to the Mayor tomorrow evening.

To gather himself together, and get his mind focused on the present job, Max manufactured a theatrical cough, and cleared his throat, as he cleared his mind to learn whatever he could from Carlo's rambling story. What he learned was: Nissa had found work in one of the great houses along The Lakeview, but Carlo did not know which one. She lived alone in the old city. She never talked about either her coworkers or her employers. She rode the ferry to Summer every morning and back to the docks every evening. She was given Sundays off, and only once had she agreed to share a picnic dinner.

"We ate by the lake. There's a field, just past the firehouse near Tassiter Lane. The men play soccer there some evenings but not Sundays, and it's peaceful, and beautiful, the little towns across the lake, farmhouses just visible on the hillsides, the way the sun gilds the water. I roasted a chicken and we had grapes, too, with two of Gabrielle's tarts. Nissa has a good appetite," Carlo announced proudly, his face bright with the memory of the afternoon. Then his smile faded. "But . . ."

After a long minute, "What does your father think?" Max asked.

"What does my father have to do with it?" Carlo demanded. "She's sworn me to secrecy—and I'm breaking my word to tell you, which I wouldn't do if I weren't so . . . so worried about her. Besides, my father—he saw her the first time and decided she looked like a gypsy. A gypsy, just because she's a stranger and she carried a carpetbag. My father would think the worst because he doesn't know her, doesn't know her family, and once he makes up his mind . . . Gypsy is what he calls everybody who looks at all different, everybody he takes against, he said she must have bad blood, he said she has to be up to no good or why would she be alone. He doesn't know I see her, and I'm not going to tell him. I hope I'm not wrong about telling you but . . . If I only knew that she was safe . . . She doesn't have to let me love her, she doesn't have to care about me in return, I only want her not to be so sad. And afraid, because I think she's afraid. Can you help me, Mister Max?" Carlo asked again, peering into Max's face.

"I don't know," Max said honestly.

Carlo went on as if Max hadn't spoken. "How much do you charge?" He took out a purse, ready to pay. "You can try, can't you?"

Max was curious, he couldn't deny it. He was curious not about the woman but about his own ability to discover who she was and what, if anything, troubled or endangered her, with no clues other than her regular ferryboat ride to work to go on. This was a real detective job.

"I could try," he said.

Carlo opened his purse eagerly.

"All right," Max said. "I'll see what I can do, if I can do anything. The usual fee is twenty-five to start and another twenty-five if I succeed. I can contact you through Flora Bunda?"

Carlo gave him the coins. "Yes. Anytime. She's a real friend. Can you start tomorrow?"

"It may take me some time. I have other cases," Max told him.

After a brief pause, Carlo said, "That's all right. I already feel better, just knowing you're there to help Nissa. I won't keep you any longer," he said. "I know you're busy." He shook Max's hand again eagerly. "Thank you." And he walked quickly away, heading across the street toward the docks, and in almost no time disappearing into the fog. All Max could hear was his footsteps.

Max folded the notebook closed and went quickly across the front of the theater to his bicycle, which he was relieved to find just where he'd left it, the white basket glimmering in the shadows. Rather than frighten himself with wondering—had what he'd heard come from inside the theater, and had he really seen someone moving beyond the shadows of the alley?—he mounted his bicycle and rode toward home.

He didn't notice the dark figure flattened up against the front wall of the theater. The stocky figure didn't step back out onto the road until the last whirring sounds of bicycle wheels on cobblestones had faded into the distance.

When Max arrived at the dinner table, Grammie and Ari had long since finished eating and were sitting in front of their empty plates, while what was left of the chicken stew had grown cold in its pot as they waited for Max, and the dumplings on top of the stew looked slimy and sodden and not like anything you'd ever want to put in your mouth. Max was greeted with anger.

Not that anybody yelled. Not that anybody pounded a fist on the table to demand to know just where he had been and tell him this was unacceptable behavior. In fact, nobody said anything.

Max slipped into his chair. He served stew and dumplings onto his plate. He took a drink of lukewarm milk.

Nobody spoke.

Max broke the silence. "I'm sorry. I was—"

"I don't care," Grammie said.

Ari looked reproachful, saying, *How could you be so inconsiderate?* without uttering a single word, the way dogs can.

"You'll be sorrier once you taste those dumplings," Grammie observed, not unhappily.

Max didn't try to explain, if this was the way they were going to be. He said "I'm sorry" again, and Grammie said, "I hope you'll at least let me know next time. And don't try to tell me there won't be a next time. I know better."

Grammie sounded more discouraged than angry, really.

"I will," Max said. "I give you my word."

Grammie nodded, but did not smile. "That's always been good enough for me," she said, then watched him eat the cold glop, not letting him get away with leaving anything on his plate. Probably, Max thought as he forced himself to chew, she figured that the cold dinner was punishment enough. She was right about that, he admitted to himself, forcing the last gluey mouthful of dumpling down his throat.

Only then did Grammie tell him: "I got a letter today, which I didn't open. From Andesia."

12

In which Max gets a letter from a king

The heavy envelope with its bright stamps was addressed to Miss Aurora Nives at 17 Brewery Lane in Queensbridge, but Grammie hadn't opened it. "I knew where it was from," she explained, turning the elegant envelope over to show Max the wax seal with its design of sharp mountain peaks with an *A* included, or trapped, within them. They had last seen that design on the golden brooch that arrived at 5 Thieves Alley in April, in the packet with two first-class tickets on the nonexistent *Flower of Kashmir.* Max alone had seen it since then, and only once. The frightening, annoying button was still hidden in his drawer. But here was a letter. Perhaps this message would be clearer.

"It's his handwriting," Max agreed. His father's thick dark letters spelled out Grammie's name and address. Max turned the envelope over again and touched the seal with his fingertips. Now that a response had actually arrived, actual word from his parents, he was not all that impatient to open it, as if he didn't want to hear what it might say.

"What are you waiting for?" Grammie asked.

"Should I leave?" Ari asked.

"No," Grammie and Max said at the same time, and then, "I'm just . . . ," Max mumbled, and Grammie admitted, "I know, it's . . ." Neither of them said what they were thinking: that this had nothing to do with privacy and everything to do with reality. This communication made everything more real, and what if it contained bad news? Or dangerous news? They weren't sure they wanted to be alone, just the two of them, with what it might contain.

Then, resolutely, Max took his dinner knife, wiped it clean on his napkin, and slit open the envelope.

The writing paper was as heavy as the envelope, the gold engraving at the top of the page had that same three-peaked design, the handwriting was his father's. There could be no doubt. Max read the letter through, silently and quickly, anxiously. Then he read it out loud.

"Dear Miss Nives," he read, *"I was pleased to receive your letter, trapped here in the palace as I am by our mountain winter."* Max looked up. "Winter?"

Ari echoed Max's confusion. "But it's summer."

"Not in the Southern Hemisphere," Grammie told them.

"In the Southern Hemisphere, the seasons are opposite to what they are in the Northern Hemisphere."

She announced this in her schoolteacher voice, so Max knew it was a fact, but he was surprised to learn it. He would have spent some time wondering at the strangeness of that, but at the moment what the King of Andesia had written was more important. He read on:

I am afraid that I cannot recommend my country for a family vacation. Here in Andesia there are only a few inns, and those are not suitable for ladies and girls. Also, it is a long, rough journey to my country, traveling overland from Maracaibo, especially hard going when you leave Machiques behind. So that, although it would give the Queen and me great pleasure to welcome guests from our old country (for guests, as everybody knows, can be as entertaining as theater) and although we could promise you a most rapt audience for all the news you might bring, Andesia would not be a safe country to visit.

Max looked at Grammie. "Where is Maracaibo?"

"On Lake Maracaibo, Venezuela," she told him. "I've seen Machiques on the maps, when I was looking for Andesia; it's inland."

"That's wild country, isn't it? Jungle. Mountains," Ari said.

"Is he telling me not to come?" Max asked.

"Finish reading," they answered.

Max read on:

The Queen is flattered to hear that you think she is beautiful. I must say, I think the same, and she is clever, as well, and kind. The people of Andesia have grown very fond of her in the short time we have been here. "Her Excellency likes people," they say, and they are right. "His Excellency listens politely" is the best they can say about me, I'm afraid.

You asked if I always knew I was a king. No, I did not. I was taken by surprise, I can tell you, when fate (as people put it) rapped on my cabin door—or you might say it rapped on my numb-skull. Certainly, the crown came gift-wrapped. But I have always liked adventures and this is certainly a big one for me, even if my country is small and poor and we who live in it are trapped among the high mountains. For we must all play the roles we are assigned, must we not?

The letter was signed *William, King of Andesia.*

When Max finished reading, there was a long silence in the kitchen. Then Grammie held out her hand and he passed the letter to her. She studied it for a while before offering it to Ari, who only shook his head and looked from one to the other of them. "What does he want you to do?" he asked.

"I don't know," Max admitted. "There's something funny . . ."

"Agreed," Grammie said. "But I can't put my finger . . ."

"I need to think," Max said, looking down at the envelope. His father had addressed it to Miss Aurora Nives as if she were a schoolgirl, even though he knew perfectly well who she was.

"Yes," Grammie agreed, staring down at the letter she held in her hand.

"Let's talk at supper tomorrow," Max suggested.

"If you're here," Grammie said, a not-so-gentle reminder.

"I promised, didn't I?" Max said.

13

The Water Rat *Jobs*

• ACT II •

SCENE 1

The next day, Max was outside early and painting—although, really, he barely saw the tall white clouds billowing up into the blue sky, like sheets hung out to dry on a windy day, and he could not have said exactly how he had arrived at the shades of blue he saw on the paper before him. His hand and eyes were at work but his mind was elsewhere: on the letter from Andesia, mostly, which advised him not to visit but seemed also, somehow, to be saying more, but *what* more, Max could not understand. He had read the letter over so many times that he had it memorized, like lines in a play. The oddness in it flickered just in front of him, but when he reached out he couldn't capture it, or even touch it. Usually, when Max painted, his mind cleared and ideas arranged themselves in his brain. Usually, after an hour or two in front of his easel, he knew what to do. But not that morning. The disturbing sense that he was missing something in his father's letter kept distracting him and refused to move aside, until at last he gave up.

He rinsed his brushes, closed the box of watercolors, removed the red beret, and wrote a quick note to Captain Francis, saying that Carlo did not need worrying about, the Solutioneer was sure of it, and Captain Francis could send his final payment to 5 Thieves Alley, for which Mister Max thanked him.

He went to the library to tell his grandmother that he might be late for dinner, and ask if she would please, if he was late, keep it warm in the oven for him. He thought that would make her smile, and it did. Then he went back home to pick up a pad of paper, two pencils, and his red beret. He had time before his final meeting with the Mayor to take the evening ferry around the lake and at least find out what this Nissa looked like.

Carlo had said that she took the ferry every workday morning from the city docks up to Summer, and made the longer journey from Summer back around the lake in the evenings. Max decided to ride the five o'clock ferry, along with people who worked in Queensbridge but had homes in one of the lakeside towns, where the streets were quieter, if not so lively, and house prices were lower, even if there were not so many houses to choose among. There was the definite risk that Carlo or Captain Francis would recognize him, maybe as the Solutioneer or maybe as Max Starling, so he decided that his painter self was his best disguise and walked to the docks carrying a large sketch pad and wearing not only his red beret but also the smock-like blouse worn by the old Nurse in *The Queen's Man,* a style of dress unusual enough to be thought artistic, he hoped. He was an artist, out for an evening ride in hopes of capturing a scene, or a face. If he stood close beside the wheelhouse, Carlo wouldn't notice him, being busy helping passengers on and off the little boat, and the Captain would literally overlook him, besides being fully occupied keeping his eye on the water, or on the docks. Max thought he'd be safe.

He joined the workers streaming onto the boat, clerks from stores in the New Town, a few bankers and doctors and lawyers who had built themselves big houses with views over the lake but did not own carriages yet, young men and women who worked in offices, and a few well-dressed shoppers carrying wrapped parcels and wearing broad-brimmed hats decorated with gauzes and laces, flowers and feathers. The ladies claimed the white benches on the foredeck and the men milled about. Carlo was too busy taking tickets to pay any particular attention to an artist. Captain Francis was up on the bridge, listening to the chug of the motor and giving a final check to the various gauges and valves, to be sure *The Water Rat* was ready to make this trip. This was the busiest time of the afternoon, as crowded as the morning route when these same people took the ferry to their workplaces.

Standing alone and undistracted by the rumble of the

motor or the hum of conversations, Max looked out over the bow, intent, serious, for anyone to see. Every now and then he made a few marks on his sketch pad. He was thoroughly in character. Most of the passengers gave him no more than a passing glance, although a lively group of young men who wore the trousers and shirts of office workers nudged one another, and pointed him out to one another with sidelong glances, and laughed.

Max ignored everybody. He was making art.

The first stop on the route around the lake was the town of Summer, at this season a busy little village of cafés and restaurants, gift shops and small stores offering the latest styles for men and women, as well as a dockside boat rental business. Most of its restaurants, hotels, and boardinghouses were open only in these warm months. The town filled to bursting when the royal family came to stay, and now, when they were due to arrive in two weeks, every store on the plaza had been decorated with bunting, and at every door and window flowers shone in the evening light.

Beyond its wide lakefront plaza, Summer was a town of twisting lanes and low stone fences overgrown with jasmine, primroses, and clematis vines, which sent out waves of fragrance and color all summer long, to greet the little ferry as it landed. Several passengers got off but only half a dozen people waited on the dock to cross over onto *The Water Rat,* all of them women, most of them servants from the large houses along The Lakeview. These wore full blue skirts and loose white shirtwaists, now wrinkled and stained by a day's labors.

Some had knotted shawls around their shoulders against the early morning chill and the evening temperature drop. Only one of the women wore a hat—a small, dark cloche—and gloves, and a short fitted jacket as dark gray as her stylishly cut skirt.

A quick glance at Carlo's face as he handed this young woman on board confirmed Max's guess. This was Nissa. The young woman's face, in profile, was so entirely expressionless that it had to be a mask, so there was no way Max could guess at her feelings about the young ferryman. She kept her eyes cast down, as if fearful of losing her footing, and she held her head bent. She freed her gloved hand from his assisting fingers as soon as she stepped off the short gangplank, and moved along to the bow of the boat without a backward glance. Once there, she stood motionless at the rail, looking forward, as the ferry pulled away from Summer to round the Promontory.

On its perch at the very end of the Promontory, the summer palace was clearly visible from the ferry, a long, low white building with curved red tiles on its roofs. From its many terraces, the King could overlook the entire lake, westward to the town of Brookside, north to Graffon Landing, south to the lights of Queensbridge. Its many windows shone gold in the lowering sun, as if the building knew what a treasure it was to the royal family, the holidays being a time when, for week after long summer week, the royal children could be more boys and girls than princes and princesses of the realm.

Nissa, however, seemed uninterested in the palace. Her

attention was fixed on the small waves that rushed by the prow as the ferry cut its path through the water. One passenger left the boat at Passway, and he wore the felt cap of a countryman, its single pheasant feather pointing up, toward the mountains. Max guessed that he was a farmer with business in Queensbridge that day; a wagon waited at the dock, probably to carry him home. The tiny village of Passway had grown up on the only cove on that section of lake, where hills crowded right down against houses. It was really no more than a landing place, with one inn, which housed also the post office and a general store to serve those who lived on the widespread farms. A single road led out of the village, up into the hills and then, more steeply, up into the curve of the mountains that rose without foothills along the northern lakeshore.

The ferry went on, circling the lake, stopping at Graffon Landing, where nobody got off or on; and Bosca, where a throng of employees from Mr. Bendiff's factories, wearing smocks with an elaborate *B* embroidered on the back, made a talkative, happy load for two stops—standing back to let the few Brookside passengers get off and the few Brookside citizens dressed for an evening in the city get on—until they themselves exited at Notton, the newest and least expensive of the Queensbridge suburbs, just far enough beyond the outskirts of the New Town to require its own ferry stop.

Nissa left the boat at its final stop, the docks in the old city. Carlo watched her, but she kept her head bent and did not look at him. Once Carlo had turned back to his labors, Max folded his sketch pad closed and followed the young woman. He wanted a good look at her face, to see what expression it wore when she knew Carlo could not see her.

Nissa was slender, in her fitted jacket and swinging skirt, and she walked with quick grace, her head sometimes raised to look around her but not, Max thought, to enjoy the shop windows, or the variety of people on the streets. No, Nissa looked around her the way a squirrel down from its nest to find food looks around itself, ready to bolt up the nearest trunk to safety. She looked up and around, quickly, briefly, then down again. It wasn't until she was emerging from a tea and coffee shop that Max actually saw her, but when he did he understood how Carlo's heart had been so immediately and completely won.

It was her eyes, he thought at first, but almost immediately noted also the round chin and broad forehead, her short, straight nose, and the spun gold hair under the cloche. Her eyes were simply what you noticed first. Nissa's large, round eyes were set deep into the delicate bones of her face. They were a smoky green color and her lashes were golden, and their expression struck him, as sharply as an arrow. The wide innocent eyes of the young woman looked out at the world in sad surprise, as if she had not yet forgotten that she once hoped for good things, things now forever lost. Once Max had seen her eyes, he could see that there was a haze of sadness all around her. The drab color she wore could have been mourning. But her hair was the color of spring sunshine and the little smile with which she looked back at the tea merchant, who had called some pleasantry after her, seemed more suited to a person for whom the world is a pleasant, easy place to live, a person who would brighten any room she entered, who would have a life full of gladness but yet—such was her gentle goodness—would arouse no envy.

An interesting character, thought Max, an interesting story, probably. Also, a story she kept secret, from Carlo and, Max guessed, from everyone. He had seen her face and, like Carlo, he wanted to help this young woman, whatever her trouble. Secrets, he had learned, were the very soil that sorrows grew most easily out of. He already knew what his next move would be: he would be waiting in Summer when she arrived for her day's work. If he knew where she was employed, he might be able to figure out some way to be introduced to her.

That settled, he hurried back through the streets of the old city, to outfit himself for his meeting with the Mayor.

14

The Mayor's Job

• ACT I •

SCENE 5 ~ THE SOLUTION

Mayor Richard Valoury arrived at the stage door accompanied by Officer Torson, and Max was glad he'd thought to wear the tinted glasses. The light in the alley was dim, but he didn't underestimate Sven Torson's curiosity. As the heroic spy from *The Queen's Man,* in his long dark overcoat and wide-brimmed hat, wearing tinted glasses and a silly long white silk scarf, waiting behind the little wooden porch, he was probably not going to be recognizable. He looked nothing like the gardener, Mister, whom Officer Torson had met only twice before.

In fact, both the Mayor and Officer Torson were so wrapped up in their own concerns that if there *had* been anything suspicious about this Solutioneer, they wouldn't have noticed it. Without any polite chitchat, without even introducing Officer Torson, the Mayor strode up to Max and demanded, "Well? What have you discovered?"

Max reported the conclusions he'd drawn: "I believe the culprits are boys, school age or slightly older, probably. I suspect they are forcing the small shop owners to pay for protection."

"Protection from what?" asked the policeman.

"From the damage they'll do if they aren't paid off," Max answered.

Mayor Valoury turned to Sven Torson. "It's what we were afraid of."

"But now we have some idea who to look for," the policeman said.

"Can you tell us any more?" the Mayor asked. "Because time's running short. If anything is going on that might in any way endanger the royal family, we have to warn the palace."

"Of course," Max agreed.

"If we can't keep the royal family entirely and absolutely clear of danger, danger of any kind, it means soldiers everywhere," Officer Torson added, in case this Solutioneer didn't understand all the consequences. "Soldiers cause trouble and they don't always help."

"Generals like to be in total control," the Mayor added. "The army doesn't care about ordinary citizens. Not like a mayor does."

"And how could the royal family have their usual holidays, free from public duties and cares for these summer weeks, if there were always soldiers around? Never able to just take a stroll, have an ice cream, fly a kite in the meadows, hunt in their forests, or even go out on the lake, just for a morning's fishing? Never able to be as private and free as the rest of us."

"I see the difficulties," Max said. "I wish I could have been more helpful."

The Mayor turned to look at Officer Torson, who had turned to look at the Mayor. They nodded at one another, as if approvals had been asked, and given. Then they both turned to the Solutioneer, a slender figure, almost invisible in the poor light in his long dark cloak, with his hat pulled so low that you could barely see his glasses, and why would he wear tinted glasses in this light, anyway? It was the Mayor who made the request.

"Actually," he said, "you *could* give us more help. We think. If you were willing."

"How?" Max asked.

"The shopkeepers are all too frightened to talk," Officer Torson began. "And we need to smoke these hoodlums out. *I* can't do it because everybody knows . . ." He hesitated, apologizing, "I've got a reputation for—" He faltered.

"Honesty," the Mayor finished when the policeman seemed unable to say the word. "Integrity. They know he'd never be susceptible to bribes or to—" and the Mayor faltered.

Max guessed that the Mayor had kept secret from the policeman the threats that had been made against his family. Without hesitating, or thinking, he turned to demand, "You didn't tell him?"

Some secrets were so dangerous that they should never be kept.

"Tell me what?" the policeman asked.

"Not yet," the Mayor mumbled.

"You have to," Max said.

"Tell me *what*?" the policeman demanded.

"I know," the Mayor admitted to Max. He turned to Officer Torson. "I'll tell you as soon as we're done here."

"That you will," the policeman said, not at all the way an underling usually speaks to his superior.

Mayor Valoury turned back to Max. "Officer Torson is known to be too honest and I'm too public a figure, and unmarried, too. Besides which, it would be much more dangerous to threaten me, or try to blackmail me. Not that there's anything they could blackmail me about," he added quickly.

Max was afraid he could guess now what was going to come next.

"So I thought . . . that is, we wondered if . . ." The Mayor turned to the policeman again, as if for assistance, but Officer Torson only said, "My family? The children?" in a shocked voice.

"We thought that if you were to go to the shops that have been attacked and tell them the rates for protection were going up, that they might then turn to the police for help. Be willing to give us some information about the hoodlums, descriptions, names."

"Of course," warned Officer Torson, who was honest even

when it might work to his disadvantage, "if you do that, the hoodlums might hear about it. You'd be like bait in a trap."

The Mayor continued his argument. "We have to identify them, and take them into custody, and bring them to trial. The trial wouldn't be until fall, so that the royal family need not hear even a whisper about it, because—it would be truly disastrous for Queensbridge if they lost faith in the lake as a safe place. If the guilty parties are in custody, and we put out the word to the shopkeepers, quietly of course . . . We'll pay you, of course. For the extra time. We'll pay double the usual," he offered, trying to read the expression on what he could see of Max's face.

They hadn't asked Max how he had reached his conclusions. They agreed with him, so they didn't wonder. They didn't know, therefore, that he had already tried something very like their plan, and without success. "But I—" he began.

The Mayor interrupted. "Also, it seems to me that the city needs to have a private investigator permanently available. He'd need his own office, of course, and we would provide that. We're going to be decentralizing the city library, opening smaller libraries in different areas of the city, and perhaps even one or two of the lakefront villages, libraries that will be more convenient to more of the people, so there will be office space available in the city library building," he offered.

Aha, Max thought, distracted by this information. *That's what's—*

"You'd be doing your city a real service, and your King,

too," the Mayor continued. He was using any argument he could think of. "As well, I would be able to recommend your services to anyone who needed them, without specifying how it is I have come to know your excellences, of course. It wouldn't do for this situation ever to get out, in any way."

It was a plan, and if he revisited some of the vandalized shops it could work, Max thought. If what he had deduced about the protection racket was correct, that is, and he was pretty confident about that. Just what might happen when the criminals were being smoked out, he had no idea. That was one thing that made him hesitate. He didn't want to risk his own secrets. Another thing that made him hesitate was his grandmother. Because if anything happened to him . . . If he made himself a target where something might happen to him, or where he might be exposed as Max Starling, twelve-year-old abandoned child, Grammie was the one who would be the most hurt by that. And now that he might have discovered what had been worrying at her, the secret she had been protecting *him* from, he wanted to spare her further worry.

On the other hand, Max *did* want to finish this job up well, and help the Mayor, and the city, too. Then, too, if he succeeded in stopping these criminals he could ask that Grammie keep her job. He could probably think of some way to make that request that wouldn't give away his relationship to her.

And maybe he could even think of a safe way to discover who the boys were. He wondered what Tomi Brandt, who roamed all the streets of the city, might know. He wondered what Pia might say that would get him thinking in new ways, if he told her about it. This problem *could* be solved without putting himself at risk. Maybe. Possibly. Most problems had more than one solution, after all, more than two even, more than three sometimes. And wasn't that what he was good at? Wasn't he, after all, the Solutioneer?

"I will need some time to think about this," he said to the two men. "I'll be in touch. It won't be long," he assured them, and walked away, with no more emotion than the Miser had shown, leaving his poverty-stricken neighbor after having refused the request for help, at the end of the first act of *A Miser Made Miserable.*

Sven Torson called after him, "I'll watch out for you, day and night, if you'll do this," then Max heard him demand, in an entirely different tone of voice, "Just what is it, sir, that you should have told me?"

Striding along the docks with his coat billowing behind him, turning up into the winding streets that would take him to Thieves Alley, Max was lost in thought, wondering how to find Tomi, who just might know something. Max knew how little chance he had of approaching Tomi without revealing his secret. Tomi had seen through one disguise already. Could he trust Tomi Brandt? On the other hand, was there any other way the Solutioneer could approach this problem?

15

The Mayor's Job

• ACT II •

SCENE 1 ~ THE CAPTURE

Max didn't sleep well that night. The next morning, he couldn't concentrate on his painting. His mind jumped from one thing to another, like a frog trying to find his dinner, hopping from one lily pad to another, chasing one bug after another, always leaping and landing and looking hungrily about. There was his father's letter and the problem of how to find some not-dangerous way to discover who was threatening the shopkeepers of the old city. There was the question of Nissa, and how to discover her secret, and also the question of whether he would be wise to try to talk to Tomi Brandt, or if it would be wiser to continue keeping his own secrets. Not to mention, now that he knew what she had been keeping from him, what he should say to Grammie.

Not to mention *why* his father had written that kind of letter, which was probably because it was dangerous for someone—for Max? for his parents?—to write the plain clear truth. And there was that maddening button.

Hop. Hop. Hop. And not one fly in range of his long tongue.

The Mayor's request at least was not an elusive mystery. However, Max didn't know if he owed his first loyalty to his grandmother, in which case it was honorable and responsible to decline the job, or to the city where he lived, in which case the honorable and responsible thing was to agree to be the bait in the Mayor's trap. He knew what the heroic Lorenzo Apiedi would do, but he thought he also knew what the Absentminded Professor would say, being, as he was, a humanist and believing, as he did, that the most important thing in life is to harm no one, especially your own family.

Unfortunately for Max, he could see the wisdom and rightness of both of these points of view.

Maybe he should try to find Tomi Brandt, after all, go into the old city and look for him . . .

He didn't bother with any disguise that morning. That morning, he was a boy on a bike, in a boy's dark trousers and a boy's cotton shirt, with a boy's blue cap on his head. He was twelve-year-old Max Starling, not Mister Max, the Solutioneer.

In other words, he was a little careless.

If he couldn't have any ideas about how to solve any of the problems facing him, Max said to himself as he pedaled vigorously along the narrow street, he could still be sure that the Starling Theater was safe. He didn't think it was in any danger but checking would give him something useful to do. After he had seen that everything was all right with the theater, he decided, he would walk to the baker for a roll and stop at the cheese store, so he could have a quick sandwich for his midday meal. He hoped that while he walked something about his feet landing squarely on the ground in a regular rhythm, *thunk-thunk-thunk,* would jar ideas loose in his brain. He hoped that if he was looking around him at the people on the streets and the goods displayed on carts and in shop windows, an idea might come out from hiding and introduce itself to him.

At the theater, everything looked as usual, which was just what Max expected. He leaned his bicycle against the wall and made a slow tour all around the building, just to be sure, across its blank rear face, through the alley by the stage door, across the chained and padlocked front entrances, and back to the office doorway where his bicycle waited under the high bathroom window farther along the alley. Satisfied, he got his roll and a chunk of cheese, and sat down on a doorstep to enjoy lunch, looking at the people who moved along in front of him but not really seeing them. If he were to agree to be the bait in the trap, he wondered how Officer Torson planned to guarantee his safety, and he wondered just how that trap would be laid. Also, he wasn't sure how he would keep the scheme a secret from his grandmother, and he wasn't even sure he should. He chewed and swallowed and tried to think of another way to discover the identity of the three extortionists.

It wasn't until he glimpsed a stocky figure and felt a rise of hope that he realized that he was actually expecting to accidentally run into Tomi Brandt. Certainly he'd glimpsed the boy often enough—too often, he'd thought, worrisomely often—in the weeks since he'd left school. Max wondered about confiding his secret to Tomi, and asking for his help. Tomi wasn't a gossip. His sense of honor meant—probably—that he could keep a secret. That is, if it seemed honorable to him to give his word. He took two steps toward the stocky figure, thinking of what to say first.

But it wasn't Tomi. It was some boy Max didn't know and had never seen, with a shaggy head of corn-yellow hair, oddly black around the ears and forehead, as if he had colored it to appear in a play and failed to wash it completely out. But why would a boy color his hair? And really, the boy didn't resemble Tomi at all, except in his build. Max resumed his seat and his lunch.

After he had finished his sandwich, Max sat for several minutes, still half expecting to see Tomi. But Tomi didn't appear, and the only other idea for identifying the culprits that Max had come up with involved asking Pia to ask her father to bribe one of the shopkeepers, pay him more money than he could resist, to identify the boys. Given the sound of that letter to the Mayor that so boldly threatened harm to

Sven Torson's family, Max wasn't sure even Mr. Bendiff had enough money to buy that information. He needed to walk some more.

Also, he needed not to be worrying at that problem, like a dog worrying a bone. He distracted himself from the Mayor's problem by thinking about his parents.

What did they want him to do? Or did they want him to do nothing?

When Max saw that he was about to cross in front of the berth where *The Water Rat* rested—and he wasn't wearing any kind of disguise!—he turned quickly up a side street, heading away from the docks and into the heart of the old city. He walked along at a brisk pace, by cafés and bars and boardinghouses, food shops and notions shops and stalls that sold used clothing, making his way back toward the more residential sections, and the little square, and the Starling Theater. No longer lost in his own thoughts, he was puzzled by the looks he got from some of the people on the streets, who stepped aside to let him by before he even thought to ask them to move, or offer to move himself. Apparently there was something in his face or in his gait that made people want to step aside and let him pass.

It was all making Max uneasy, and he was glad to step out of Barrow Street onto Park Lane, where two-family houses replaced narrow buildings with their shops on the ground floor and apartments stacked above. Here, fewer people were out on the roads. He could hear his own footsteps again, but curiously blurred, a *thunkity-thunkity* sound, as if there were an echo.

It was then that he realized he was being followed, and being followed by someone the people walking toward him didn't like the look of. He studied the street ahead, looking for an open door, checking to be sure there was someone else in sight. These houses had small yards, for children to play in. It was a neighborhood where families could enjoy a summer evening sitting on their own front steps, conversing with friends who passed by. The streets were cobblestoned like the others, but almost empty now. Too empty, Max thought, listening to the footsteps behind him—more than one pair?—and unable not to notice that the three or four other people approaching him also kept their distance, and kept their eyes on the ground right ahead of their own feet, as if worrying over getting safely by him.

Were the footsteps coming nearer? Max wondered, when he was closed in on.

Somebody crowded him from behind and somebody came at him from the left, to walk right at his side, almost forcing him into the center of the road. Max had already turned to look at the person crowding into him on his right, a boy, an older boy—Max took it all in in a swift, troubled glance—broad-shouldered and muscular, a nose that had been broken at least once, with dark hair and a whistling mouth.

Why was he whistling? He hadn't been whistling a minute ago, had he?

Max couldn't stop to think, or to ask what was going on, because he was being kept moving forward by the three other bodies, as if they were a gang of four boys out together, not one boy walking alone in the custody of three strangers.

Max glanced quickly to his left. That boy was younger, probably his own age, or no more than a year or two older, and he was the stocky boy Max had seen earlier, mistaking him for Tomi. That boy, too, did not look at Max, but his expression—as he watched an approaching businessman who moved to the other side of the street—was alert and intelligent. He had bright blue eyes and his eyebrows were as corn-yellow as his hair. And who was crowding up against Max's back? Didn't he feel slighter? Smaller?

Max saw and wondered all of this in the first seconds that flashed by, as he realized just what was going on. He tensed his muscles to just stop. Dead. In his tracks.

Then the boy on his right stopped the whistling long enough to mutter, "I've got a knife," before he went back to his lively melody.

Is he whistling a hornpipe? Max wondered stupidly as he felt something sharp pierce through the cotton shirt covering his upper arm. His left arm flew protectively across his chest, but he kept on walking, although more slowly, now resisting the pressure at every step—as he tried to think.

Panic, he was discovering, is not the best soil to grow clear thinking out of.

Four blocks ahead, Park Lane came to an end at the little square in front of the Starling Theater. Two chattering women approached the boys, heads bent together, and Max wondered what would happen if he cried out for help. The whistler didn't lose any breath worrying about that; he just dug the knife a little deeper into Max's upper arm.

Probably, they could cut his throat and run off before either of the women figured out what was going on. So Max concentrated on the greenery ahead, where the fountain sprayed water up and a fine mist drizzled down. If he could pretend to trip, there, at the fountain, and make a run—leaving the boys momentarily taken by surprise—and reach his bicycle? On a bicycle he could get away. On a bicycle he was much faster than anyone on foot. Max had played a stumbling suitor in *The Adorable Arabella,* whose clumsiness made him sympathetic to the audience, although not so sympathetic that they hoped he'd win her heart. The clumsy suitor was more a clown than a lover, but that experience, Max hoped, would come in handy. In his imagination he practiced the stumbling fall.

Three blocks to go. The street ahead was briefly empty and a bag was put over his head and Max stumbled for real. They caught him from both sides.

He could see nothing. Everything he could hear was muffled by the same thick material that kept all light out. The air inside the bag was stale and smelled of—what?—of straw, and ashes, and something acrid as old smoke.

Max's boots slipped on the cobblestones now, and he heard the boys laughing, as if they were all involved in some rough game together, the kind of shoving and pushing game

96

boys like to play. He tried to keep his bearings, tried to make a mental map, because wasn't it always better to know where you were? They were still holding his arms. From outside, it would have looked as if they were helping him stay upright.

Max was having trouble getting enough air into his lungs, but they held his arms too tightly to allow him to lift the bag off his head.

They turned sharply left and walked on for a while—how long? Fifty steps? Seventy-five? He didn't think to count until it was too late. They turned him right and walked him along, then again right, and after a while left, and after another while left again, and quickly left, and he was totally confused. He gave up trying to do anything more than stay on his feet.

At least the knife no longer pricked into him.

Disoriented, consumed by anxiety, Max heard a metallic rattle, like chains—was he going to be chained up? Like a dog in a cage or a prisoner in a dungeon?—but before he could finish any of those fears he felt himself being shoved down two shallow steps until he fell, fell hard, down onto a wooden floor.

16

The Mayor's Job

• ACT II •

SCENE 2 ~ THE CELL

Hands grabbed Max's arms and he was jerked to his feet, then pulled along—how far? He had no idea, he could only feel: feel fear, feel blind, feel choked for breath, feel off balance. With his head in a thick cloth bag, he couldn't even sense any difference in the air around him. He thought he was inside, but if he was in a large empty space or a narrow one, he couldn't tell. All he could tell was that the three bodies continued to crowd close around him, forcing him to keep moving forward.

Finally—after what had seemed only minutes but could have been much longer, he couldn't keep track, he couldn't *think*—they jerked him to a halt, and hands shoved at his shoulders. He was forced down, onto hard ground—wood? stone? dirt?

His arms were pulled forward and his wrists tied tightly together.

Max couldn't even find two words in his head and he had no idea what he might say if he could say anything. His heart was hammering in his chest and he was glad to be sitting because his legs were shaking. Everything was blank, and stank of—something, something acrid and nasty as turpentine, and maybe it *was* turpentine? But the voices were clearer here, inside, wherever here was. There was a disagreement going on and for some reason—why should it be so?—this quarrel between his captors cleared Max's head. Maybe he would hear something helpful as the two voices argued.

"Aren't we going to take the bag off before we set him loose?" asked a blue voice, as calm as Grammie's baked custard.

The question was answered by a jagged dark voice. Purple, Max decided. "I've maybe changed my mind about doing that."

"Hang on, Kip," said the blue voice. "We're just going to scare him off. That's what we said, that's the plan. He's plenty scared by now, I'm sure of it."

The purple voice, Kip, said, "Not so scared he can't hear you telling him my name, thank you very much." When he was angry his voice got sharper, and heavier, more dangerous.

"You changed the plan," said the blue voice. "I was so surprised, I didn't think."

"No, you didn't, did you, *Colly.*" Kip's voice was suited to meanness. "I can see his ears flapping inside the bag, *Colly.*"

"I said I was sorry. But *do* we leave the bag on? Just because he hears what might be only our professional names."

Kip laughed. "You're not stupid, I'll say that for you. I'm thinking now—maybe we'll keep him prisoner a day or two, a week. Let him know we mean business."

"We can't kidnap him. That's what it is, Kip, kidnapping, and that's a serious crime."

"More serious than arson? Than taking protection money? Who're you kidding, Colly? Because it's not me, I promise you that."

"And besides, what would we feed him?" the blue voice asked, a little sullen now. Colly and Kip, Max repeated to himself, as if he was in danger of forgetting those two names, or their voices. But why was the third boy silent?

"Who says we'd feed him?"

"Even you have to admit murder is serious."

"I know that even the word frightens *you.* But think for a minute, Colly. Use that famous brain of yours. If we just leave him here and he dies, it's not like we killed him. But if it happens to happen? Think about it. Anyone else who's getting the idea of horning in on our little business will know better without us having to even raise a finger."

The blue voice said, "I couldn't let you do that."

The purple voice laughed. "Why don't you turn me in right now, then? Turn Blister in, too, and—oh yes . . ." His voice grew even heavier with mock surprise, as if he had just realized this. "And of course yourself, too. See what happens to your life if you do that. See if you ever get to do anything better than work in an ink factory. Give back all those coins you've been saving up—you may pretend you're spending like me, but I've been watching. You don't fool me. Not for a minute. Nobody fools me, do they, Blister?"

"Nosirreebob," said a third voice, a wobbledy, watery, colorless one. "Nobody couldn't never. Not you."

Could Blister be anybody's name?

"We'll leave him here for the night," Kip announced. "And the reason I know you won't do anything, my softhearted friend, is that you want to get away from Queensbridge more than you care about what happens to someone you never even met. Who was trying to shove you aside and take earnings out of your pocket, and you might think about that. Because it was a pretty stupid thing for anybody to try to do," the purple voice said, and a finger ground deep into the muscles at Max's neck. "I bet you're sorry now."

Max debated not responding but decided that would be foolish. He didn't trust his voice, however, so he only nodded his head within its stinking bag. Although, he realized, nodding, it wasn't entirely true. He'd smoked out the gang, hadn't he?

"Leave him?" Colly sounded surprised. "Here?"

Where was he, Max wondered, that the one person who sounded . . . normal, or maybe just uncriminal, in the gang was surprised at the thought of leaving a prisoner alone there?

"Why not? His hands are tied and we can tie up his ankles. He should be safe enough."

"With a bag over his head?" demanded Colly. "And no water?"

"You have a better idea? You agreed he needed some scaring off."

"With no way even to take a piss? For how long, Kip?"

Max was beginning to think that this Colly boy was an all-right person.

"Why not leave him in the bathroom, at least? There's only that one window nobody could escape out of. The door has a key and nobody will hear him if he shouts."

"If I do that, will you shut up?" Kip demanded. He was out of patience.

"Hands tied," Colly answered. "And no bag."

"Great. So he can identify us."

Colly said, in his blue voice as bright and expectant as an actor onstage, giving a cue to another actor, "He won't look. He's too scared to look. Aren't you?"

Max knew what to respond. He nodded.

"What's your name, prisoner?" Kip demanded.

Max said nothing.

"You've got a name, don't you?"

Without thinking, Max shook his head, and if he *had*

thought he would have known that that would make Kip angry.

"If you try to identify me I really will have to kill you." The voice was a dark, infuriated purple and its words were greeted with a silence that must have meant looks exchanged between the three of them.

Max waited.

"You don't think I can do it," Kip muttered.

"I do. I know you could," Blister said quickly. "You can do anything. You can do whatever you want, Kip."

Colly was less sure. "I'd hope you wouldn't be so stupid. I'd think you'd prefer prison to the gallows."

"And you'd know about the gallows, wouldn't you?" Kip answered, sarcastic and purple-voiced, like a king on his throne, so sure that he can do whatever he wants that he lets himself do anything. "Oh, sorry, Colly. I forgot she was your mother. I hope I didn't *hurt your feelings.*" Kip sneered the last three words, and then Max was knocked against so roughly that he fell over sideways. Noises flowed around and over him.

"Colly, stop," pleaded Blister. "You know you never can never"—thumping sounds—"you know he's"—grunts now, *umpphh* sounds, and cursing—"he's got a knife, Colly! Remember!"

Silence. Max was jerked up onto his feet.

"We'll mount a guard over him for the afternoon," Kip's voice announced. He was panting a little.

"You know I work the evening shift," said Colly, also panting.

"That's why you'll be the first guard. Blister will be here just before four-thirty, plenty of time to get to your big, important job, stirring turpentine into soot."

There was another silence. Then Kip gave another order: "We meet back here at seven tomorrow morning."

"You know I can't get away that early," Colly said, and he sounded tired, a faded blue voice.

"At nine, then. Understood?" Kip demanded.

Colly didn't speak, but he must have nodded because Max was pulled up onto his feet and then pushed, stumbling, forward until he tripped over a low doorsill and could barely keep his balance, while the bag was jerked off his head. He got only a brief glimpse of three boys—their shapes, their faces—before the wooden door was slammed shut and he heard a key turn in the lock.

He almost—in the relief of seeing again, in the relief of breathing clean air—gave it away. He almost turned to grin at the three faces as the door closed behind them. Because the bathroom into which they had locked him was in the Starling Theater, a tiny room that had one narrow window, high up on a wall, one stained sink, and one porcelain toilet, with a water tank above and a flush chain hanging down.

He knew where he was. He knew the building around him and the streets around the building. They had walked him in circles to confuse him, but in fact he was not that far from where they had grabbed him.

Max sank down onto the toilet seat, his legs watery with relief. Not that he knew of a secret passage out of this tiny room. Not that there were weapons concealed in the water tank. Not that he could climb up, somehow, to reach the window, which was in any case too small to squeeze through. Not, in fact, that there was any reason to think he would escape. But he knew where he was and, for no good reason, that enabled him to remember *who* he was.

He was the Solutioneer, in search of a way to report his discoveries to the Mayor. And he was Lorenzo Apiedi, the young hero of *A Patriot's Story,* unafraid of anything his captors might do to him. (This last was not strictly true, but Max had had a lot of practice being someone else, so it was partly true.) But mostly, right then, he was Max Starling, boy captive, and he needed to use the toilet the Colly boy had kindly made available to him.

Afterward, he flushed and went to the sink to wash his hands as best he could with his wrists lashed together. Then he bent over to drink from the faucet. Finally, he sat down on the floor, his back against the door, to try to form some kind of a plan.

All he needed was for the gang to set him loose. Unless Kip was serious about killing him, both to silence him and to rid them of what they supposed was competition, he would be set free in the morning. So all he had to do was wait.

Maybe.

Because while Max thought that Colly and the third boy—Blister? Was his name really Blister?—had no desire to hurt him at all, he wasn't at all sure about Kip. Kip was the wild card. Like Important Banker Hermann in *The Worldly Way,*

Kip cared only about what he wanted, and he didn't care how he got it. Kip was dangerous.

In *The Worldly Way* it had taken the combined efforts of the truehearted sawmill manager (played by William Starling), the sympathetic old bank teller (played by Bartleby Nye, their character actor), and a clever young carpenter (Max Starling) to defeat Important Banker Hermann (also played by Bartleby Nye). In this production, however, Max would have to play all three parts.

Drama involved both words and action, but Max couldn't *do* anything. As far as action was concerned, his hands were, literally, tied. But he could talk—if only he could think of what to say.

Whatever he said, he would speak as the truehearted manager, sure of the rightness of his cause (and Max *was* that) and confident of his courage (even if Max wasn't). His question came as much from curiosity about what the answer would be as from the desire to speak in character. "Where am I?" he called out.

There was no answer.

Max thought for a few minutes, then called again, "Colly? If you're there, tell me: Why is it that you have a job but you also extort money from these shopkeepers?"

Colly's answer was muffled by the closed door. "Can't hear you."

Max put his face next to the door. "You have a job, right? But you still force people to pay you for protection. Why are you doing that?"

"Why do you?" Colly's blue voice answered quickly.

"How do you know I *do*?" Max asked right back.

Colly was silent.

Max waited.

Colly's voice laughed. "I never see the coins from ink-making. They're paid to my grandfather. You could say, looking at it a certain way, that I'm a slave." There was no self-pity in Colly's voice; he was just making an observation.

Max was finding this boy quite interesting. "So this protection income . . . ," he began, and let his voice trail off.

"Escape money," Colly said. "If I can get away—maybe even out of Queensbridge? If I could go back to school—I don't care if I'm older than the others. What do I have to be proud about? But an educated person has a better chance at a job and I'm good with numbers, I always have been. I could have a good life." He was silent for a minute, then, "I don't know why I'm telling you this," Colly said.

"Well," answered Max, the Important Banker seeing a clever way to turn things in his own favor, "maybe so that I can offer you a better deal if you let me out?"

Colly laughed, sharp and blue, like the icy waters of the lake in winter. "That's not the kind of person I am. And if that's the kind of person *you* are, I'd be trading in Kip for someone just as bad. Or maybe worse. At least I know what Kip is like."

"You can't blame me for trying," Max said, although clearly Colly did.

"Besides which, I told Kip I was in with him. I gave him

my word. Unless he decides to kill you, of course," he reminded the prisoner.

Colly had nothing more to say.

Max shifted his position, leaning back against the door, to think. Deep within the empty building, the quiet was complete.

Max considered the plaster walls. He stared up at the window. He studied the faucet curved over the sink and the short chain hanging down above the toilet. Then, playing the only role possible at that moment, which was the Absent-minded Professor, who was always thinking his own thoughts whatever might be going on around him, he wondered how he would go about painting a skyscape of what was visible through the window, how to paint the glassy sheen so that anybody who saw the picture, even without a wooden frame to give them the clue, would know that they were looking through a pane of dirty glass at the sky over a city. The bathroom was on the same side of the theater as the private entrance, beside which Max's bicycle still waited—or so he hoped; the bicycle was about his only chance for escape, if he could get that far—and it was closed in by the building next door, so that there was, really, no sky visible, just light from the sky. It was a real painting problem.

After what felt like a long while—although he couldn't be sure—he tired of that subject and turned his attention to the Pythagorean theorem. He held all the different steps of the proof together in his imagination. He constructed squares on the sides of a right triangle, visualizing the parallelograms and triangles, and then he recited the necessary proofs of congruence to himself, one after the other, deducing the relationship of the three lines of the original right triangle and ending with a silent, victorious *QED:* $a^2+b^2=c^2$.

Then he wondered—for how long, he couldn't tell—how he might get himself out of this situation, or if all he had to do was wait. The worst thing would be the hunger, but there were worse things than hunger, and Max did not want to think about them. Although he wondered if he was foolish not to.

Of course, this made him think about his parents, and their journey to Andesia. How had they traveled? Had they been prisoners or accomplices? Had they wanted him with them or had they been glad that he was safe, as they imagined, at home?

Max didn't want to think about his parents. He didn't know *what* to think about them.

If it had not been summer, he could have made an accurate guess at the time by the quality of light in the window, but he only knew that it was coming up on four-thirty in the afternoon by the sounds of Blister arriving. Blister's steps stopped and he asked, in a breathless and colorless, watery voice, "Am I late? Don't be angry."

"You're in good time."

"Kip said I was going to be late."

"You know Kip," Colly's calm blue voice said. "He likes to—"

Blister interrupted him. "If it wasn't for Kip, I'd be dead meat. For the crabs."

"That was years ago."

"I've seen meat the crabs got at," Blister persisted. "And he lets me live in his yard. And he gives me food when he can. You shouldn't say bad things about Kip."

A silence greeted this remark.

Blister said, "Not to me anyway."

More silence.

"Even if it's true, but where else would I go?"

"It's a big world."

"He'd find me." Of this, at least, Blister sounded confident. "He doesn't think you're a good gang member anymore, Colly."

Colly laughed. "I never was. But thanks for the warning. I'll watch my back."

Max heard footsteps go along the corridor again, but this time the person was walking away. He thought he heard Blister lean up against the other side of the door, and he stayed seated, listening hard. He pictured a boy out there, alone in a big, empty building, the empty rooms along the corridor, the empty stage stretching unseen in front of him, and beyond that was row after row of empty seats, with the high dark space over the stage, lights dangling down . . . Emptiness closed in around Max, but it was a familiar emptiness. He could imagine how it might feel to Blister.

The clever young reporter in *The Worldly Way* had the trick of asking questions that threw people off balance by suggesting that he knew more than they wanted him to. So Max asked, "How long ago was it that Kip saved you, Blister?"

"I never said," Blister's voice protested from the other side of the door.

"But what happened?" Max asked.

"I can't remember. I never remembered. I was little and he pulled me out of the water and he says I didn't have a name, but that was a long time ago, years and years. But I must have had a name, don't you think?"

"Maybe not, if someone threw you into the river," Max said, as unsympathetic as the young reporter had been to Important Banker Hermann, who was trying to persuade him to conceal the truth of things, or scare him into cooperating, or bribe him to not write the story. "But why did Kip pull you out?"

"They wouldn't let him have a dog. They said he was too mean so he said he'd have me instead. At first, he hid me in the cellar but then I got to live in the shed because they washed their hands of him," Blister reported. "Like they washed their hands of me," he explained. "In the river."

"So where am I now?"

One of the other things the reporter was good at was switching topics so suddenly that the Banker had given away one of his secrets before he realized it.

But Blister had been told what to do and he did what he was told. "I can't tell you," he said. "Kip doesn't want me to talk to you," he added, sounding so watery and pale that Max actually felt sorry for him.

Max leaned against the locked door, listening and thinking, and after a while he asked, "Did Kip say that I can't talk to *you*?"

Blister took a minute to think about that. "No," he finally answered, and his voice had a watery smile in it. "He didn't, did he?"

Max had been raised in the theater and knew the power of words. "I could tell you a story," he offered. "Or sing you a song or recite a poem for you." If he could get Blister to relax his guard again, he might learn something to his advantage. At the moment, that was the only thing Max could think of to do, the only plan he could come up with.

It took no time for Blister to decide. "A story," his voice said. "With animals in it."

"Wild animals or tame ones?"

"Animals that live in a shed," Blister said.

Max chose "The Bremen Town Musicians," and he used all the dramatic skills he'd learned. His voices weren't very good, he knew, but his descriptions were—of the four animals and how each came to be fleeing for his life from a master who planned to get rid of him for being old and useless, of the little house where the robbers lived, and of the great fright the four animals gave to the robbers. "After that, the robbers were never seen in the forest again," Max concluded, "and the four friends lived there together for all the years that were left to them."

After a long silence, Blister's voice said, "I like that. Do you know one about another dog?"

The only story Max could think of was Aesop's fable about the dog in the manger. This struck him as an uninteresting choice but Blister enjoyed it. "He could have slept *under* the manger. Or he could have let the ox eat and then jumped back up to sleep on the straw that was left. Couldn't he?" There was much less hesitation this time before he requested a story about birds, and Max related the one he had read recently in his study of Greek myths, the sad tale of Icarus, the winged boy, which included not only Daedalus, the father ("I don't have one," said Blister, his voice even more colorless and watery than usual), but also the Minotaur trapped in his labyrinth (at which Blister giggled, before suggesting that he was going to build one of those for Kip and then *he'd* be the one bringing bread and leaving it in the doorway).

"A cow," Blister asked next, without hesitation.

"A cow?" Max racked his brains but had no idea. "Why a cow?"

"They're nice," Blister explained. "I saw a cow at the dairy shop. She had her baby with her."

The only cow Max could remember at that moment, in that situation, was in a nursery rhyme. "Hey diddle diddle," he recited, echoing the warm and gentle voice in which his own mother used to tell him nursery rhymes, "the cat and the fiddle. The cow jumped oooo-ver," he said, dragging out the *O* sound and—since he couldn't make the gesture with his hands—moving his chin up and around in an arc, "the moon."

When he'd finished the short poem, Blister asked immediately, "Again."

The voice from beyond the door asked "Again" and "Again" so many times that Max—after reciting for the twelfth or perhaps the twentieth time, he had lost count, "and the dish ran away with the spoon"—refused to repeat it.

He waited to hear Blister's response to the refusal.

The voice coming through the door was so faint and watery he couldn't distinguish the words.

"What?" he asked. "What did you say?"

"I said, I remember. I remember that cow. From before."

"Before what?" Now Max was simply curious.

"Before Kip. I wasn't sure . . . I couldn't remember . . . There really was a before Kip, wasn't there?"

Max was about to tell Blister that of course there was a before Kip and (hoping that after all these stories the boy would want to do what Max asked) to suggest that Blister unlock the door and allow Max to take him to an after Kip, when something thumped in the corridor.

The floors in the theater were wooden and footsteps thundered well on them. Max didn't need Blister's cry of "I'm sorry, Kip! Don't—!" to know what was going on.

"I *knew* I couldn't trust you," Kip's purple voice said. "I'm disappointed in you, Blister. I'm going to have to do something bad to you. I don't want to but you've made me have to. To help you remember to do as you're told. Again."

"I'll remember, Kip, I will. Honest, I promise. He tricked me," Blister said.

Kip ignored the other boy. "I'm going to be sure everything's as it should be in there," he said, and the key turned in the lock.

Max backed away, toward the throne. Maybe he could reach up and pull down so hard on the chain that the water box above would rip out of the wall and surprise Kip enough that Max could get through the door before Kip realized it. Maybe.

The door was pulled open and a figure looked in it.

Kip was the big, broken-nosed whistler, not the corn-yellow stocky boy. He stood in the doorway and smiled at Max while Blister—his dark hair sticking out wildly—crouched against the wall opposite, his legs pulled up protectively against his chest.

Kip *looked* ordinary enough. He wasn't a giant or a monster. He wore his brown hair short and he had round dark eyes. His smile showed a lot of teeth and it seemed frank and friendly, until you noticed the one snaggletooth, which made you look more carefully into the brown eyes to see how they gleamed with meanness, waiting, watching, close on each side of the broken nose. Kip had a dangerous look to him. You couldn't guess what this boy might do.

Kip was scary and Max was frightened.

The boy saw this, and it pleased him. Without taking his eyes off Max, he said to Blister, "I told you not to talk to him."

Max watched Blister. The boy looked at his knees to say, "Wasn't. I wasn't, Kip." Then he looked up to see how this had been received, cringing a little in anticipation of its having been received badly. He looked down again, to tell his knees, "It was him talking to me," and looked up again. Kip gave him a quick, sharp glance, and Blister backed down. "I'm really sorry. I won't ever again."

"Go away, Blister. Go back to your kennel and wait for me." Kip turned to Max but continued to threaten, "It'll be the worse for you if you're not there when I'm through here."

Blister didn't look at Max, or at Kip, either. He scrambled up and skittered away down the dark corridor.

Kip's smile didn't change. "I don't know anything about you," he said to Max. He put his big right hand into his jacket pocket and closed it around something.

Probably, Max thought, the knife. "Where am I?" he demanded desperately. Maybe he could get Kip talking.

It seemed he might have guessed right. Kip's smile widened. "It's our hideout—a place nobody but us knows about," he said. "So no one will ever find you here. There's no hope for you. No use in not telling me what I want to know."

Lorenzo Apiedi at that point would stand up straight and boldly defy the tyrant, Max knew, but something told him that it was smarter to let Kip see how frightened he was so that maybe Kip wouldn't come at—

Then an idea came to Max, came fully formed and complete, and he didn't even *want* to think about it.

He lowered his head and ran straight at Kip. Like a bull, or a goat, he rammed his head against the larger boy's chest. He would take Kip by surprise, knock him over, and be running down the corridor before Kip figured out what had happened. Max knew this building; he had at least two directions to go off in and three doors to escape through. If he could just get to his bicycle, he could get away.

In his mind, he had already wormed past a surprised and stumbling Kip and started down the hallway when he felt the thump of his weight jammed into Kip's stomach and the other boy's instinctive thrust of both hands, to push Max back, off, away.

It was Max who stumbled, surprised, and lost his footing, and cracked his head against the hard porcelain of the throne.

He was knocked out for only a few seconds, but he had been the dead body at the end of *The Queen's Man,* the murderous younger brother slain in a sword fight by the Queen's spy, as played by William Starling, often enough to know how to stay limp and take shallow breaths, shallow and invisible breaths. Max knew how to play dead and that was what he did.

Although he couldn't help but wish he'd landed facedown.

"Stupid git," Kip muttered.

Max didn't move.

After a few seconds, Kip spoke again. "You're not fooling me."

Max didn't move. He was dead meat, he was a cooked noodle, he was a cloak hanging on a hook.

"I'll bring you back to life," Kip said.

Max heard heavy steps coming close. He tried to think of what to do if the boy decided to test Max with a sudden jab of the knife, to force Max to react. But Kip kicked him instead. Hard. In the hip.

This was so unexpected that Max didn't have time to react to the blow. He might have been surprised, but the shock of the blow froze him. He continued being dead.

Then came a long silence. He sensed Kip, standing above him. He could feel the boy's presence, hear his breathing. Sometimes, Kip uttered a few words, thinking aloud: "—stupid Blister's fault," and "—can't be dead, I didn't do nothing," and, finally, "I'll see better in the morning." Then there was the sound of heavy footsteps and the door, closing. The key turned in the lock.

For a long time after that, Max lay unmoving.

17

The Mayor's Job

• ACT II •

SCENE 3 ~ HELP! HELP!

All Max could feel was relief that he wasn't lying on the floor spouting blood from a knife wound. That had been a real possibility, Max knew. Blister's fear was only one sign of what Kip was capable of. The men who owned the shops, that butcher for instance, would never have been so frightened by Colly and certainly not by Blister. Most of the time, when people are that cowed into submission, there's a good reason.

That there are people in the world who have no sympathy for others, who can't seem to imagine how it feels to be helpless and weak, Max knew. He also knew that there are people who enjoy being unkind and even cruel. He knew this not only from his own experience but also from the plays he had performed in. His father often claimed that the villain was a more interesting role than the hero, more complicated and bold, but those were villains like Robin Hood, as much heroes as villains in their own stories, or Important Banker Hermann, who only behaved badly around money. Villains like Kip—and Max suspected that in real life, most villains were closer to Kip than Robin Hood—you could neither admire nor enjoy nor sympathize with. Certainly, you never wanted to meet up with them and have to worry that they would take out their knives—for no good reason, because what good reason *could* there be for slicing someone up?—and cut pieces off you. Or kick you, when you were lying unconscious on the floor.

For a long time, Max enjoyed that feeling of relief, of not lying in his own blood with no help in sight. No help in sound, either, he thought, and laughed at his own joke, and sat up.

The light at the high window was still bright, so he knew it wasn't much past suppertime, which meant that he wouldn't yet have been missed. No one would notice his absence until Grammie gave up waiting at a table where his seat was, once again, empty. He wouldn't blame her if she thought he'd gone off somewhere, again, breaking his word to her. She would be as angry at him as worried about him. Max couldn't guess *what* the Mayor and Officer Torson would think when he hadn't gotten in touch with them as he had said he would. He could only hope that they would suspect something.

But even if they did suspect something, what would they do? And when would they do it? So few people had a clue about what Max was up to . . . He was as snared in his own secrets as trapped in the bathroom of the Starling Theater.

He could only hope that Grammie would be worried enough to start looking for him, and that sooner or later she would think of looking in the theater, and that her later would be sooner than nine in the morning. This, he knew, was unlikely. But if she did come to the theater, and if she looked down the neglected alley by the private entrance and saw his bicycle, she would recognize it.

Unless, he thought grimly, Kip had noticed the bicycle and stolen it.

Max could feel it, the speeding up of his heartbeat and the dryness in his mouth, the panic rising again as he realized that there was no escape from this trap and that Kip and his cohorts would be back in the morning. His only realistic hope at this point was that they would all arrive together. He didn't want to have to face Kip alone. He didn't think the boy was fool enough to really think he'd killed his prisoner, but he might want to come back early and alone to do something about that.

At those unnerving thoughts, Max's panic rose like a river slowly, slowly rising to overflow its banks and sweep everything away in a flood.

He had to stop thinking like that, he knew, but he didn't think he could.

Max took three deep, calming breaths, and let each out slowly, as he had learned to do before stepping onto the stage.

He stood up, and used the toilet again. He washed his hands, then leaned over to take a long drink of cool water from the faucet, and to splash his face, too.

He was hungry and the water gave his stomach something to do.

Then he sat down again, to wait, leaning against the wall with his legs stretched out. Time passed, but he couldn't measure how much, or how slowly. Eventually, the little window gleamed gold. To give himself something to do, and to keep panic at bay, and to have the company of his own voice, he recited lines from plays, then the titles of all the plays in the Starling Theatrical Company's repertoire with a complete list of the cast of each. Over and over, the way Grammie had taught him to fix them in his memory, he conjugated Spanish verbs, first *amar* and *tener* (to love, to have), the most regular, then the irregular verb *ser* (to be), each verb in each of the four most common tenses: present, future, imperfect, and past. He repeated the few nursery rhymes he still remembered, and that made him wonder about Blister, and what it might mean that he recognized "Hey Diddle Diddle." It meant a lot to the boy, that had been obvious. And what kind of life would you have to be leading for something so insignificant to mean so much?

After that, Max recited as much as he could remember of poetry he'd memorized for school. He remembered much of "Elegy Written in a Country Churchyard" and all of "The Highwayman," which was a lot more fun to perform, although, he realized, listening to his own voice saying the elegy a couple of times in order to retrieve lost lines, "the paths of glory lead but to the grave" had a real ring to it.

Finally, because he had run out of other things to tell himself, he recited his father's letter. "Dear Miss Nives," he said, speaking into the shadowy air of the small room, "I was pleased to receive your letter, trapped here in the palace as I am by our mountain winter." He went on, reading it aloud from memory, comforted by the sound of his voice and by his father's voice, too. He recited the letter over and over, until the words no longer carried any meaning but were just familiar sounds.

It was on the tenth recitation—or maybe the seventeenth; he hadn't kept count—that he heard it. "When fate (as people put it) rapped on my cabin door—or you might say it rapped on my numb-skull . . . ," he was speaking, when he heard it. He sat up. He gathered his knees to his chest, grinning. "Certainly, the crown came gift-wrapped," he said slowly, listening. How many times, he asked himself, did that word appear in his father's letter, in one way or another? He counted: six times. This was not likely to be a coincidence, one word appearing six times in a very short letter, and only twice not in disguise.

Max was so excited that he had to stand up and walk, back and forth, three paces, turn, three paces, turn, listening to the whole letter one more time, making sure he'd caught everything.

It *was* a coded message. He had sent off a coded message

and his father had sent one back. He couldn't wait to tell his grandmother.

He stopped pacing. In order to tell his grandmother the news, he would have to get out of this situation. In order to get out of this situation, he was going to have to get out of this small room. In order to do that, he was going to have to free his hands. The necessary steps lined up, like a geometric proof going backward.

But right then, Max was entirely distracted by the discovery he'd made in his father's letter. Maybe the word *entertaining* was also a clue, he thought, because not long after that his father used the word *theater.* Maybe those two words were a clue William Starling put in to direct his son's attention to the fact that the letter had a hidden message.

Was there more? Max wondered. It would be like his father's extravagance to stuff a letter full of secrets. He thought about what his father had written, wondering about every bit of information, from the weather and geography reports to the answer to the question about being King, and the Queen's pleasure at being thought beautiful.

So, Max realized, there was a message from his mother, too, in this letter. How could he feel so cheerful, given the fix he was in? But he did.

He wasn't surprised that his father could report his mother's popularity, but it was unexpected to hear that his charming, exuberant father wasn't equally beloved. In fact, that was a very odd thing to say about your King, wasn't it? "His Excellency listens politely"?

Max slapped his bound hands against his forehead. How could they have missed that? And missed also "Her Excellency likes people," which was, if you thought about it, either a silly or an ungrammatical thing to say about a queen. "Her Excellency likes her people," that would make sense. Nobody would even think to notice if a queen liked people in general. They'd say she was a kind and loving person. "His Excellency listens politely," "Her Excellency likes people": HELP, HELP. Trapped, trapped, trapped, trapped, trapped, trapped. Max hit at his forehead again. He had to get out. He had to tell Grammie. They needed to make a plan.

The first step was to free his hands. Max looked down at his bound wrists and only then did he notice how little light was coming into the room from the high window, and see how the window was now silvered. The long summer day was definitely ending. That meant it was already quite late.

Grammie would be worried. Angry, too, maybe, but it was the worry he had hopes of. Worry might lead her to do something. If she called in Officer Torson, for example, or sent Ari out to look for her wandering grandson. Max concentrated on the rope that bound his wrists across one another, the right wrist tight on top of the left. They had wound it around several times in a figure eight formation. Max studied his wrists and wondered how Kip had gotten ahold of the rope.

Cut it from somebody's clothesline, he guessed. Probably his own mother's, and let her laundry fall into the dirt, too.

He couldn't wriggle his hands free, couldn't slip one free from under the coils. Two or three attempts at that convinced him. He then started pulling his wrists apart, trying to twist them at the same time, to stretch the cotton rope. He thought that might be having an effect and it didn't hurt so much he couldn't bear to do it. It would take a long time—he couldn't guess how long—to stretch the strands of rope enough so that he could slip a hand free, but he had time. He had all night.

However, freeing his hands was only the first step and he had no idea how to escape from his prison . . . unless he could rip the flush chain down from the water chest above the toilet and use it like that medieval morning star weapon, to break the glass and then, somehow—how?—reach up to the window.

Panic rose in Max's chest, again, and dried his mouth. Still twisting his wrists, he turned on the water and bent over to drink, so awkwardly that water splashed all around, even down onto his shirt, where it soaked in. The cool, heavy wetness on his shirtfront and the clothesline wrapped around his wrists made Max think of shirts hanging out to dry, and sheets, and trousers, their weight pulling the line down—he could see it, he had seen it a hundred times—the way a clothesline was stretched by water and weight.

He turned the water on harder and stuck his wrists under it, soaking the rope with water as he twisted his hands, pulling his wrists away from one another to stretch and weaken each strand, so as to pull apart the fabric strands that had been wound one around the other to form a rope.

And after all, it didn't take so very long for the strands to have loosened enough. By then the room was quite dark. The only light came from the silvery rectangle gleaming high up in the wall, but Max didn't care. He turned off the water. He slipped his hands free and rubbed at his wrists, wondering how to tackle the next difficulty—

Did he hear something? Out in the corridor?

Max froze. Listening.

Footsteps? It sounded like someone moving cautiously.

Five doors lined the corridor, and this little bathroom's was the fifth. The first opened onto a room full of props and costumes, the second onto a large dressing room, lined with dressing tables and mirrors, for the actors, the third onto a large dressing room for the actresses, and the fourth onto a smaller room with its own clothes rack, and two soft chairs as well as the dressing table, for the principals. Max heard a door opening, and, after a few seconds, closing. That was the sound that had first attracted him. He heard another door open. Almost opposite the bathroom door, a short staircase led up to the backstage area. If he could get to that staircase . . .

Who was out in the corridor? Searching.

Should he shout for help? Or would that be the thing that would get him into serious trouble?

Max positioned himself beside the sink so that when the door was pulled open he would not be immediately visible. His hands were free but he draped the rope around his wrists, as if they were still bound. If it *was* Kip out there, he meant Max harm, and Max intended to fight back—the first step, with surprise on his side, being to get possession of the knife.

And—he decided, picturing it—dropping the thing into the toilet bowl.

He heard a muffled grunt—of surprise?—beyond the door, and tensed. There was the grating sound of the key in the lock. The handle gave a squeak. The door was cracked open and then pulled back, slowly, quietly, and Max saw someone in the shadows. He tensed every muscle.

"Eyes?" a voice whispered.

Max swallowed. "Tomi?" His own voice was a croak. Was it Tomi? Could it be Tomi? How could Tomi be here?

"Ha!" Tomi cried as he switched on a flashlight and shone it at Max. Then he turned it off again, to save the charge on its zinc-carbon battery. "I *knew* it was you I was seeing. That *was* you, that Bartolomeo, wasn't it?"

"What are you doing here?"

"More to the point, what are *you* doing here?" the other boy answered. The flashlight glowed again, illuminating Max briefly, before the room went dark again. "Are you tied up?" Tomi asked. "What's going on, Eyes?"

"Max, my name is Max," Max answered.

"I know, but what's happening?"

"Let's get out of here, then I'll tell you," Max said, and added, "I need to let my grandmother know I'm safe and I'm pretty hungry, too." He was grinning now; he could feel that smile all over his face. He grabbed Tomi's shirtsleeve and pushed the boy back into the dark corridor, giddy with relief. Not so giddy, however, that he couldn't think. "Wait," he said, and turned back to push the door closed, grope to find the handle and the key below it. He locked the door.

"What are you—?" Tomi started to ask.

"Come this way," Max said. "I've got a bicycle. I hope—"

"How do you think I knew you were here?" Tomi asked, from behind him. "Did you know the chain at the entrance has been cut? That padlock's useless. Can you slow down a little, Eyes? *You* might know where you are but I don't."

Max slowed to a fast walk. He didn't really believe any of the gang would be returning at this hour—whatever precise hour it was. Tomi stumbled a little behind him, giving himself intermittent flashes of light to see by, but Max hurried forward until he stopped at the door. Before he pulled the bolt to open it, he asked, "Will you call me Max?"

"What?"

"Max. It's my name." He slid the bolt and opened the door.

"I *know,* I didn't think you—" They stepped out into the night air. "Where are we going?" Tomi asked.

"Are you coming?" The bicycle rested silently against the wall of the theater.

"Are you kidding? Do you actually think I'm going to let you out of my sight before I find out what's been going on? You were supposed to sail off somewhere. In April," Tomi reminded him.

"Aren't you expected at home by now?" Max asked. He had his bicycle by the handlebars and there was just light enough to see Tomi's face. The other boy looked relaxed, and amused, about the opposite of how Max thought he himself probably looked right then.

Tomi shook his head. "Usually, these days, I'm at the firehouse all night, and nobody at the firehouse pays much attention to me."

"Get on, then. I have to—"

"Aren't you going to get rid of that rope?"

"It's a souvenir," Max said, and laughed, and heard the edge of hysteria in his laughter. "Get *on.* I'll explain when we get there."

"I hope it's a good story," Tomi said, and he mounted onto the bicycle seat, taking a firm grip on Max's shoulders.

18

The Mayor's Job

• ACT II •

SCENE 4 ~ EXPLANATIONS

They raced through the winding, empty streets. Gilded by the occasional streetlamps that stood at intersections, the rounded surfaces of the cobblestones gave off a dim glow. No lamps shone in the buildings they rushed past. Max thought it must be deep in the night, possibly even approaching dawn, although there was as yet no lightening of the eastern sky. He didn't like to think of how worried and angry Grammie must be. "What time is it?" he asked.

"Somewhere between dark and midnight," Tomi said from over Max's shoulder.

"How can you be so sure?" Max demanded.

"I know things," Tomi answered, with laughter in his voice. "What's your hurry, Eyes? You've got away now, and

I'm not any too eager to smash my face on stones, but you're acting like we're being chased."

Max wasn't about to admit to this boy that he was worried about the upcoming scene with his grandmother. A father might have been different, even a mother, but a grandmother for heaven's sake . . . All he said was, "I asked you, call me Max. Which is my name."

Tomi just laughed. "I know. I like winding you up, that's all. What's with you, anyway? I think you have to tell me, now that I've saved your life."

Max disagreed. "Probably not my life."

Tomi laughed again.

Max dropped his bicycle onto the ground beside his own back door, the house dark and silent behind it, his eyes on the lights that shone in Grammie's kitchen windows. He was almost running when he got to the steps, Tomi at his heels. He burst into the room. "I'm sorry—"

Grammie rose from the table, where she and Ari sat in front of mugs and a teapot. Her face was pale and expressionless.

Max braced for trouble. "It really wasn't—"

But by then she had thrown her arms around him and was holding him close, the top of her head just below his nose. "You're here," she mumbled into his shoulder. "You're safe. You can't know, I was that worried . . ." She stepped back and looked up at him. Behind the glasses, her eyes swam with tears. "I am so happy to see you."

"I thought you'd be angry."

"You gave me your word," Grammie told him. "I knew something must have gone wrong or you'd have been here."

Max could only smile. *Now* he could feel simply glad, and relieved, and grateful to Tomi. *Now* he could begin to wonder what to do next. Everything was all right, now. He stepped farther into the warm, bright room and said, "This is Tomi Brandt, he's in my class at school. Tomi? My grandmother—"

"But you're the librarian," Tomi said, sounding a little puzzled. "You're Mrs. Nives."

"And you're out in the middle of the night," Grammie answered in her teacher voice. "What kind of trouble have you gotten Max into?"

"I didn't—"

Max smiled even more broadly as he interrupted Tomi's protests. "And this is Ari. He's my math tutor. Among other things."

The two shook hands.

"Well, then," Grammie said. "Are you two hungry? Thirsty?"

"Yes!" said Max, so vehemently that they all laughed.

By the time they had finished the loaf of brown bread and the chunk of sharp white cheese, and the frittata Grammie set down on the table, large enough to feed all of them ("I wasn't hungry before," she admitted, adding, "Even Ari didn't eat much"), and another pot of tea, Max had finished telling them his tale, and it was Tomi's turn to explain that he'd sighted the bicycle and noted how it was hidden in the alleyway, so he'd come back, as the afternoon and evening wore on, to check on it. "I was already suspicious," he explained to Grammie and Ari. "I recognized that bicycle—and that gardener, who said he'd found it. I barely saw his eyes but they were that burned-meat-on-a-spit color and . . . I was suspicious."

"You're the only one," Grammie remarked, studying Tomi. "You must be a noticing person. I haven't seen much of you in my library."

Tomi avoided that subject and went on to say that when the bicycle was still there beside the empty theater building and it was so late in the evening, he thought something might have happened. "Something not good, to Max, which is who I thought it was, or even this Bartolomeo character, if he was real, which I doubted. It's just that—there was something not right about it all. And then I checked the entrances and found the chain was cut—"

"You went into the empty building? Alone?" Ari asked. "You must have good nerves."

"I'm training to be a fireman," Tomi announced.

"You must be a good friend, too," Ari went on.

The two boys were sitting side by side at the table. At Ari's observation, they turned to look at one another. Neither of them spoke. They were, however, in perfect agreement: Adults didn't understand the way things went at schools, among kids; they didn't remember what friendships were like, and who you were never friends with however interesting you might find him.

"I've been hearing things about a Mister Max," Tomi said in a teasing, hinting, questioning voice.

That reminded Max. "Did you know about the protection racket? About these three . . . ?" But he couldn't think of the right word for Kip and Colly and Blister. Not boys, certainly, but in two cases not really criminals, in his opinion. "I thought you might know something. I wanted to ask you about that but then they—got me."

Grammie reached out to put her hand over his wrist, but she didn't say anything. She didn't need to say anything. Max knew what she meant.

Tomi answered thoughtfully. "I know *about* Kip, so I've seen Blister. Colly used to be in school with us, don't you remember? A class above? Maybe two classes? He left school when—you must remember *that,* the woman who killed her husband. Do you remember it, Mrs. Nives?"

"I'd like to forget it, but yes. And she was hanged for it. A sad story."

"I've only seen Colly a few times, since," Tomi said. "He works in Sterne's ink manufactory; he's been there a long time. What did they want with you?" he asked Max. "Kip's . . . He's always been a bad one and he's getting worse. If Blister wasn't such a cringer—and if you didn't have to take on Kip to get ahold of him—somebody would have taken him in. But he's such a sad sack, and sort of disgusting, nobody—"

"But didn't Kip save Blister's life? That's what he said. He can't be all bad if he did that."

"Kip pulled a box out of the water and the kid was in it,"

Tomi told him. "Besides, does one good deed make up for sixteen years of . . . He steals things, especially from weaker people. He was always terrorizing the smaller kids at school, before they expelled him. They say he'll use his knife with no provocation and . . . He was drowning a dog when he pulled Blister's box out. Or a cat, it might have been a cat, but it wasn't his own, either. The poor kid who owned it was right there, trying to . . . Kip's really mean, Max. He's worse than mean—he's dangerous."

"I know." Max had the bruises to prove it. "But not for Blister. Not entirely," he said, seeing Tomi's expression. "He's an arsonist, and a vandal, too. Those three are—"

"So you've found out for sure that that's what's been going on?" Tomi asked. "Everybody suspected there was something, we all wondered at the firehouse . . . There was too much of it for a coincidence, but nobody would say anything; there was . . . You knew there was some secret, and you thought you could guess what it was, but nobody was talking about it. If you've proved it, we should go to the police." Tomi was already half up out of his seat.

Max raised the hand that wasn't holding a mug of tea. "Wait, Tomi. Wait, I have to think. We need to make a plan."

"No," Tomi said eagerly. "The police will arrest the three of them, they'll tell the Mayor, and he'll make sure the trial is quick, and public. That way, everybody in the old city will know they don't have to be afraid. You don't know what it's been like, Max, with people trying to pretend nothing is going on. Everybody is frightened. Nobody trusts anybody."

"But I do know," Max said. "The Mayor already knows, too, just not *who*—" He was going to have to explain everything to Tomi, or the boy would go dashing off to ruin the Mayor's hopes, meaning to help but not helping one bit. The opposite, in fact. "Listen," he said, and he told the story—well, some of it, the relevant part of it. He started almost at the very beginning, with missing the boat and the entrance of Mister Max onto the stage.

"I should have known," Tomi said. "Or at least guessed."

"Why would you?" Max wondered, but went on before Tomi could answer.

He skipped most of the middle of the story and anything involving his parents, then concluded with the Mayor's desire to keep this particular problem a secret from the royal family, which meant from popular knowledge, which meant—especially—from the newspapers. "We don't want the kind of hullabaloo that they whipped up over the whole *Miss Koala* business. That's why they hired me, to figure out a way to stop the extortion *and* let people know it's over and do it quickly. Eventually—in the fall—they'll bring the gang to justice. But you know," he admitted, as that word, *justice,* rang in his ears like a bell, "I feel sorry for Blister—"

"He certainly sounds like a miserable little fellow. A wretch," Ari agreed. "Do you think somebody tried to drown him? Like unwanted puppies or kittens? Or maybe his people were on a boat that sank. Or he could have just fallen overboard. But then, what was he doing in a box? Was it a wooden box?"

"I don't know. Nobody knew anything about him. Nobody came looking for him that I ever heard of," Tomi said. "But how can you stop them and let people know it's safe again and at the same time keep it a secret, Max?" He looked at Max with interest; he wasn't laughing now. "Have you really been earning a living as a detective?"

"Solutioneer," Max corrected, flushing with pleasure at the boy's tone.

"Living by yourself?"

"If you don't count a tenant—that is, me—or that his grandmother's only a garden away," Ari said.

Tomi looked at the three of them, and then again at Max. "So what's the plan here?" he asked, grinning with pleasure and excitement. "What do we do next?"

"I'm afraid we *have* to call in the police," Grammie said.

"And send Blister to prison?" Max asked. "I don't want to do that. Hasn't his life been hard enough already? He never had a chance."

"He's still an accomplice," Grammie pointed out. "He was there, even if he's little more than a whipped dog."

Max didn't have to say anything. He just let Grammie listen to her own words.

It was Tomi who clinched it. "She only pushed him down the stairs," he said. At the blank expressions that greeted this statement, he explained. "Colly's mum. Well, actually, she whacked him with a wooden chair and he was at the top of the stairs . . . They lived on the fourth floor," he said. "He liked to gamble, Colly's dad. He gambled everything and he wouldn't stop, and when he didn't have wages of his own to bet with, he took what she earned. Washing sheets, and ironing them, to earn enough for food and rent for the three of them. She didn't mean to kill him," Tomi said. "She confessed right away and she was sorry, and she said she deserved to be hanged and the parents—his parents? They told the judge he was the prop of their old age and without him they were lost." Tomi turned to Grammie. "Don't you remember, Mrs. Nives?"

"I remember," Grammie said, now thoughtful. "I thought she was spineless. I suppose she must have loved him, but still . . . She didn't protect her child. Or herself, but a child . . . They never said in the newspapers that it was an accident."

Tomi shrugged. "Newspapers," he said. "They like to stir people up. Stirred-up people buy more newspapers."

"Why was she hanged, then?"

Tomi shrugged. "She'd threatened him before, apparently. The neighbors testified that they'd heard them fighting, on many occasions. She admitted to doing it and his parents wanted revenge for their son's life. Popular opinion turned him into a model citizen, just a little weak about gambling, and people were afraid of what might happen if wives started thinking they could kill their husbands. Everyone said she didn't care about anything anymore. Not even about Colly. She just—nobody spoke for her, she had given up, and—" He was silent for a few seconds before he said, "The grandparents took Colly in and people said they were good and generous, but they took him out of school. As soon as they could. Colly was *smart,*" Tomi said. "It was all so— It wasn't *right,*" he concluded.

By then, Grammie was nodding.

Then Tomi's voice changed. "Kip, however—Kip's another story, an entirely different one. It *would* be right for Kip to go to prison. Except," he added morosely, "that when he comes out he'll probably be worse than before."

"Is there any way to punish Kip without punishing the other two?" Max asked, and he looked around the table.

Nobody could think of any.

"It's hard to learn how to be brave," Grammie said slowly, "when someone is always there to take advantage of how powerless, and weak, you are." She looked at Max first, then Tomi, then Ari. "I always admire the courage of little children, even if"—and she smiled at some memory—"a lot of the time it's pretty foolhardy."

"What if Colly gave back the money he's taken?" Max suggested. "His share of it, I mean. He said he was saving it up so he could start a new life, and go to school to learn a trade to earn a living. It would be a real punishment for him to give it back."

"And leave him there with those grandparents?" Tomi asked. "I wish we had room but we already have too many people and not enough beds. There's food enough for us, but nothing left over, so I can't offer. And you know? I agree with Mrs. Nives about—I sort of admire Colly for making a plan, to do something to change his life."

"I don't know that I said *that,*" Grammie objected. "I

wasn't saying I admire extortion and threatening people. And I was thinking about Blister, actually."

"It's a lot the same," Tomi assured her, as if they were both grown-ups, with equal amounts of experience.

Grammie humphed.

The four of them looked from one to the other, trying to figure out the way through or around or even under this problem.

"I wish . . . ," Ari began, but did not finish the thought.

"I know," Grammie said. "I know exactly. The law and something more, too."

Max, for his part, was remembering how it felt to be a prisoner in that small room, with no way to get out. He remembered the odd shine of light on the high window, which made him think of the darkness when a bag had been tied over his head. It had stunk inside the bag, stunk of turpentine and something dry and acrid and flavorless. He thought: Colly's future must look like that to him, like being locked in a tiny room with a stinking bag tied over his head, blinding him, choking him. He thought: Blister's whole life has actually *been* like that. "There must be *something* we can do," he said urgently. "There has to be some way to do this right."

"I better make a fresh pot of tea, and would anybody like snickerdoodles?" Grammie asked, rising from the table, followed by a chorus of "Yes please." Without turning around, she said, "I wish Pia were here."

"Me too," Max said. He remembered the knife Kip had pulled out, the sharp shine of its blade, and he imagined blood spurting out from his arm—or stomach? He shivered, and tried to drive that image from his mind by trying to imagine what Mr. Bendiff would have said if Max had gotten his daughter kidnapped, but the image kept returning.

"Who's Pia?" Tomi asked curiously. "Do you have a girlfriend, Eyes? Or a sister? Because I never heard that you have a sister."

But Max didn't answer. He was beginning to have an idea.

19

The Mayor's Job

• ACT III •

THE GRAND FINALE

Kip wasn't a fool. He had a backup plan, which was: If he'd actually killed the stupid git last night, he'd see to it that Blister took the blame. He knew Colly wouldn't buy it, but he also knew how badly Colly wanted to escape. Kip had already figured out that he was about to break ranks. For Colly, the vandalism had been difficult, the arson almost impossible, and this kidnapping was more than he could swallow. Originally, Kip had been looking forward to really scaring their prisoner, terrifying him. He imagined bringing the knife closer and still closer to his captive's ear, maybe even taking a little nip off it, or maybe scarring his cheek before coming closer and still closer to that soft skin under the chin that hid the jugular vein—and watching him get more and more frightened, beg harder and harder, maybe weep and wet himself . . . before Kip sliced the rope and let him scarper down the hall. Now, he admitted to himself that Colly wouldn't have permitted that.

The gang was about to break up, he knew. That little moneymaking business was about to fold. The only question was, if there was a dead body waiting for them in that bathroom, whether Colly would be interested enough in saving his own skin to turn a blind eye. Kip guessed that he would.

So Kip made sure they all met at the same time in the little square and slipped into the empty theater together. Then, when he had unlocked the door to the bathroom, he made sure with a quick shove that it was Blister who went in first.

Just in case.

Just in case there was a body lying on the floor. Blister would believe whatever Kip told him, and Kip would say that when Blister had stumbled into the room he'd knocked into their prisoner and caused him to crack his skull. Blister would believe it was all his fault, and when the police found the body—because dead bodies started to stink after a few days—Blister would confess. And how could anyone say that wasn't what had happened, if Blister was confessing?

Kip shoved Blister into the room and shouldered Colly aside, keeping Colly behind him. He heard Blister stumble, and fall heavily. Kip was so busy maneuvering Colly that it took him a second or two to grasp what Blister was saying, and register what he himself was seeing.

Blister was asking, puzzled, "Where'd you put him, Kip?"

He turned on his knees to raise bloodstained palms toward Kip.

There was a wide puddle of blood on the floor. What was a puddle of blood doing on the floor?

"Kip?" Colly had wormed his way past Kip, and when Kip looked at his partner in crime, he saw both shock and fury. "What did you do to him? What have you done with him? Is he dead?"

Kip didn't know what he was hearing, or seeing. How could he, when the scene before him—red blood pooled on the wooden floor between toilet and sink, the bowl of the sink smeared with blood—bore no resemblance to the scene he had left behind him last night, the unconscious body, legs splayed, eyes closed.

"I didn't—" he muttered, and then he figured out what had happened. He turned on Colly, blind with rage, fists drawn back. But before he hammered that sneaking traitor into a pulp, he made sure Colly knew he'd figured it out. "You've set me up, you're your mother's son, you—you're not going to get away with—" And he let fly with his right fist.

The only reason Colly could duck the blow was because Kip was distracted by the sight, in the corner of his vision, of a man, who stepped forward into the center of the small room, one hand on the hilt of the long sword that waited in its scabbard at his side. Kip wheeled to face him.

The man was young, and tall, red-haired. He looked like one of the elegant, handsome fops Kip had seen on the streets of the New Town, going into restaurants, riding by on high-stepping horses, wrapped around in fur-lined coats, but his eyes were cold and the smile on his lips was not friendly, not kindly, not amused. "You'll be Kip," he announced.

At the look in his eye and the tone of his voice, a cold hand reached up from Kip's stomach and he said nothing.

Blister didn't speak, either, but Colly wouldn't stop talking. "Where is he, Kip? If there's any chance he's alive, every minute counts—I should have known better than to believe you—" Colly stopped, swallowed. His face was pale. The summer-corn yellow of his hair could not warm the fury of his blue eyes. "You better tell me," Colly warned, and tensed his muscles to throw himself on Kip, and beat it out of him.

Kip could have laughed at Colly, and he would have except that his mouth was frozen. The stranger drew his gleaming blade to lay it flat across Colly's chest and force him back against the sink, saying in a voice that sounded amused, "I'll take care of this, youngster"—all without taking his eyes off Kip.

The man could see the fear in Kip's face, and Kip could see how that pleased him.

"I never—" he started to say.

"Shut it," the stranger ordered.

Kip shut it.

Colly did not. "You don't understand," he said desperately. "There was a boy here, he was—we—but Kip must have—he has a knife and I don't know, he maybe even killed him and we have to find him, in case he's still alive."

"I never!" Kip cried.

"This wasn't what was supposed to—" Colly insisted. "There's no time to—you *have* to tell me, Kip."

"I said, shut it!" the stranger repeated, and this time he speared Colly with one of his looks.

In the silence that followed, Blister murmured, "There's a lot of blood." He was still crouching on the floor. "Where did all this blood come from?" He looked up, bewildered, and then Kip saw it cross the simpleton's face, the idea that Kip had done this, with the knife Blister had so often seen flash in front of his own eyes. "You shouldn't have," Blister blubbered.

"Oh, I don't know," the stranger said.

Kip turned his full attention onto this man, ignoring Colly's muffled groan.

"It might even be that I should be grateful to Kip," the stranger said. He saw their confusion and he was enjoying it. "Not that he would have known that. Not that anyone will ever know it. Not that the world will see me as anything but a brokenhearted cousin applying his handkerchief over the coffin while his grieving and now childless uncle meets with the lawyer to rewrite his will." And he laughed, a quick, cruel, happy laugh. "Kip's done me a favor and I'd do him one in return by sending him off to the French Foreign Legion, except for one thing."

The stranger waited and waited and waited until at last Kip had to ask, "What's that?" He'd heard about the French Foreign Legion. Who hadn't? An army for hire, men who'd fled their own lands and lives for one reason or another, usually to save their own skins, men trained in the art of battle, trained to be ruthless, heartless, merciless, so that anybody who came up against them arrived already terrified. The French Foreign Legion had always sounded pretty good to Kip. He wondered what one thing kept the stranger from sending him there, but he was afraid he knew the answer.

When the man spoke, however, Kip was surprised. "A soldier in the Legion has to be one of his unit, one finger on a hand, not a fist of his own. The men of the Legion stand together or fall together, and anyone who isn't willing to die for his comrades, or with his comrades, makes a weak link in the chain. You always take the lion's share, that's the way you like things. I don't see you being willing not to be top dog, and I certainly can't imagine you standing firm in a chain when the chain's in trouble. Which is too bad for you because it means I'm going to have to turn you over to the police, who, I'm sure, won't take long rooting out your little extortion racket— You're surprised? You didn't really think you were getting away with it, did you? It'll be the law for you, then the courts, and then the hangman." He smiled at Kip.

Kip didn't bother trying to look like he was smiling back. He couldn't think and smile at the same time. He didn't know just what had really happened here and he suspected that it was the murderer himself standing there, in a fancy red jacket with two rows of gold buttons down the front and more gold buttons on the sleeves, with the kind of sash across his chest that only powerful men wore, with a sword he obviously knew how to use already out of its sheath, with—most alarming of all—the obvious intention of finding someone else guilty of his own crime. If this man ran Kip through with that sword, the law would sing his praises, for bringing down a murderer (what did the law care if he was innocent?) and ending the extortion, too. Kip was trapped.

When you were in a trap, you got yourself out of it.

"I've got a policeman waiting for you in the corridor," the stranger announced. "If you'd care to let us know where you've stashed the body, I'd be grateful."

Kip looked at the man. How grateful? he wondered, and was about to ask that when the man spoke again.

"Not grateful enough to do you any good," he said—with that smile. He smiled like someone who didn't care about anybody else, who was so sure of his position in the world and his power to get whatever he wanted that all the other people were no more than beetles, running around underfoot, to be stepped on. With a satisfying crunch. "Or maybe I would be. Do you want to risk it?"

But Kip *couldn't* tell him where the body was, and the man knew it.

"No? Not willing to help us out here? That's too bad, Kip," the stranger said, although his voice didn't sound like he thought it was too bad at all.

Kip took off. He'd take his chances with the policeman in the hallway and let Colly and Blister take their chances with the law. He whipped around and was through the door, the knife out of his jacket pocket and ready. He threw the door shut behind him but didn't lock it. He couldn't take the time. He almost didn't notice the figure, two figures it was, stationed beside the stairs up to the stage door.

Kip ran right at them—the policeman and his girlfriend! A country girl, by her red embroidered skirt and braids. What a fool she was, to let a policeman court her when everyone knew policemen got the worst of everything. But what a piece of luck for Kip that this policeman was the kind whose girlfriend followed him onto the job. More luck that she was a screamer, howling away like that. Of course the fool would take care of her first, protect her. Kip only had to shove at him with one big hand and threaten her with the knife held in the other, to open the way to the stairs, out the door to the alley, and the street, and the docks, and—he hoped—the French Foreign Legion.

What Blister understood was: There was blood and the boy was gone and the rope his hands had been tied up with lay in the blood like a long, twisted noodle. Blister understood right away that Kip was in trouble, with his knife. Blister didn't like kneeling in the blood, and his palms were smeared with it, but he didn't want to move. He had to twist his head to see what was going on.

The trouble was, Blister didn't know what Kip would do. Except that what he would do was probably going to hurt because when things didn't go the way Kip wanted, Blister ended up black-and-blue. He cringed away, and down, as if Kip wouldn't be able to see him, and waited for the blow. The trouble was, when Blister was frightened he couldn't think at all. When he was frightened, everything swirled and wound and blew around him and he couldn't understand any of it. The trouble was, Blister was almost always frightened.

Something was different with Kip. Blister wasn't surprised when Kip shoved Colly—hard—into the man in the red coat, but he didn't expect not to get a good kick as Kip ran out of the room. There was so much fear in the shadowy little room at that moment that Blister gulped for air. His mind swooped and darted, unable to land anywhere and rest.

But he didn't like this blood on his hands.

"Can I wash my hands, Colly?" he asked. He didn't want to look at the man in the red coat. Blister thought that if he didn't look at the man, the man might not notice him. He knew this was one of his stupid ideas but he didn't dare change it. He looked only at Colly.

Colly did dare to look at the man and then he said, "Sure, go ahead." So Blister stood up and stepped out of the blood on the floor. The water in the sink was cool and in no time his hands were clean again, and the water was swirling around down into the little round drain, turning from pink to clear.

Colly was talking to the man now, and talking about Blister. "You can't pin this on Blister, you know. Blister didn't do anything. I don't think he knew anything. I think Kip acted alone, because *I* certainly didn't—I wouldn't ever—Although, why should you believe that? But Blister *couldn't.* Anybody can see that."

"What better use can he be put to?" the man asked.

Blister had a use?

"You know that if I turn him loose he'll just find himself another master. If you're so smart, you'll have figured that out."

Colly didn't say anything. But Blister didn't think he'd found Kip. Kip had found him, and saved his life. But now his life had been saved already and he didn't need anyone to save him again.

After a while, the man said, "Somebody has to be found guilty and your leader has scarpered, so if it's not Blister, that leaves just you, doesn't it?"

Colly was silent.

Blister decided—all by himself, he decided it; he felt himself deciding—to keep silent, too. He was trying to think and it was not a quick and easy process.

The man said, "That leaves just you, Colly. When the body turns up. And I expect that nobody would be surprised to learn that you were a murderer."

Colly said, "She was defending herself—and me, too—and it was an accident that he fell down the stairs."

The man laughed. "What are you now, a lawyer?"

"I could be," Colly answered, and he didn't sound at all frightened.

Blister saw that the sword had been returned to its sheath, so maybe Colly didn't need to be frightened anymore.

"My mother didn't have money for a lawyer and that's probably why they could send her to the gallows. If I were a lawyer, things like that wouldn't happen to people like her."

The man was staring at Colly, and something about him

had changed. Blister didn't know what. The man's coat was just as red and his boots just as high and shiny and he stood just as straight as before, but he was different.

This was all because of that boy they had tied up and left here, and now there was only blood. Blister knew *he* hadn't come back to do something to the boy, and Colly said *he* hadn't, and Kip denied it, too. So what had happened to the boy? "Where is the boy?" Blister asked.

Then he clapped his hand over his mouth, sorry he had spoken.

"Good question," the man answered, not at all angry.

"In one of the other rooms?" Blister suggested. He explained to the man, "This is our hideout, because the people that own it went away for a long time. There isn't any electricity or gas, but we don't come here when it's dark so that doesn't matter. But there are more rooms . . . One is filled with costumes. Even swords, and three have mirrors. Could the boy be hiding in one of those rooms?"

"Probably not hiding," Colly told him, as if he were warning him. Warning him about what? "Who are you?" Colly asked the man.

The man smiled, although not in a mean way now, and told Colly, "You'll find out if and when you need to." He looked at Blister and said, "I know a man who isn't young and his wife isn't young, either. He has a herd of goats, up in the hills, and he could use a boy to work with him. His own sons have gone to live and work in the village because the work of the farm is so hard, the winters so long and cold, the paths so steep and dangerous. The old man needs someone strong and brave. That boy would have a warm home and all the food he could eat, and he would work for a master who has rough manners and a kind heart." He kept on looking at Blister, as if waiting for the answer to a question.

Blister understood, but he had to admit, "I'm not strong. I'm not brave." He held out his hands, palms up, to show the man how helpless he was.

"Maybe," the man said. "Then again, maybe you can be."

Blister thought for a minute, no longer. "Do they have a dog?"

"They have two dogs. The dogs guard the herd from wolves and watch over the house and the old couple. They herd the goats, and they'll find a goat that's gotten lost. They sleep by the fire."

Really, Blister had decided as soon as he heard they needed a boy. He was a boy and he needed a warm home and food. "How do I get there?" he asked.

Colly interrupted. "Are you sure?" he asked Blister.

Blister nodded. "I've decided," he told Colly, but he didn't know how to explain to Colly how exciting it was, to decide that something would happen and then it happened.

"I think you're right," said Colly. "Good luck, Blister." And Blister could tell he meant that. Colly asked the man, "How does he get there?"

The man opened the door and called out, "Girl?"

There were quick footsteps and a girl with two long white pigtails, wearing a bright red skirt with yellow flowers and green vines, came into the room. She curtsied to the man, who told her, "Take this boy with you, in the carriage, down to the docks. Put him on *The Water Rat* for Passway. Tell Carlo to wait at the dock until he is met."

"Should I—?" she started to ask, but with a stern look the man silenced her.

"Blister," he said then, and Blister stood up straighter. "There will be a man sent to meet you. He will know your name and he will take you up to the village where the goatherd will come to fetch you. The goatherd is named Joseph Ruvid. You can call him Uncle Joseph so there won't be any questions. Have you got that?" he asked.

"Uncle Joseph," Blister said. "Yes."

"He'll probably want to name you something new," the man said.

He waited, so Blister said, "Something new, yes."

The man said, "I want to be sure: Do you really want to do this?"

Blister nodded, then thought of something he wanted to say so he said it: "Thank you."

"You're welcome," the man said matter-of-factly. "Off you go then, girl." He handed the girl a purse and told her, "Give this to Carlo; he'll see that everyone is paid."

"Yes, sir," the girl said, and she curtsied again. "Come on then, you," she said to Blister.

Blister took two steps to follow her out of the little room. Her shirt was as white as clouds.

"Blister?" the man called after him.

He turned around again. Maybe it was not going to happen, after all.

"Tell the man who meets you to give you a bath. First thing. Tell him, it's an order," the man said.

"Yes, sir," Blister said, as the girl had done, but he knew boys didn't curtsy. He went into the hallway after the girl. A policeman was there, sitting on the stairs, his back against the wall, his hat pulled down over his eyes. Probably asleep, Blister thought. No wonder Kip got away so easily. But Blister wasn't getting away. He was going away, because that was what he had decided.

Left alone with the handsome, redheaded, princely man, Colly resigned himself to another run of bad luck. *He* knew he hadn't murdered anyone, but who would believe him? He figured that this man didn't want to accuse Kip—whose father was a silversmith with commissions from important people. He wouldn't want to accuse Blister, who was such a sad story that the newspapers would probably turn him into a hero. That left Colly.

All of Colly's life, bad luck had tripped him up and trapped him.

All Colly had had, from the age of seven, was his own desire to put himself in a position to live the life he would choose for himself. He had thought that going to school would give him a way to do that, but school had been taken away from him. Then he'd thought that working, at however low and unpleasant a job, would give him a few pennies to gradually pile up until they were enough to let him set out on his own—but everything he earned was paid to his grandfather, to cover the cost of feeding and housing him, they said. Even the spare hours of his day were not his, but belonged to the chores his grandparents required of him.

All Colly had ever been able to keep, of his own, was being a person who did not whine and complain, who gave an honest day's work for his pay, who performed his chores reliably and well. Colly was a person who played fair, and he was proud to be that. There wasn't anything else he could be proud of, but most of the time, that was enough.

Then that, too, had been taken away from him, when he had chosen to go along with Kip's scheme to get shopkeepers to pay protection money. To be honest, and Colly always tried to be honest with himself, nobody had taken anything from him in this case. He'd given it away, his pride or his honor or whatever it is that you surrender because you've convinced yourself that the future prize makes present bad behavior good. Or even OK. Colly had done this to himself, he knew that.

He looked at the red-coated man, at the colorful medals displayed on the broad blue sash he wore across his chest—an awful lot of medals for such a young man, he thought—and understood that he deserved whatever bad luck awaited him.

Colly squared his shoulders. He couldn't complain about fair. He'd gambled that he wouldn't get caught—as foolish as his father—and he'd lost. He looked right into the proud face, ready to hear whatever the man had to say to him. But first, he wanted to say it clearly, whether he was believed or not. "I didn't kill him. That boy."

"But you *did* exact protection money."

"Yes. I did do that," Colly answered, not allowing himself to look down.

"Are you sorry now?" the man asked.

At that question, all the worry, and relief, and dread, and fear that Colly had been feeling for the last several hours exploded in him, like a boat on the lake bursting into flames. "Of course I am," he answered impatiently. "How could I not be, when I was sorry even when I was doing it? But sometimes you have to do things you don't much like doing, with people you don't much like, to get what you need."

"I don't know about *have to,*" the man protested mildly.

Colly shrugged. The man was right, of course.

The man waited, but Colly had nothing more to say. His boat had blown up, and sunk.

The man waited some more.

Colly said, "Why don't you just call in your policeman and have me arrested."

"For something you didn't do?"

Colly shrugged. "Well, if the body never turns up, how can anyone say I murdered him? And if it does . . . I should have stopped Kip, I know. Somehow. Turned him in before he had a chance to . . ." He made himself keep looking straight into the man's brown eyes and made himself say it, "I didn't think he'd actually use the knife, but that's no excuse, not really. I knew Kip was getting greedier and meaner."

"You weren't greedy?" the man asked coldly.

Colly shrugged, because he hadn't refused to take his share of the coins. That was true. But he didn't like being the mouse to the man's cat, so he said, "I don't know what you're up to. You said Kip had done you a favor, so why are you delaying things like this?"

The man said nothing, just smiled, and Colly started to wonder. He looked at the blood on the floor of the small bathroom and the bloody rope curled up in it. You'd have thought some blood would have been spread around, in whatever struggle there was—because wouldn't there have been some kind of a struggle? And if the body had been dragged out of the room, or even if Kip had picked it up and carried it, there wouldn't be just a kind of puddle on the floor. Besides, didn't blood dry pretty quickly? Wasn't that how scabs formed when you had a cut or a scrape? Why was this blood so red and runny? Was it fresh? If it was fresh because Kip had just murdered their captive only minutes earlier, Colly didn't believe Kip would have met up with them that morning.

The pieces did not fit together. The more Colly thought, the less the pieces fit together, until he asked, "What's going on here? Who are you?"

The man kept smiling, and now it was the kind of expression Colly remembered appearing on the face of a teacher at one of the questions Colly asked. Now the man seemed not so powerful, or cold, or cruel, or even unfriendly. "Who are you?" Colly asked again.

The man sat down on the throne and stretched his legs out

in front of him. His boots gleamed with polish, even in that dim room. He adjusted the sword at his side and instead of answering Colly's question, asked one of his own. "What do you remember about the boy you kidnapped?"

An odd question, but Colly had no reason not to answer. He tried to remember, to picture the boy, walking along the street, then stumbling on the roadway when they had the bag over his head, and his surprised expression when they'd snatched the bag off.

And now Colly wondered why he'd been surprised, not scared or confused or lost.

"Not much," he admitted. "A normal, ordinary boy—brown hair, tallish, the usual pants and shirt. He didn't move like an athlete but he was coordinated enough. I can't really remember him," he realized. "Except . . ."

The man waited patiently.

"His eyes, he had—" Colly pictured them, trying to remember. "His eyes were a weird, non-eye color, kind of . . ." He tried to think of what else he had ever seen that was the same color. "Where I work, the ink factory?"

The man nodded as if he already knew this. But how could he know this about Colly?

Something was going on, Colly guessed, and it was not a happy thought. How badly will all this turn out? he wondered.

"We use charcoal in the ink. The charcoal comes in these brown hemp bags that, after a while, with use and reuse, turn a black and brown and gray color. His eyes were like that." Colly thought some more, then had to say, "That's all

I can remember about him." Then he went on the offensive. "But I don't think he *is* really your cousin and I also don't think he was someone standing between you and something you want." Having said that, he waited to hear how the man would respond.

Colly had no plan to try to get away. He had the dismal suspicion that even if he tried he wouldn't succeed, that eventually he'd find himself back in the presence of this man.

The man said, "I find myself wondering if you are different from the other two."

Of course I am, Colly thought impatiently. When you are expecting the ax to fall, you can't enjoy the wait. But he spoke with rock-bottom honesty—because what was the point of trying to fool himself, or this man. "Not so's you'd notice." He had done what he had done. He was responsible for what he had done.

He thought: This must be how his mother felt, after the death of his father, caught in a trap she had made herself and with no fight left in her.

He said, "If you're not going to tell me anything, then I wish you'd get on with whatever you're going to do to me." In case the man doubted it, he added, "I'm not going to plead guilty to murder, whatever you do."

"I should hope not," said the man. He looked closely at Colly. "But what about the other crimes?"

Colly shrugged. He couldn't deny those charges.

The man waited.

Colly knew what he was waiting for. "You want me to

say I'm sorry—and I am, because those people needed the money, maybe not the same way I need it, but they earned it and I didn't. But there's no point in me saying I'm sorry because if I thought it would work I'd probably do it again. Or something like it because . . . just because," he concluded. That was all he was going to say.

"You should be in school," the man said.

That was obvious, although what it had to do with his present situation, Colly couldn't guess. "Who *are* you, anyway?" he asked.

"Someone who thinks you're worth taking a chance on. So"—and the man rose to his feet—"can you go on living with your grandparents?"

"Is there anything you don't know about me?" Colly wondered.

"Do you want to keep your job in the ink shop?"

"What do you think?" Colly laughed.

The man had yet another question. "Are you willing to repay the money that was taken from your victims?"

"I'd have to work for years," Colly pointed out. "I only took a third."

"You'd only be asked to return what you took. But would you do it?"

Colly hesitated. The only thing that had made it possible for him to be part of Kip's thuggery was the pile of coins that grew larger every week. If he didn't have the coins, what he had done became even worse, and it was already bad enough as far as Colly was concerned. This wasn't an easy question to answer, even if he knew full well that the money didn't really belong to him. "I guess. I know I *should.*"

"There are other jobs, for boys who know how to work," the man assured him. "How do you feel about washing dishes?"

"I've had lots of practice," Colly told him.

The man nodded, and changed the subject. "Where's your hoard of coins?"

"There's a room down the hall, full of costumes. You know this is a theater? I put them into the pockets of jackets. Not all together, in case Kip . . . I can get them for you."

"Actually," the man began, but instead of finishing that thought, he stepped into the doorway to call, "Tomi?" and before Colly could wonder about that, who should step into the bathroom but Tomi Brandt.

Colly couldn't think *what* Tomi Brandt had to do with this man. In fact, for a moment, he was so surprised that he couldn't think at all. Then he turned to the man to ask yet again, "What is going on? Who *are* you?"

"Someone your grandparents will be afraid of," the man said, this time with a smile that made him look young. "Meanwhile, you and Tomi can go about repaying your victims, and don't you think that you might also apologize to them?"

Colly shook his head. He knew what would happen. "At least one of them will want to turn me over to the police. And if none of them do, when my grandparents hear about it, they'll do it. You don't understand how much they . . . They really want . . . What they really want is to get the best, the biggest, revenge they can on me. Because there's no one else to blame, and punish," he explained. "I'd rather you just turned me over yourself," he said, and pointed out, "You know where to find the coins now."

"So you *don't* want to go on living with them?"

"What choice do I have?"

The man didn't argue with him. He stood thinking, but not for long, while Colly and Tomi waited, patient as horses, for him to say whatever he decided to say. Finally, he nodded. "After you and Tomi gather up the coins, you can tell him how much to give to each shopkeeper, and, Tomi, if you'll take care of that?"

"With pleasure."

"You can also inform them that there won't be any more payments asked of them. Tell them the Mayor has taken care of the problem. And here"—he reached into his own purse to take out a silver coin—"I think we should give that to Bert Cotton, with thanks for his generous help."

"When I got the bucket from him this morning, he sounded like he was so glad to be part of it he wouldn't need any more thanks."

"Tell him, we thank him anyway. I'll be paying a call on your grandparents, Colly."

Without a word, Colly led Tomi out into the corridor and down into the costume room, stupefied and amazed by the morning's events, the utter turnaround and flip-over that had happened in his life. He did no more than glance at the policeman leaning against the far doorway, standing on guard in a lazy and relaxed manner, his cap low on his forehead. He barely recognized himself in the mirror that stood just inside the costume room door. His hair was still the same corn yellow, but the eyes that met his looked like they belonged to someone he had never seen before.

When the two boys had left the hallway, Max slipped away, going out the stage door and across to the small square, where he sat and waited for the others to join him. As writer and director of the scene just enacted in the bathroom, he was entirely satisfied with how it had played out. His actors had done their jobs well. Even Ari had been convincing. Those who had—all unbeknownst to them—been assigned roles had stayed in the character he had predicted. Word would have begun to spread when Tomi asked Bert Cotton for a bucket of blood from slaughtered chickens, so Officer Torson might already know the good news. Kip was probably on his way to where—as Grammie had announced—he'd either be killed or find some useful training for his violent impulses. Blister and Colly would be better off, and that pleased him even more than ridding the city of Kip. Nobody could say for sure if the rough life of a goatherd would offer Blister the chance to learn a sense of his own worth, but it might, and Max was confident that given half a chance, Colly would make his own way. Who knew? He might even become a good lawyer, the wiser for his unhappy childhood, and maybe even a judge with a broad streak of mercy in him.

In less than an hour, three lives had been entirely changed, and by him. Well, by the Solutioneer, and with help, but it was *his* plot they had acted out, *his* story, and they were *his* lines, most of them. This must be how his father felt, Max thought, onstage, taking his bows, as if there was nothing he couldn't do next.

Now he could write a letter to the Mayor announcing that the extortionists had been discovered and dealt with. He expected the Mayor would be so glad to know there would be no publicity at all about it that he'd gladly pay a large bill. Everything was turning out as Max had hoped, and planned.

But Ari, he thought—looking at the silent theater in front of him, waiting for his troupe to join him—Ari said he couldn't act. So what had been going on there?

20

In which secrets are revealed

Ari was the first to join Max. They sat side by side on a bench and listened to the plashing of water in the fountain, looking out on the quiet street and the blank face of the theater. Ari undid his belt and set the sword at his feet. "Well," he finally began, but before he could continue, Tomi and Colly emerged from the stage door and separated at the end of the alley. Colly ran off, but turned back at the corner to call, "Thanks! I don't understand, but . . . Thanks!" And he was gone.

"I've got the list," Tomi reported to his two companions in the plot. "That was fun, Eyes." He grinned. "We all envied you your parents, with their theater, and missing school the way you could, and we were right to be jealous." He looked across to the empty building, and grinned again. "I guess I should get started," he said, but all he did was shift from one foot to the other. "You better replace that chain, but it *was* fun. Wasn't it, Ari?" he asked.

Ari, who was staring curiously at Max, admitted, "It had its moments." Then he gave a little laugh, so Max knew that Ari, too, had liked being a part of the performance.

"You were really believable with Kip," Tomi added. "Are you one of their actors?"

"Eyes?" Ari asked Max. "Is that what they call you at school?" He asked Tomi, "Is it a friendly name? Because it doesn't sound all that friendly."

Before either Tomi or Max had to answer those questions, Pia hurried up the street, her face as red as her skirt after the long run back from the docks. She didn't have enough breath to say anything, but she didn't need to speak. The expression in her eyes, as she stood panting and looking from one to the other, said it for her—part mischief and a lot self-satisfaction. When she finally had enough breath, what she said was, "I wish—I'd been in—the room. I heard—most of it, but"—and now her breathing had entirely steadied—"I wish I'd been there to watch it. You were brilliant, Ari. With Kip, I mean."

"It's true," Max agreed. "What was going on? Because you said you can't act."

"That wasn't acting," Ari answered. "Unfortunately."

"What do you mean?" Pia demanded.

"Why unfortunately?" asked Tomi.

Ari's smile was uncomfortable, even embarrassed. "Bartholds have tyranny in their blood, so—"

"You're a Barthold?" Tomi asked, shocked and alarmed and pleased all at once. "Don't tell me you're the next *Baron,*" he added.

Pia, who already knew exactly what Ari was, had her own question. "Does this mean you're going to come out of hiding? And everyone will know who you are? That would be great news because my mother is already green with envy that I go to the castle and that I've met the Baroness. She'll have two cows if I tell her I know *you.*"

Being in the line of fire of Pia's attention like that made Ari rise to his feet and strap the sword around his waist again. He pulled the red jacket down so that the gleaming buttons were lined up straight, and carefully adjusted the sash. "I should talk to those grandparents," he said, not looking at anyone.

"Aren't you going to answer me?" Pia demanded.

"Answer which question?" Ari asked, and before she could start off again, he turned to Tomi. "Do you know where they live? Can you show me?"

"Sure, and then I'll set about going to the shopkeepers, which will also be a lot of fun." He turned to Max. "Thanks for doing this, all of it," he said, with an earnest expression. "If anyone asks me, can I tell them it was you? Mister Max, I mean. The Solutioneer."

"Give the Mayor credit, too," Max advised.

"Oh, I know how things go. I will. See you around?" Tomi asked.

"Sure."

"No, I mean it," Tomi said.

"So do I," Max answered, and discovered, unexpectedly, that he did.

With Ari and Tomi gone, only Pia remained. She stood in front of him, expecting something. Max waited for her to leave. He really wanted to be alone so that he could . . . could feel entirely glad, just for a few minutes, all by himself. But Pia sat down and looked at him expectantly.

Max stood up. "Thanks for your help," he said. "I don't think Blister would have gone off with just anyone," he added, even though he didn't think that was entirely true.

She allowed a small smile of satisfaction to curve her mouth. "We did it, didn't we? You never said *how* you're related to the people who own the theater," she told him. "You *are* related, aren't you?"

Max didn't answer.

"Never mind, I can find it out for myself," Pia said, and with that pronouncement, exited.

For several long, satisfying minutes, Max didn't move. He stayed where he was, looking at the theater's glass doors but not really seeing them, smiling to himself. Then he remembered Tomi's warning. Like any unhurried policeman, however disorganized his uniform might appear to an onlooker, Max went up to take a look at the chain that secured the front entrance. That was when he saw what waited for him.

He didn't have to go up close to know what it was. He

recognized from several paces back the round shape and the gold color, long before he could distinguish the three peaks stamped on it. He didn't have to take it down from where it had been stuck on the glass with—with chewing gum? Who used chewing gum to stick something gold onto glass?

Crossly, Max pulled the chain free. He unlocked the padlock, re-wrapped the longest section of chain around the door handles, fitted the padlock through two loops, and snapped it shut again. With Kip out of operation, the theater would be safe again.

Crossly, he picked up the remaining length of chain and pulled the gold button off the glass. He had to scrape the gum off the glass, too, which made him no less angry. He jammed the button into a pocket and carried the chain in his hand as he stomped off to Thieves Alley.

The good feeling he'd been floating along in, the feeling of his own courage and cleverness, was gone. Maybe he *had* solved the Mayor's problem and saved the city, but that wasn't good enough, was it? This button felt like a mocking message, each of its three sharp mountain peaks sticking a pin into Max. Apparently his father believed that Max should have done better. Apparently he was getting impatient.

Max knew what he wanted to do with this message, but he decided instead to just toss it into the dark back corner of his drawer to join up with the other button. Max wasn't going to let his father steal this morning's show from him.

Max had agreed to join Grammie for a picnic lunch behind the city library, to tell her how things played out, but there was still time before then to go home and feel content, feel pleased with himself, feel proud. This was the most difficult job he had undertaken and he had completed it successfully. There had been luck involved, granted, and he had had a lot of help for sure, but still . . . Also, he hadn't had a paintbrush in his hands for much too long. He was curious to see if he could paint the sky as seen—seen but not really visible—through dirty windowpanes. He didn't know if he could paint from memory and he doubted that he could, but he looked forward to trying.

Gentle rains in the night had left the grass and leaves and flower beds glistening in midmorning sunlight. Birds chattered and chirped to one another as they went busily from branch to grass to bush, clouds floated sedately across a pale sky, and Max would send a large bill to the Mayor's office, enough to live on all summer. He still had the job of Carlo's girl waiting, and it looked like a real challenge for the Solutioneer. Moreover, he had discovered the secret worry Grammie was hiding from him and had figured out the secret message in his father's letter. For just an hour he could let himself forget exactly *what* that message was. For just what was left of the morning, he planned to be proud of his success, and relieved to have escaped harm, and not to be worried about anything.

After a long and peaceful hour, he gave it up. It was the glass he couldn't get right, especially the way unwashed window glass affected light. He couldn't make it look like the daylight sky *or* the nighttime sky, both of which he remembered clearly. He was going to have to ask Joachim about how to produce that effect, and he looked forward to that conversation, the two of them working on a painting problem.

His stomach reminded Max: Grammie was expecting him. He quickly washed out his brushes and spread the three unsuccessful pictures out on the kitchen table. Maybe when they had finished drying they would look more as he had envisioned, but he doubted that. Then he went upstairs to find a pair of short trousers, of the kind worn by little boys, and one of the plain blue collarless shirts such boys wore during the summer. His best disguise was to look even younger than he was, Max had decided. At least, for the moment. He went out as a schoolboy on the loose for the summer.

Grammie began the picnic by pouring him a mug of lemonade from a big thermos. ("I want to hear everything, step by step, blow by blow, inch by inch. You'll need to keep your throat moistened.") Then she unwrapped two thick meat sandwiches for him, plus a much thinner one for herself. ("I need to practice eating less. Maybe I'll try gruel, to save wear on my teeth, to save wear on my purse.") Lastly, she set out two bright, plump oranges and a plate of chocolate walnut cookies, telling him, "They're not Gabrielle's, but you used to think mine were pretty good."

"I still do," said Max, taking one and eating it in two bites.

While he ate his way through the sandwiches, Max made his report, giving Grammie all the details she could hope for, from the sound of Kip's feet pounding down the hallway to

Colly's farewell thanks, and including Ari's surprisingly good performance as the merciless Baron Barthold. Grammie was paying such close attention to his story that she seemed to forget the sandwich waiting on the bench beside her.

At the end, she was silent for a long while. Then, "You did well, Max," she said. "You did really well."

He nodded and felt his cheeks grow warm and kept his eyes on the orange peel he was stripping away. Why should praise for something he was proud of make him feel embarrassed? he wondered. Still, he had the urge to change the subject, so he asked her, "What do you mean, gruel? Why would you want to eat that?"

"I wouldn't want to," Grammie assured him. "Although I might have to."

"I know what gruel is," Max told her. "It's watery porridge. It can't be very tasty."

"Not tasty at all," Grammie agreed. "Or so I understand. I haven't sunk to gruel yet, in my life," she promised him. She looked beyond him to the library building, where it stood behind its guard of tall oaks.

"What *is* going on, Grammie?" Max asked. He already knew but he thought that it was better for her to tell him her secret than for him to reveal that he had found it out.

His grandmother took a deep breath and looked straight at him, her eyes brave and blue behind round glasses. "They want to retire me," she said. "The Mayor and the Council, they think I'm too old, now, and there's a younger person they want to hire who is— I can't deny that he's more qualified to be head of the new kind of library system than I am, and I won't deny that the new system is a good one. But it means I have to retire and I don't know how I'll earn my living." She took off her glasses and rubbed at her eyes. "I'm sorry, Max." She picked up her sandwich, only to put it down untasted.

"It could be that you don't have to retire," he told her, immediately explaining, "I can tell the Mayor. He's going to be feeling awfully grateful to Mister Max right now."

"He *should* be," she said.

"I could ask him to keep you on," Max offered. "For my payment. I'd like to do that."

Grammie smiled, just a little lifting at the corners of her mouth. "If that isn't . . . You're . . . It's very kind to think of doing that, Max, and I'm grateful, don't think I'm not grateful, but—"

"You're a *good* librarian," he said.

"I know I am, but they're right. I am getting older. I'm not in touch like this younger man is. Also, I don't have university degrees; I'm not so well educated. I'm just well read. And there are parts of the collection I haven't built up, I do know that, because I don't know enough. And—I can tell you this, you'll understand—I'm not so sure I really *want* the job anymore, except for earning a living. I certainly don't want it if they don't want *me,*" she announced, with a hint of her old spirit.

Max knew he should tell her. There was, really, no reason not to. In fact, there were at least two good reasons in favor of telling his grandmother that he'd found his father's fortune, which both of them had thought was just one of William Starling's colorful and boastful extravagances. The first reason was that it would ease her mind and free her from worry. The second was that right off, when they knew his parents had disappeared that April morning, Grammie had assured him that she would take care of him, and never mentioned the sacrifices she would have to make to stretch her salary to cover a second person, when it barely covered her. Of *course* he ought to tell her.

But Max didn't want to give up the secret. Having that secret gave his independence the kind of support that the thick stone pilings gave to the bridge that carried carriages and motorcars and pedestrians over the river.

But he had to tell her. He knew that, and besides, he still had one secret left, didn't he? Because he wasn't going to tell his grandmother about the buttons and add to her fears and worries. Not that the buttons were anything he wanted to have for a secret—but Max guessed you didn't choose the secrets you were given. They just landed on you, *boom!*—or in the case of the buttons, which were pretty small, they landed on you *tick tick*. Max smiled to himself, and said, "Grammie? I don't want you to get all bossy at me about this, and you have to promise not to ask any questions . . ." He waited for her response.

She was puzzled, and told him with a teasing smile, "You have my word."

"Because I found the fortune."

Her face was blank. With surprise? With failure to take in the meaning of his words?

"My father's fortune. It actually exists. I actually found it, and—there's a lot of it, enough so neither of us has to worry. *If* I can't earn enough by myself, I mean, because I'd rather earn my own living, and yours, too, by myself. If you lose your job, I mean."

"It's real? You found it? Where?"

"In the frame for *Arabella.*" Max told her this because she should know, just in case.

"And it's real? How much is there?"

"You promised you wouldn't ask questions," he reminded her, so she answered her inquiries herself:

"I guess you wouldn't say it was enough if it wasn't." She looked back at the library building again. Max also looked at the library, but he studied the way the leaves on the oaks broke the sky up into blue fragments, to give Grammie time for this news to sink in.

She picked up her sandwich and ate it, still thinking over what she'd been told. Once, she chuckled to herself. "Banker Hermann engaged to Arabella," she said, and chuckled again. "He *told* us that, in the note he left for you, didn't he? It was a clue. That father of yours . . ." Grammie finished the sandwich and, after a couple of cookies, she started to peel the orange.

Max was glad he'd told her.

Then, of course, because she was Grammie and couldn't

help herself, she said, "Just one more question? Will you answer just one more?"

"Maybe." He grinned.

"How did you figure it out?"

Max had to laugh when he thought about that, and then he admitted, "It was something Pia said, plus something in that note he left, and then the idea just . . . came to me."

"She is certainly useful, that girl. Isn't she?" Grammie poured them each more lemonade, and waited for whatever else Max might have to say, because from the look in his eyes she guessed there was more. Max had brought his sketch pad with the letter from the King of Andesia and the postcard tucked safely into it. He spread them out on the bench between them.

"I want you to listen—really listen. Listen," Max urged, and took a deep breath. Slowly, pronouncing each word clearly, he read the letter out loud.

Grammie concentrated on listening.

When he finished, "Again," she said, like a little child. She was staring blindly into the grass at her feet, concentrating on his father's words. He started again, but after the first words, *"I was pleased to receive your letter, trapped—"* she interrupted him.

"That's one."

He read on and she kept count. She only discovered four of the six, but that was enough to convince her, and she didn't have the advantage of a small, dark room to help her pay the closest possible attention. At the end, she looked at Max. "Trapped," she said.

He nodded.

"He's offering information about how to get there, too. Is he suggesting that the Starling Company make a tour in Andesia? When he puts *guests* in the same sentence as *entertaining*?"

"I didn't think of that. But right after, he says *not safe,* so he can't be. Can he?"

"Obviously, he doesn't want us to rush blindly in. He's definitely saying it's dangerous. You know, it could be that he's advising us not to try to go."

Max considered telling his grandmother that there was no *us* in this, that they were *his* parents, *his* problem to solve. But that could be settled when he had determined on a plan. There was no need to quarrel right now about that. For now, he quarreled about his father's meaning.

"If you look at what he says, though—and it makes no sense, really no sense, what they say about—"

"Oh good, you're still here." It was Pia's voice, and Pia was hurrying up to them. They'd been so intent on what they were doing, they hadn't even noticed her approach. "What's that?" she asked, reaching out for the letter. "A new case?"

"Job," Max muttered, snatching it away and folding it closed. Grammie slipped the postcard under his sketch pad.

"What's the big secret?" Pia demanded. She looked at their faces. "You don't want me here," she announced, correctly. "Why don't you want me? What're you hiding?" Now she was glaring down at them, her dark eyebrows drawn together.

Pia wore a summer dress. It had tiny white spots on a blue background, which goes by the name of dotted swiss. Her white-blond hair was out of its usual braids and hung loose down her back, held off her face by a blue hair band. She wore white socks, folded down to make a cuff, and white sandals. She didn't look happy.

"Don't you look nice," Grammie remarked.

"Don't change the subject," Pia answered, "and no, I don't think I do. I look like a stupid doll dressed up to be taken to lunch with her mother and some *other* mother and her icky daughter. Can I have a cookie?" she asked, reaching out.

"Won't that spoil your lunch?" Grammie asked, with a quick glance at Max that asked for advice, but Max was busy thinking of how to get rid of Pia.

"It'll be some fancy cold soup and chicken salad with grapes and nuts in it and only one tiny roll for each person," Pia said. "And my mother will be all fluttery and flattering and she won't even notice that all they want is to get a favor from my father. Nowadays, it's always about the restaurant, and what night the royal family will be dining there, but *she* thinks she can make them into friends. I don't want to go," Pia concluded unhappily.

Finally, there was something safe for Max to say. "Where's your mother now?"

"Looking at a magazine. I told her I needed some books

to read. She said—you know what she said?—that I have to leave them in the motorcar when we get to Clarissa's house." She waited for Max and Grammie to respond to both of those appalling pieces of information. When neither did, she went on. "And she bought herself a brand-new R Zilla hat for the occasion and she can't get into the motorcar with it on her head." Pia laughed at that memory.

Grammie said, "It's only lunch. It won't last long."

"But I'll hate every minute. I don't know why she didn't take my sister instead, except that they pretended that Clarissa wants to show me her ant farm. *Formicarium,* we're supposed to call it, and that's the excuse for inviting us but nobody believes it. And everybody likes my sister and my sister likes everybody liking her, she's a much better guest, so I don't see why, do you?"

They shook their heads.

Pia stood waiting, the half-eaten cookie in her hand.

Waiting for what? Max wondered.

"I could run away, when we get back to the car. I could come back here and meet up with you," Pia offered. "And help out with whatever it is."

"Wouldn't your mother be angry?" Grammie asked gently.

Pia explained, "She's going to be angry anyway because I'll talk too loudly and say the wrong things and once they've learned that my father isn't telling anyone, not even the chef and Gabrielle, when the royal family is coming, they'll just be waiting for us to leave, anyway. And that'll make her angry, too, but she'll decide it was something I did. So I *could* run away."

There was only one way to stop Pia. "No," Max said.

"No what?" she asked.

"No helping on this job," he said. "I don't need your help."

"So it *is* a case. I knew it. Why can't I help?"

"It's private."

"I'm your assistant. You said. I helped with Madame Olenka; you said I did a good job. I helped this morning. You should let me help now."

"Not on this one, Pia," Max repeated.

She glared at him, and then she glared at Grammie, too, and dropped what was left of the cookie down onto the ground. "Then I guess I'm not interested in being your assistant anymore, if you feel that way," she said, and she stomped off.

At the door back into the library, she turned to call to him, "You'll be sorry."

Max doubted it.

"And if you think anybody would mistake you for a little boy, you're kidding yourself," she called back.

But Grammie asked Max, "Don't you want to catch up with her and—maybe, apologize?"

"For what? She's the one butting in where she isn't wanted. She owes *me* an apology."

Grammie sighed. "I know, but . . ." She sighed again. "You're two of a kind, cut from the same cloth, peas in a pod, the both of you." But she was already uncovering the postcard and Max was unfolding the letter, and for both of them Pia had already been sent to a back corner of the stage, a minor actor in a scene where Max and Grammie had the leading parts.

Max pointed out the "Help! Help!" message and Grammie had to agree with him. "They definitely want us to do something. But what can we do?"

"I should go there," Max said.

Grammie looked at him, but didn't speak. She kept looking at him.

Max started pacing up and down the path. He felt that he should be home packing, now that he knew what he should do, and if it was winter in Andesia he'd need . . . but Grammie just kept looking at him. She had no expression on her face.

Max sat down. "You think I shouldn't go without a plan," he told her.

She looked at him.

"You think I shouldn't go without a good plan," he said. "Because it's dangerous."

"Yes," Grammie said. "We need a plan."

"I need to think," Max said. He was feeling a little desperate now and he could feel his brain starting to skitter around, like some drop of water dancing on a hot griddle. He was the Solutioneer, he reminded himself. This was his business; he was good at thinking up ways to solve problems.

But this problem was about his parents, and that was

different, the way yesterday's problem of being locked into the bathroom of an empty theater had been different. He was better at setting about solving other people's problems than his own, Max thought, and that made him smile. Not that he thought it was amusing, not a bit of it. This was an ironic smile, the kind more often found on grown-up faces.

Well, Max was certainly more grown-up than he'd been just a few weeks ago. He stared at his shoes and concentrated his thoughts. "The reason I noticed the *Help*s?" he said to Grammie. "It's because what he was saying didn't make sense. What I'm thinking now is: neither did a lot of what he said in the postcard."

They reread the postcard silently, attentively. Then Grammie read out loud, *"The rich oft underestimate beauty's lasting embrace?"* She turned it into a question.

Max pointed at the words and read off, "T-R-O-U-B-L-E. And it's not Shakespeare."

"No it isn't," Grammie agreed thoughtfully. "Although it is WS, our WS, who certainly thinks he can be called Great."

"So the postcard is a warning," Max concluded, "and a reminder about the fortune and how to find it."

"Which you have," Grammie said.

"And now he wants help, because they're trapped."

Grammie looked full into her grandson's face to ask, "But how can we help, Max?"

21

The Water Rat *Jobs*

• ACT II •

SCENE 2

Max put his bill—for five hundred!—into the mail that afternoon, and wondered if he was being greedy. Actually, he knew he was being greedy; what he really wondered was if he was being *too* greedy. He'd see what happened and, meanwhile, the afternoon mail brought two requests for the Solutioneer's help, so even when he had addressed Carlo Coyne's problem he could be sure of having something to keep him busy. He and his grandmother each had their assignment. Grammie was gathering information about traveling to Andesia and he was working on his list of possible reasons for a boy—or a young man, or a middle-aged detective, or a minor city official, or anything else he needed to be—to show up at the King of Andesia's palace door.

Grammie was thinking about that, too, but they had agreed it was too soon for talking. They needed to think, first. They sat together on Grammie's back steps at the end of that long June day, reading their letters and the newspaper, and not mentioning what was foremost in both of their minds.

"I won't be doing *that,*" Max announced as he crumpled up a letter from a Hilliard School student who wanted Mister Max to stop his little brother from following him everywhere and ruining all of his games with his friends. "Doesn't he know how lucky he is to have a brother?"

Grammie looked up. "I thought you liked being an only child."

"I do," Max said, because he did. "But I'd like to be an only child who has a brother."

Grammie humphed, and returned to her reading of the Positions Vacant notices.

Max's other letter was from a lawyer whose daughter had fallen in love with, and wanted to marry, "a handsome enough fellow, but he says he's a Romanian count and I don't know where his money comes from." Could Mister Max undertake to find out something about the man? "My daughter is a silly, vain girl, natural prey to fortune hunters and I'd be tempted to just let her find out how wrong she is about this Count Wenceslas, if it wasn't my own fortune at risk."

Max didn't like the tone of that man's voice, or the way he talked about his daughter, either. He already felt sympathetic to the girl but he asked his grandmother, "Do they have counts in Romania?"

"I'm not sure. I can try to find out. Do you want me to?"

"Yes, please," he said.

Max slept long, deep, and dreamlessly that night. When he finally woke up, he could see by the sunlight in his room that it was late in the morning and he remembered—surprised that he had forgotten them—two things. First, he had a painting puzzle to discuss with Joachim. Second, he had the mystery of Carlo's girl, Nissa, to work on. That is to say, there were two things to be done in that day, both of which he would enjoy doing. He got out of bed feeling energetic and clever and generally cheerful.

He drank down a glass of milk for breakfast and jammed the small notebook used by Inspector Doddle into the rear pocket of his trousers, before he put on his red beret and set his painting gear into the bicycle basket. At Joachim's, after Max and his teacher had spent a solid hour trying out every way Joachim could think of to get the effect Max was looking for, Joachim announced, "I knew it couldn't be done. Watercolors are the wrong medium for glass."

"Let's have some lunch," Max suggested, having realized the same thing a while back.

"Since you refuse to learn how to use oils . . . ," Joachim grumbled, but there was a note of satisfaction in his voice. "It's hopeless for you. Oils can capture glass, the look of it."

"Are you hungry?" Max asked. He looked down at the large golden dog, who, seeing that the two had stepped back from their easels, had gotten to her feet in hopes of a walk, or maybe a snack. "Sunny is. Aren't you, Sunny?"

"You mean that *you* are," Joachim told him. "Go ahead and get yourself something, but I've just lost an hour of good light trying to help you and—See that purple cosmos blossom? Imagine it in my new style. I'll call it *June Afternoon.* It would be easier to get that flimsy, papery look of the petals in watercolors. In oils it's going to take real . . ." His attention returned to the important thing.

Max went into Joachim's kitchen, but once there he took out the little notebook to write, *Painter.* An artist might certainly want to travel in South America, in the mountains, and paint the magnificent skies over those peaks. An artist is a solitary kind of person and often strange, at least in comparison to the way most people behave. Most people, just for one example, do not care exactly what color a cloud is. For most people, a cloud is a white puffy cloud or a gray rain-bearing cloud, and that's good enough. But for an artist, the many shades and tones white puts on during its long journey to black are distinct and different and (this perhaps strangest of all) endlessly interesting. Beneath *Painter* Max added *Mountaineer* and *Prospector*—although to go to Andesia as a prospector might get him in trouble with whoever owned the mines that were already there. He wondered if there were some gemstone he might be digging for, something you could only find one at a time and rarely, something it would be safer for a lone prospector to be looking for. Were there gemstones in those mountains? He made a note to ask Grammie to research that for him, too. Then he set about finding some lunch for himself and turned his mind to the Solutioneer's next job.

He would be waiting for Nissa the next morning, in Summer.

Nissa knew how slippery waterside planks could be and she always stepped carefully, even cautiously, onto the landing. "Thank you," she said to Carlo Coyne, without looking up into his face. He had handed her off the ferry with the easy courtesy that was one of the first things she had noticed about him. She kept her attention on her feet and her balance until she heard the little boat chugging away from the dock, and even then her glance didn't linger on any of the bustling women in fresh white blouses or the hurrying men, many wearing the broad straw hats and red bandannas of gardeners, who moved across the plaza ahead of her. These laborers had grown more numerous with each passing day, as the establishments and homes of Summer readied themselves for the arrival of the Royal Family. They hurried right off to their various workplaces, but Nissa could linger.

Nissa was not a daily servant. She had time for a cup of coffee at the waterfront café, seated at one of the small round tables set up on the broad stones outside its entrance, and time to read one of the newspapers the café provided for its patrons.

Now she did notice, with alarm, that there was a workman who had not left the plaza with the others. But he was kneeling beside a bicycle, busy with some problem with the chain, it seemed. Or maybe—he rose to his feet and seemed to be fiddling with the straps that held a large white-and-black basket—it was a problem with the handlebars? It would be hard on him if he had to lose a day's wages, Nissa thought. She hoped he could repair his bicycle and get himself to his job; she had learned how necessary even a few coins could be. Her heart trembled for him, in his trouble. He looked young, too, younger than she'd first thought. Young people, she knew, could be left defenseless and alone.

Her heart trembled for a different reason, however, when she noticed that this laborer left Summer just behind her, wheeling his bicycle south along The Lakeview. She told herself there was nothing to fear. She might be walking unaccompanied but this road was busy with foot traffic and carriage traffic and even, sometimes, motorcar traffic, since the owners of the great houses along The Lakeview liked to have their motorcars as well as their well-matched, high-stepping pairs of carriage horses. The woman who employed Nissa—rather a foolish person, although Nissa suspected that beneath her sillinesses and her vanities and her way of clothing herself in feathers and ruffles, she had a practical head and a good heart—said frequently that the speed of a horse was the fastest she cared to go in her lifetime and if her husband wanted to charge around at twelve miles per hour, he could travel alone. Which, of course, the man did. He was a businessman. If he could get halfway around the lake in under three hours, why would he choose not to?

Her father had often said, arriving suddenly, departing

without notice, “Time is money, Nissa. Never forget that. Time is money.” And her father had not even been a businessman. Nissa had remembered everything he told her and she remembered that advice especially, now that she needed to. She was earning her living doing the one single thing she knew how to do, which was to be a lady, in order to buy herself time—time to adjust, time to think, time to find her own true self, no longer her father’s daughter.

In her haste to get away from the man, Nissa stumbled and then took a minute to adjust the strap on one shoe, and to compose herself. It wouldn’t do to arrive at the house looking anything but calm, competent, and confident. The bicycling laborer rode on past her and she felt immediately less worried. It was just her foolishness, thinking everybody could recognize her. Moreover, why would anybody have any idea that she could be found here, at this lake, on this road, at this hour? She had allowed her nervous imagination to frighten her, that was all. Nissa settled down to enjoy the rest of the pleasant walk. After all, it was Carlo Coyne who had handed her off the ferry this morning and would hand her onto it again this evening.

But when she saw the same laborer wobbling slowly on his bicycle back toward her, she was immediately afraid. His face was shadowed by the brim of his straw hat, as if he didn’t want to be seen. She quickened her step. It wasn’t far now to the gatehouse where the gardener’s wife would be at home.

The man approached her and dismounted clumsily from his bicycle. He spoke with his head bowed, as if embarrassed.

"Missus," he said, "can you say? I look for"—he hesitated, trying to recall something complicated—"Bin-*deefa*? To work," he concluded. "You find for me?" He glanced up and she saw that he was in fact young, but then she saw his eyes and was distracted, before they were hidden again under the brim of his hat, eyes the color of the sea-stained granite blocks of a harbor jetty.

"Oh," Nissa said, a little confused. "Well, yes, I can." She had relaxed, at hearing his words and seeing his eyes. "It's there, this is the wall, there's an entry just around the corner"—she tried to show with a gesture the curve of a road—"and a little stone gatehouse." She pointed, then wondered, "Have they asked you to work there?"

"Work I hope. I dig. I build stones"—he made a piling motion with his hands—"build woods"—a hammering motion—"work hard. First clean face, boots? Yes?" And he turned away from her, as if, having found out what he needed to know, he had no further interest in her, and went across to the meadow that separated the roadway from the lake water.

That suited Nissa. She did not want to arouse anyone's interest. She liked this lake, with green hillsides rising up around it and the wall of mountains to the north. She liked the busy city of Queensbridge, with its well-stocked library and large park, where she could sit alone and read. She had found employment with a family whose worst vices were vanity and self-indulgence and that, moreover, included at least one lively intelligence—and probably two, she guessed. Six days a week she traveled over water that, if it wasn't her familiar restless ocean, still had the smells and sounds she had grown up with. And she was handed onto and off the ferry by a young man as sturdy and steady as the little boat his father captained.

Nissa left The Lakeview and walked slowly up the long, graveled driveway, past the gatehouse, calling, "A good morning to you," to the woman in the open window. She admired the tall oaks and leafy chestnut trees, the long green lawns and bright flower beds, the sparkling glass windowpanes and the welcoming doorway. As she waited for the door to be opened to her and to hear the butler's courteous "Good morning, Miss Nissa. Mrs. Bendiff is still at breakfast," she wondered if she should have warned that laborer that, as far as she knew, he would not be needed there.

Max watched Nissa walk away from him, through the gateway and up the long driveway. He was dumbfounded, he was dismayed, he was distressed, disturbed, disgruntled, and entirely displeased. The Bendiffs? The Bendiffs! Nissa worked for the Bendiffs, but what job could she do there? He'd never seen her, the few times Mister Max had left a message for Pia, to ask Pia—and now the full understanding of his bad luck struck him. He was going to have to ask Pia for information, ask her for help.

Pia would, of course, gloat. Max didn't know if he'd be able to listen to her gloating without kicking her permanently out of his business, good riddance to bad rubbish. He rode away down The Lakeview, going home to become Mister

Max in Inspector Doddle's clothing and then ride back, to deliver his request, hoping all the way that he could listen to Pia's gloating long enough to learn something.

That, however, turned out to present no difficulties after all, because Pia sent an immediate response. No, she would not meet him at the ice cream shop. "No," she wrote. "Not on your life and besides, it's not Gabrielle's anymore because she left already to start her job at *B's,* and you're supposed to know everything and be so smart but I guess you don't."

Max did not groan aloud in front of the boy who had carried Pia's message. The message wasn't this boy's fault. He just dropped a coin into the outstretched hand. Pia was treating Max as if he had no right to keep anything private from her, keep things safe from . . . her nosiness, he thought, from her way of pushing her opinions into his business. Because solutioneering was *his* business. Too bad for her, Max thought. If she thought he needed her to find things out, she was far from right. She had been useful and he wouldn't deny that, not to her, not to anyone, but she wasn't essential.

Max considered how he could go about discovering more about Nissa. Carlo had told him everything he knew and Pia refused to help. His only other information source would be the young woman herself. But how could he persuade her to talk to him?

Had he finally been set the problem he wasn't going to be able to solve? The secret he was not going to be able to winkle out? Max hoped not, because Nissa had won his complete sympathy. He would have wanted to help her even if Carlo

Coyne hadn't hired him to discover what it was that needed doing. But all he could think of to do was to follow her again.

And so Inspector Doddle, in his round pork-pie hat and his worn blue satin vest, plump-bellied and patient, took the afternoon ferry up to Summer and settled himself onto a bench in the square to watch rain clouds approach from the west and slowly cover the sky. Max knew the sky was not as dark as it looked through his tinted glasses, so he didn't worry about being rained on during the long trip around the lake, back to the Queensbridge docks. Instead, he bought a newspaper and turned to the page of international news, to worry about his parents while he waited.

There was little news from South America that day, which was not unusual since it took an earthquake or a revolution for news from those distant lands to travel so far. Max leafed through the rest of the pages, reading items about the old city and the New Town, about preparations for the royal holidays (increased ferry runs, a welcoming committee, the route the King's procession would take from the train station to The Lakeview), about business events (the opening of *B's* in less than a month, a new line of inexpensive but thoroughly stylish hats offered by Tess Tardo, the closing of a ship's chandlery due to the decrease in the number of commercial sailing vessels), and social events (a photograph of two women wearing gauzy summer dresses and wide-brimmed summer hats, one with a fat white *Z* that ran like a lightning bolt down the crown to join two proud egret feathers, with a small curtain of tiny pearls hanging down from its wide brim, the other a plump gauzy affair, scattered with small flowers). Max wondered what made those two women newsworthy and he read that one of them, the one with pearls on her hat, was the wife of Hamish Bendiff, of Bendiff's Jams and Jellies, proprietor of the eagerly anticipated new restaurant, displaying her R Zilla hat as she exchanged recipes with the wife of Lawyer Cobbles, whose head bore one of the creations of Tess Tardo, recognizable by the signature flowers, at a garden party held at the hillside villa of Lady Adelaide, Chairwoman of the Mayor's Committee for the Benefit of the Poor and the Needy.

So that was Pia's mother. She looked ordinary enough to Max, light-haired and a little plump, pretending not to notice the camera that was photographing her, but placing one hand on her hat and smiling at her companion, as if at the oldest and best of friends.

Maybe they were friends, although Pia's mother looked as if—without the huge hat and the pretend smile—she would be a cookie-making, homework-helping kind of mother, ready to wipe your tears or applaud your tree climbing and spend hours teaching you how to jump rope or ride a bicycle or roll a hoop. In the photograph, Mrs. Bendiff looked like a person who had been given the wrong role in the wrong play, but wanted to perform it well.

She also looked like a person who shouldn't be the mother of a daughter like Pia, a girl who wanted to be doing only serious, important things, and to always do them her own way.

Max was so lost in his own thoughts that he almost missed Nissa's return to the wide plaza. The young woman went directly to the same café table she'd sat at in the morning, and did not look around. As far as he could tell, a cup was set down in front of her without her even asking for it, as for a regular customer, and in fact, the woman who owned the café joined Nissa at the little round table. Max was not close enough to hear what they said to one another in their brief conversation, but he got the impression that they were comfortable together and, since Nissa had more than half an hour to wait before the ferry was due, he guessed that this was how she ended every working day, with a cup of coffee. She took out a small book and read and did not once look at him but Max got the feeling, from the angle of the back that was turned to him, that she thought someone might be watching her, and he knew, from the way she carefully stood as far from him as she could get during the ferry ride, that she had noticed him. So he bustled noisily off in his own direction when they debarked at the city dock. He didn't want Nissa to think she was being followed.

Also, he needed to get home to see what costumes were available to him. He should become a regular at the café, but in what role? An artist? A restaurant cook? A day laborer? City official? Who would a young woman like Nissa be most likely to trust enough to exchange a few polite words with? She was willing to talk with the café owner and she also apparently trusted Carlo. Maybe that was a clue.

Max thought about how Nissa and Carlo had met. He imagined the scene as if it were a play he was seeing, the fearful young woman boarding the ferry and the earnest young ferryman paying his attentions to her. What was there about Carlo that would have made Nissa feel safe?

Carlo, Max realized, had a reason to be where he was. Carlo worked on the ferry. He was supposed to be there, you'd expect him to be there, he had an identity. Carlo had a recognizable position, so he was what he seemed to be, what he said he was. He was not some secretive stranger. The same could be said of the café owner, with whom Nissa also seemed to feel comfortable. Nissa seemed uneasy about anyone who didn't have an obvious reason to be where they were. So, if Max was going to try to talk with her, and to persuade her to talk to him, he needed a job. Or, rather, he needed to seem to have a job, since his work as the Solutioneer would probably *not* make her feel unnoticed, and unthreatened, and safe.

Carlo thought that Nissa had some secret she was keeping. But Max thought that more likely the secret was keeping her. Nissa seemed to him like the canary in the cage, stalked around by cats whose sharp-clawed paws might dart at her at any moment. But what job could he have that would put him naturally into her path? How could he insinuate himself into the Bendiff household, and what work could he do there? It was really irritating that Pia had chosen this exact moment to refuse to assist him, just because he and Grammie claimed a little privacy.

Back home, Max changed into trousers and a shirt to join Grammie for dinner. He was not having any ideas, good or bad, about the problem of Nissa, so he shifted his attention to the other ongoing question—which had certain similarities to this one, didn't it? He opened his detecting notebook to the page where he had already written down three occupations that might take him to Andesia and added two to the list, *Geologist* and *Troubadour.* Then he folded the notebook closed and crossed over to his grandmother's house. Surely he could learn to play a guitar well enough to be a credible troubadour and enough Spanish to sing in that language. Couldn't he?

22

The Water Rat *Jobs*

• ACT III •

It wasn't until Thursday that Pia showed up. Max was alone in the house. Ari was helping Gabrielle move her boxes into one of the apartments that Mr. Bendiff had created out of the Workhouse Master's residence for his chef, his sous chef, and his pastry chef. These employees praised his generosity, but Mr. Bendiff believed it was the employer's responsibility to see that his workers could live comfortably. Also, he said, it was a practical matter, saving him the cost of a night watchman. Mr. Bendiff was like a king and Max wondered how a boy would get in to see Mr. Bendiff, if he weren't already known to him. It would be good practice for Max to make an anonymous entry into Mr. Bendiff's presence, somehow, and now that he'd thought of it, he started to wonder just how it could be done. How did you make your way past the obstacles surrounding someone so important and busy that he was like the treasure hidden at the heart of a maze?

At the moment, however, Max was enjoying the quiet of a solitary morning of vocabulary memorizing followed by reading a few of Aesop's fables in Spanish. A knock on his door interrupted his concentration on the story of the oak that stands firm, and is blown down, while the reed that bends survives the windstorm. Before he could stand up to go down the hall and open it, or even call "Come in," Pia burst into his kitchen. She had the red peasant skirt she had worn two mornings ago at the theater over her arm and she glared down at him to say, "I had to bring this back and, anyway, I wanted to tell you that it was really stupid so I'm going to pretend it never happened."

Max couldn't think what to think, except that this was just like Pia. Pia was always perfectly herself, he thought, and even if that self was so annoying that he often wanted to bop her a good one, he liked her being so true to it. He guessed this might be Pia's idea of an apology, and it turned out he didn't care about their quarrel. "All right," he answered.

"So, what was it you wanted to see me about?" Pia asked. "Can I have a glass of water? Do you have any cookies?" As she asked, she was already reaching down a glass from the shelf and opening the cookie jar to take out two large hazelnut cookies. "Do you want one?" she asked. And then she looked at Max. "Are you laughing at me?"

"No," he said. "No, I'm not laughing. I'm just—I'm grinning at you."

Pia surprised him. Instead of being offended, she smiled broadly and sat down. She thrust one of his own cookies across the table at him. "My father does that. Everybody else gets mad but he just . . . He takes me seriously, though. He knows I mean it."

"Mean what?" Max asked.

"What I say." Pia took a big bite, chewed thoughtfully, swallowed, and admitted, "Mostly. So what *did* you want?"

Now Max filled his mouth, so distracted by deciding how to say it, how much to tell Pia and how much to keep to himself, that he barely tasted the toasted nuttiness. When he was ready, he swallowed. "This isn't my secret. So I'm not going to explain, or tell you any details. The trouble is, I don't know if you can leave things alone." And he looked right at her.

Different expressions ran quickly over Pia's face, like little waves following breezes across the surface of the lake. She drew her dark eyebrows together in displeasure and looked down at the hand holding the cookie—was she embarrassed? Her eyes sparkled with anger at what he'd said and her mouth smiled in rueful acknowledgment of the truth of it. Finally, she shrugged.

This was no answer. Max said, "I mean, can you not ask questions? Can you take my word for things?"

"You mean like whatever you and your grandmother were hiding from me?" she demanded.

Max could have denied that, but if he did he'd be making a mistake, he knew. If Pia was going to be a real assistant, she had to know how to assist and not try to horn in on everything. So all he said was, "Yes. Like that."

More expressions crossed her face, irritation and chagrin and then, with a little widening of the eyes and a sharp glance at him, curiosity. He knew what she was thinking: she was wondering how to find out on her own what it was that he and Grammie were keeping to themselves. He bit his lip to keep from grinning again.

At last, "All right. I can," she said. "I will." Without giving him more than three seconds to tell her what he wanted, she demanded, "Isn't that good enough for you?"

At that, Max did allow himself to laugh, just a little, before saying, "I need to know about a young woman who works for you. For your father, I'd guess. She goes to your house to work but I don't think she's a servant."

Pia was already nodding; she knew who he was talking about, but he went on anyway.

"Her name is Nissa. Do you know who I mean?"

Pia nodded again but, uncharacteristically—was she teasing him?—did not say anything.

"What do you know about her?" Max asked.

"In the first place, she doesn't work for my father." Pia liked being able to correct him, that was obvious. "She works for my mother. She's a social secretary—at least, that was the job Mum advertised in the newspaper. But really? She's teaching my mother how to be a lady."

Pia spat out the word *lady* as if it were peppercorns she had accidentally bitten down on and wanted out of her mouth, fast.

"Mother—she doesn't want to be called Mum, she wants us to call her Mother, but Mum's who she's been to me, all of her life."

"All of *your* life, you mean," Max pointed out unsympathetically.

She glared at him. "I told you about her, she wants her children to have the right kind of friends and herself, too, but to her that means dressing right and having the right manners, wearing the right clothes and jewels, living in the right house with the right china and crystal and furniture . . . Nissa is supposed to be teaching her how to know about the things the right people already know, what to wear, what to talk about, what to serve at parties, how your home—and children, too—how everything should look. Also about books and paintings and music." Pia laughed, mocking.

Max had to know. Of course he wondered. "Theater, too?"

"I don't think Nissa knows much about plays," Pia told him. "But she does seem to know about all the other things. She said she had governesses and they traveled with her. She told us about herself the day she came to apply for the job and Mum asked her to stay for lunch, to see if her manners were good I think. But she hasn't said anything about herself since and my father wasn't there then to ask the kind of questions he likes to ask. He's almost never home for lunch, unless Mum is having some kind of party. She isn't stupid, my mother. She almost never has a party unless he'll be there. She knows if he's there, then everybody—well, almost everybody, I can't imagine the Baroness Barthold caring, can you? But anybody else will accept her invitations, but only to meet him and talk to him and listen to him; it's nothing to do with her. She didn't always used to be like this. My sister says Mum used to be more . . . normal with herself, and all of us, before . . . When my father started Bendiff's Jams and Jellies, with all the money the brewery made? Mum was the one who made his jams, so she worked in the kitchen right beside him. She went around to stores with him, too, with loaves of bread she'd baked, to spread the jams and jellies on for tasting. Everybody was glad to see her then, not like now. She wasn't proud, then."

"But what do you know about Nissa?" Max asked. At another time he might be interested in Pia's mother's life story, but right now he had a job to do, a problem to solve. "What's she like?"

Pia shook her head. "I don't know. How could I know? I almost never see her and when I do . . . She's shy, maybe. Or maybe she's someone who doesn't talk much? Because she doesn't feel shy to me, or proud. Or even, really, as if she thinks she's a lady even if she knows all those things that ladies know. She always wears the same skirt and blouse, or maybe it's a different one because they always look freshly cleaned. She has a soft voice and—have you seen her?" But she went on before Max could answer this, "Her hair is golden and she has eyes the color of . . ." Pia didn't know how to name the color of Nissa's eyes.

"Green smoke," Max suggested, and then—too quickly for her to get started talking again—he asked, "How long has she been working for you?"

"About four weeks. Maybe three but I think four. She *has* helped Mum, I have to admit. She tells her what she should wear and she's even trying to talk her out of those R Zilla hats—but I don't think even Nissa can do that. Those hats cheer my mother up."

"What about friends?"

"Mum doesn't have *friends.*"

"No, I mean Nissa. Does she?"

Pia shook her head. "Not that she talks about."

"Family?"

Another shake of the head.

"Where is her home?"

A shrug and raised eyebrows, to say *No idea.* "I don't know anything about her, not really," Pia realized. "Do I? Except, it's sort of funny when somebody never, ever talks about herself, not even a little. It makes you wonder." She looked thoughtfully at Max. "Like you never talk about *your*self."

Max opened his mouth to return the conversation to the subject of Nissa, but Pia was already doing that. "I have to say that she explains things to my mother without making her embarrassed at all the mistakes she makes, and Mum makes a lot of embarrassing mistakes, I promise you. So maybe Nissa used to be someone important? Did she run away? Is she hiding? Who is after her? Why are you so interested in—"

Max cut her off. "Thanks, Pia. You've been a help."

The idea of insisting on finding out what was going on was practically printed in capital letters across Pia's forehead, but she pulled her braid, instead, and offered, "I could try to find out more. I could try to talk to her. I mean, I could ask her questions. I could do that if I walked with her to wherever she goes when she leaves the house; I think she might live in Summer. I could follow her, she always leaves at four. She might talk to me, anyway. She looks like someone lonely and I bet she's not used to being lonely like I am so she might want to tell me things, if I gave her the chance."

"Pia?" he said, with a warning in his voice.

"Or—" she started, then jerked down on her braid, hard. But she couldn't help reminding him, "I found out about Gabrielle for you, didn't I?"

"Pia," he said, with a little more warning.

"Oh, all right. But this means I'm still your assistant. Aren't I? If there's a case, you'll ask for my help. Won't you? If you need it."

"If I need it, I will," Max said. He was waiting for Pia to leave, now that peace had been restored between them, now that she had told him all she could about Nissa. He wanted to be alone to think over what he'd learned and form a plan.

"What're you reading?" Pia asked, and pulled the book across the table, to turn it around and read the open page. "Is that Spanish? Is that the fable about the oak and the reed? I know that one, but are you going to Spain?" She closed the book (losing his place in it, he noticed) to ask, "I thought you liked being the Solutioneer. I thought you earned a good living at it and— Would you like me to ask my father to give you a job? He always needs salesmen, to go around to places that don't carry Bendiff products and persuade them to try them in their stores or use them in their restaurants. I bet if you wanted to, once you started you'd be good at working for my father. He already likes you."

"Go home, Pia," Max said. He couldn't be any clearer. "I've got work to do."

"What work? Why can't I help?"

Max stood up and just looked down into her face. Her words were swirling around in his head, confusing him. He wanted to take his watercolors out into the garden, look at the sky, and let his brain relax and float free. All those words were like so many ropes, tying him down. Pia was exhausting. "Are you on your bicycle?"

"No, the motorcar is waiting. Your street is too small for the motorcar to drive on," she complained, but she *did* go then, and as far as Max was concerned, she could complain as much as she liked, as long as she left his house and his morning.

In *The Adorable Arabella,* the suitor who had won the heart and hand of the girl had done so by not asking for it. Frank Worthy had seemed to be unmoved by the charms other men found irresistible, and he was the one she chose in the end, perhaps because he hadn't pursued her. Frank Worthy was the role Max decided to play, to gain Nissa's trust.

And it was Pia—he couldn't deny it—it was Pia who had given him the idea. He was wishing he could deny it as he dressed himself that Thursday afternoon in a pair of long summer trousers and the blue-and-white-striped blazer his father put on for going out in fine weather. He placed Frank Worthy's straw boater on his head and studied the effect in the mirror, before covering his eyes with the tinted glasses. Max knew he should tell Pia how she had once again helped him with her rattling talk. He knew he should but he wasn't sure he would, and he didn't want to. Instead, he made sure his boots had enough of a polish for the profession of salesman.

Satisfied, Max went downstairs to pick up the small, square leather suitcase he had packed with jars of Bendiff's jams and packages of Bendiff's crackers. He added a salesman's pad before he closed the suitcase and snapped the catches. Then he reopened it, to put in a copy of William Shakespeare's *A Midsummer Night's Dream.*

He was seated at the café and reading when Nissa arrived. She took a table as far away from his as possible, but he didn't look up from his reading until the café owner came out to greet Nissa, and be greeted, and set a cup down in front of her. Max didn't know why, but he assumed that this young woman drank coffee. He looked up from his reading, but not at Nissa, although he gave a mannerly nod in her direction. He called to the woman, "Miss? Might I have another cup of coffee?" then returned to his reading. He didn't look up again until the cup arrived at his table, at which time—without even a glance in Nissa's direction—he paid the woman and thanked her for her trouble. When it was time for the ferry to arrive, Max picked up the little suitcase that had rested by his feet, replaced the book into it, and—with a vague, polite nod in Nissa's general direction—walked down to the dock.

On Friday, which was luckily another sunny afternoon, so that it didn't seem strange for him to be wearing tinted lenses, he did exactly the same thing, playing exactly the same role, Frank Worthy, a young man with more important things on his mind than any young woman. This time, however, he engaged the café owner in a short conversation. "This seems a pleasant, busy little village," he remarked, and she assured him that it was, and would become even busier with the arrival of the royal family. "They take their summer holidays here, always have, my grandfather remembered it. This is the only place where they can really relax. Here by the lake, I mean. Summer's a sleepy place in winter, I grant you. But it's not winter now," she said with a friendly smile. "Is it, sir?"

"Not a bit of it," Max answered with his own friendly smile as he paid and thanked her. The smile included Nissa, should she be watching this exchange, as he thought she was, although he did not check to see for sure.

After that, it was the weekend, when no salesman would be out at work. Max had decided not to undertake the Romanian Count job, so he had nothing to do until Monday. It was the first lazy weekend he had enjoyed since his parents disappeared. He slept late and spent what was left of the morning painting in the garden. In the afternoon he went to *B's,* where he tasted pastries for Gabrielle and admired the changes Mr. Bendiff had made in what until recently had been a decrepit and dismal home for the poor and aged and helpless of the city. Now there was a gleaming kitchen, a stylish dining room, and a courtyard hung with Chinese lanterns.

On Sunday, despite a low-lying cloud cover, Max took his paint box and a pad of heavy paper and rode up along The Lakeview, almost as far as Baroness Barthold's castle, to sit beside the lake and paint. The water was as gray as the sky and as smooth as a mirror. First he painted the sky, finishing several quick paintings that differed from one another only by a slight change in the brightness of sunlight filtered through the clouds. Then he painted the sky as reflected in the water, but those pictures were no more successful than his efforts to paint the sky as seen through glass. Max was not discouraged, however. Or, rather, he was less discouraged than interested to find that even with a subject matter as limited as the sky there were things he could see but could not paint. He was able to paint only the sky itself.

While he was eating his lunch alone beside the tranquil lake, he added *Banker* to the list he was drawing up and then—looking at the isolated farmhouses on the hillsides opposite and remembering how the Brothers Grimm had gone from house to house with their own notebooks—he wrote down *Collector of Folk Tales.*

In the cooler late afternoon air, Max mowed the grass growing up around Grammie's house and his own, then washed and changed, to join his grandmother for a roast chicken dinner. Grammie reported that "There *are* Romanian Counts, hordes of them. It seems that in Romania, the richest man in a village proclaims himself Count and nobody questions his right to collect taxes, as long as he survives and holds on to his lands. It's a bit like Andesia. Have you been reading the book I gave you?"

Max could say yes, he had.

"Did you know that I've got a book on South America's more recent history?"

Max shook his head, no, he hadn't. One look at her face and he grew worried. "What have you learned?"

"Not much about Andesia. There's never much about it, it's so tiny and remote and unimportant and—until they found the copper and silver—poor. It used to be no more than a few villages and one larger town, a total population in the whole country of about two thousand people. That was what they guessed, from the villages they could get to with horses. It's mostly hills and mountains, one plateau."

"How did they live?" Max wondered.

"The way most of the natives still do. Many of the men work in the mines. The rest cultivate whatever bits of land they can, no matter how small, and they have learned how to terrace the lower hillsides. The main food crop is maize; there are squashes and yams. Goats are a luxury, for milk and cheese and meat. There are chickens, of course, a few small herds of alpacas, for wool . . . It's a hard life, even without the mines. The Andesians don't live to be very old."

Max tried to imagine his parents in such a place: his flamboyant father, who liked to go out among crowds of people and declaim on any topic that interested him; his imaginative mother, who loved to listen, to read, or tell stories and make quiet fun of the many fools who came her way. His parents were accustomed to dressing well and living well and, especially, eating well. They were accustomed to being comfortable. Now he was even more worried. "They live in houses, don't they?"

"Pretty grand houses—well, the families who own the mines do—and the royal family has a palace. The natives live in what would probably more accurately be called one-room huts, close together in that one town. Apapa is the name of it, it's the capital, the royal palace is there. But, Max?"

Her voice warned him to look right into her eyes. It was her eyes that told him there was some bad news coming.

"The Kings of Andesia?" she said, in that same, questioning, unhappy tone of voice. "It's only been about fifty years that there has been a royal house, and in that time?"

Max waited.

"There have been twelve kings. Your father is the thirteenth."

"I'm not superstitious," Max said quickly.

"And that includes the recent four years of civil war, when

the royal family fled to Bogotá and there was no king, so it's actually twelve kings in forty-six years. And, Max? Not one of those twelve kings died in bed with his boots off."

With no question at all in his voice, Max asked, "What have they gotten themselves into."

"Their children, either," Grammie finished. "Sometimes a wife escaped."

Then they were silent for a long time, and neither of them moved, not to eat or drink, and neither looked at the other, as if each wanted to protect the other from thoughts that swarmed like wasps in each of their heads.

Finally, "What are we going to do, Grammie?" Max asked. For the first time in a long time, since just after he'd understood that his parents had disappeared from his life, he felt like a child.

But Grammie was asking him, at the very same time, "Max? What are we going to do?"

On Monday afternoon, when Frank Worthy looked up from his reading to greet Nissa with a casual "Good afternoon," she answered him. "And to you," she said, not hesitating on her way to her usual table, where she opened a copy of the *Queensbridge Gazette* and started to read.

Max had already returned to his book.

The café owner, when she brought him his coffee, had obviously decided to find out about him. "You're quite the regular," she observed.

"For the time being," Max answered pleasantly. Frank Worthy was not a chatterer. He responded frankly to questions but didn't volunteer information about himself. He let other people ask the questions.

"A salesman, are you?" She indicated the suitcase at his feet.

Max nodded.

"You're new to the area," she told him.

Max agreed.

"New to the work?"

"That, too," Max said.

"I only say that because you're so young. What are you selling?" she wondered.

Max was ready for this question. In fact, he'd hoped to be asked because Nissa was listening and she would know from his answer that he had a place in the world. Which wasn't a lie. He *did* have a place in the world, just not the one he wanted to convince *her* he had. He lifted his case onto the table and opened it, then began talking about the crispness of the crackers, the sweet fruitiness of the jams. "Everybody knows that Bendiff's products are of the highest quality," he told her as he closed it again.

The café owner agreed. "Are you asking me to place an order?"

Max answered her in just the way a confident person would. "If you want to try some, you'll ask me. Why should I pester you about it? No, I'm here to enjoy your excellent coffee and the fine afternoon, not to sell goods."

"Also," the woman observed, "the usual Bendiff representative was here just two weeks ago. You aren't their usual salesman."

"No, I'm not," Max agreed, with an untroubled smile.

"What are you, then?" asked the woman, now a little suspicious.

"I'm new, as green as they come," Max told her, with the candidness that won Frank Worthy the trust of everyone he met. "I have the idea of selling not to the shops, or to businesses like hotels or this café, but to boardinghouses and the big homes along the lake, places where they feed a lot of people. I'm not trying to oust the regular representative."

She relaxed and looked over her shoulder at Nissa to say, "That might be a good idea. It might just be a good idea. It's original, I'll say that."

Max said nothing. She went back to the customers waiting inside the café. Seeing that Nissa's eyes were on him, Max smiled and nodded and returned to his reading. Later he followed her onto *The Water Rat* and stood near to her, but did not try to talk. For her part, she did not seem disturbed by his presence and nodded a smiling farewell to him at the docks.

It was on Tuesday that Nissa first spoke because, as Max had guessed, just like Adorable Arabella, Nissa preferred not to be chased after and crowded up against with unasked-for admiration. Like Arabella, if you did not pursue her, she became interested in you. On that Tuesday afternoon, Max was already at his usual table and reading his usual book when Nissa arrived at her usual hour. The day had grown hot with steady July sunshine, and Nissa had taken off her jacket and gloves during her walk. She approached the table where Max sat and he, as if he were surprised, as if he had been unexpectedly distracted from an involving activity, looked up to see her.

"You always read that same book," she observed. Her voice was soft and low, her smile hesitant, unsure about staying on her face. She was like a fawn, Max thought, or a sleeping kitten, or the first tender green shoots in a garden. She was something you needed to be careful with.

He answered her just as his father would have, or his mother, or his grandmother for that matter, as if the one word were explanation enough. "It's Shakespeare."

She nodded. She understood.

Max stood up to introduce himself. "Frank Worthy." He kept the tinted glasses on but removed his hat. He had become Frank Worthy, and never thought for a moment that she might recognize him as anyone else.

She couldn't in all politeness now refuse him her name. "Nissa," she said.

"Will you join me?" Frank Worthy asked, pulling out a chair.

Instead of answering the question, to accept or decline his invitation, she observed, "In *Midsummer Night's Dream,* that father . . . the father would rather have his daughter locked away in a convent, or even put to death, than marry a man he hasn't chosen. What do fathers want of their daughters?"

"Obedience," Max answered. This same question had

WILLIAM
SHAKESPEARE
A
MIDSUMMER
NIGHT'S
DREAM

been discussed at the dinner table in his house, and his parents had been in agreement about it. His father had turned to Max to say, "It's lucky for you we live in modern times with wiser parents," and his mother had added, "Wiser children help." It was one of their usual conversations, with his parents contentedly contradicting one another, each looking to have the final and the wittiest word.

Nissa said, "I agree. Obedience, and blind devotion, too." Then she did sit down with Max. "Have you read the play before?"

Max could say, in complete honesty, "Many times." When he wasn't dashing about the stage as Peaseblossom or Mustardseed, or standing at respectful attention as one of the courtiers, Max had the job of cuing the actors.

Nissa looked up to wave a greeting to the café owner, then turned her attention back to Max. "I've seen it, too, in the theater."

"In Queensbridge?" Max wondered. Could this be a problem?

"No, in an entirely different place. In an entirely different life, but doesn't it strike you as a cynical idea that only magic can straighten things out? For the young couples, I mean. Because," she explained a little sadly, as if she did not wish to disillusion him, "we live in a world where there is no magic. So that the wrongs we do, the errors we make . . . they can't be corrected. Those whom we wound will remain wounded." Her voice grew entirely sad as she told him, "Those whom we have lost remain lost. Those whom we have thrown away are not to be found again."

The café owner, setting Nissa's cup on the table, had something different on her mind. "You heard what this young fellow said, didn't you? Why don't you tell your employers they should talk to him? Or the cook, all those big houses have cooks, and you work in one of those houses, don't you?"

"Oh," Nissa said, "I can't ask them to do that. Besides, it wouldn't be any use."

"Why not?" The woman pressed her point. "Why not help someone who's starting off in the world, making his own way?"

Nissa shook her head and didn't answer, but her cheeks grew rosy.

"Well *I've* mentioned you to a couple of my customers," the café owner told Max. "Jilly at the Waterside Boardinghouse, for one, and she wants you to call on her."

"Thank you," Max said. He didn't know what he would do about that. This was help he could well do without. "You're very kind," he said, because she was.

"Most people want to give others a helping hand, if it's within their powers," the owner announced, giving Nissa a look.

"You don't understand," Nissa said.

"Jilly suggested that you talk to the cook at the palace. He's already arrived, to get everything ready, because if the palace orders from you, you'll be a made man."

It wasn't the right time for Max to take out his little notebook and jot down *Import/Export Salesman.* "I don't know how to thank you," he said.

"I *work* for Mrs. Bendiff," Nissa admitted, speaking reluctantly but also a little crossly.

That changed everything. The café owner's expression acknowledged it, and so did her voice when she complained, "You never said. How was I to know?"

Nissa gave a helpless shrug of the shoulders.

"You never talk about yourself, so probably I shouldn't be surprised. So. Will the Bendiffs be taking you to dine at this fancy new restaurant he's opened? If you need a companion, you might ask me and I wouldn't say no. Or this young man here, who looks perfectly presentable even if I've never seen him without his tinted glasses so he could be a squinter. And everyone knows about squinters."

Max laughed as Frank Worthy, all confidence and curiosity. "What is it that everybody knows?"

"They're a bad lot, every man jack of them," the woman announced, and turned away to answer a summons from inside the café.

Max said, "I don't squint." He was smiling, sharing the joke with Nissa.

"Why *do* you wear them?"

"It's my eyes," he said, as if that explained everything, and went on quickly to tell her that tomorrow, Wednesday, would be his last day in Summer, or any of the lakeside villages. "I might have better luck in Porthaven."

"Don't you live in Queensbridge?"

"I don't live anywhere," Max lied easily, confident that when everybody thinks you are honest, you can get away with one untruth. "Or, I live everywhere, wherever I land at the end of the day. It's the advantage of living alone. It's a lucky thing for me that there's at least one advantage to being alone in the world," he added carelessly.

"You're alone in the world?" she asked.

It was time for the ferry and they rose from the table together and walked together across the plaza and down to the dock. "I am," Max said, and it was almost true. "Although I'd have chosen differently."

She looked sharply up into his face. "I'll see you tomorrow?" she asked as they parted to go their separate ways on the ferry.

Nissa sat down without hesitation at the table where Max waited, late on Wednesday afternoon, and started talking right away. "How did you come to be alone? May I ask?"

"Yes, of course, but I won't answer," said Max, who had been hoping for this very question. "Except to say suddenly, unexpectedly, unhappily. The pillars on which my home stood—I'm not speaking literally," he explained.

"I know what you mean," she assured him.

"—were cut out from under me."

Her eyes filled with tears, which she did not shed. Tears of sympathy? he wondered. Or tears at a memory? "Betrayed," she murmured, and her hands gripped each other hard, on her lap, and she seemed to hunch over the table, as if hoping not to be noticed, or looked at. "Abandoned."

"Left behind," Max corrected. He leaned forward and saw how she drew back, now almost huddling in the chair. His brain buzzed with an idea and his voice could ring with truthfulness as he went on. "They sailed off," he said—and saw shock stiffen her shoulders, and continued, "I thought I knew where they were going and I thought I would be with them."

Nissa sat silent, almost as if she could no longer speak. Max remembered where he had seen such a pose before, such hunched shoulders, such a bowed neck. In *A Miser Made Miserable,* when the rich man (played by William Starling) had lost everything and his poor neighbor came to offer what he could, sympathy and half a loaf of bread, shame at his own poverty had kept the formerly rich man silent, huddled in his chair before the small fire, like a schoolboy who has wet himself in front of everyone, or that Captain Trevelyn's daughter from the *Miss Koala,* or a butcher caught with his finger on the scale. Shame feared being seen, and named, and tried to stay hidden away in its darkness. Max remembered the Miser and he understood: This was shame he was looking at, and Max had guessed the source of Nissa's shame. He pitied her.

She looked at Max, and looked away, and looked at him again, and Max understood also that she wanted to speak, wanted to tell her story, and could not bear to. His own secret case was simpler. It was the safety of others that silenced him, not shame that smothered.

It seemed that Nissa had decided to take him a little into her confidence. "I guessed that we were alike, you and I. I felt there was something in common between us. I thought—I thought you were someone I could talk to."

Nissa was deciding to trust him at the very time when Max was starting to understand that, really, there was no need for her to speak. He thought he knew her name, now, and whose daughter she was.

"Because you were always reading, and it was Shakespeare," she explained, and then she smiled. When she smiled, her wide, smoky green eyes shone with tears. "I was raised with books, and music, and fine pictures, statues, museums, and if I did not have those memories now, and books to read, if I did not have the city library— Do you know the city library?"

Max nodded, but could not find any words in his mouth. Trevelyn, that was her name, Nissa Trevelyn. He would bet his father's fortune on it.

"Perhaps," she suggested, "we might meet sometime? I often read in the park."

Max shook his head. Ideas, guesses, possibilities were shooting around in his brain, like firecrackers shooting up into the sky to explode into showers of light against the darkness. He was being the Solutioneer and Frank Worthy at the same time, which was not easy. The Solutioneer was thinking of Colly, someone else whose hopes had been destroyed by parents and—this was the most useful thing to Mister Max at the moment—who minded that his education had been derailed.

But Max was also, at that time, at that table, in that company, Frank Worthy—whose understanding of people was subtle, and deep, and delicate. Only Frank Worthy had understood Arabella. Only he had guessed that she wanted the very thing everyone denied her, that is, the pleasure of desiring something perhaps unattainable, the delicious pleasures of dreaming and hoping and longing. Thus it was that Frank Worthy had won the young woman's heart. Nissa's was an entirely different case, but as Frank Worthy, Max understood what Max Starling would never have guessed—that Nissa lived in the prison of her secret, and were someone to unlock the door for her, and fling it open, or bend the bars apart with his superior strength so that she could flee, as soon as she came to rest she would build a prison around herself again. Nissa was going to have to free herself, to find, or manufacture, her own key. It was Frank Worthy who knew what to say to her.

He told her, "I don't think we will meet again. I'm going away, remember? To Porthaven."

"The sea calls you?" she asked. "Maybe it's the sea that makes the likeness I sense between us." This idea interested her and distracted her from the burden of shame that bent her down, and thus, lightened it.

Max said, "But I would like to ask you . . . I've made a friend in the old city, a boy, who would like to talk with someone who knows about books. I'd like to tell him he could come here, to the café, some afternoon, and that you could tell him what is good to read, if a boy wants to learn to be an educated man, and make his way in the world even if his circumstances have been determined to keep him down."

He had surprised her, he could see. But she was tempted and he could see that, too, tempted by the promise of talking about books as well as the chance to help a boy to overcome hard circumstances.

"He also is alone," Max added, and then said, "You'll know him by his hair, which is the color of ripe corn, and I can tell him how to recognize you. I hope I can say you'll meet him?" he asked.

"Of course," Nissa said. "Yes, of course you may. I'd like to be of use."

It was time for the ferry, then, so they rose from the table to walk together down to the dock. "You really are going to Porthaven?" Nissa asked.

"It's time I moved on in my life," Max said. "I haven't had great success as a salesman, so I may try my hand at sailoring."

"It's not an easy life. It can make you hard."

"It can be dangerous, too, I understand."

"Do you fear danger?" she asked.

"Yes!" answered Max Starling, before either of his other two roles could silence him, and then he laughed. "I'm afraid I do. But I can forgive my fear, even if I can't approve of it, or want to be in its company."

Nissa did not answer for several steps. She seemed to be lost in her own thoughts. Then she smiled up at him. "Well, at least we can travel together on this last ferry ride."

"Won't your young man be jealous?" asked Max, now the

Solutioneer. "I wouldn't want to cause Carlo to worry. I've met him, in the city, and he seems to me a fine and upright man, trustworthy. You must know he's your devoted servant."

"Carlo knows not to be jealous," Nissa assured Max. "If he doesn't, I can always tell him—and I will, because you're right about him. I hadn't thought there was anyone to be trusted, but you're right, Carlo is better than most other men. I'm glad I met you, Frank Worthy," said Nissa Trevelyn, "even if you are about to disappear."

23

In which the bag is opened and the cat steps out

On Thursday afternoon Max bicycled up along The Lakeview and lingered by the corner of Tassiter Lane until Tomi Brandt appeared outside the firehouse. When he saw Tomi's familiar stocky figure emerge from a side door, Max crossed over. Tomi was surprised to see him. "I thought you'd disappeared again, maybe for good."

"I guess not," Max answered, the Queen's Spy, the man who knew everything before anybody else even suspected there might be something to know.

Tomi was not impressed. "Not that I want you to." He grinned. "Just . . . you like being mysterious and I never know when I might see you, or someone who you might be. Whereas me"—and he gestured to the building behind him—"you always know where to find me."

"Always? You're done with school?"

"I'm thirteen now," Tomi pointed out. At the age of thirteen, the law said a boy or girl could choose to leave school. "So I'm stopping. Like you."

Max could have corrected this mistake, but was more curious about Tomi's life. "What do your parents say?"

"Mum says boys will be boys, and my da thinks you can't grow up fast enough in this world. They know where to find me, if they need me."

Max guessed from the amused expression in Tomi's eyes that Tomi enjoyed his irregular life, and this, Max guessed next, more than their common age, was why he felt at ease with this boy. "So you've decided to be a fireman?"

Tomi shrugged. "It's a trade, it's smart to have a trade, it's good to know how to put out fires, and it's exciting, even dangerous. Sometimes." That those were the times he liked best was clear.

"I have a favor to ask," Max said, and took a few steps away from the building, to be absolutely sure they wouldn't be overheard. It would seem, he thought, as if the two boys had moved forward to enjoy the lake, which shone blue in summer sunlight. A westerly breeze carried the smell of water to them. "Can I ask a favor?"

"Sure," Tomi said. "If I can. You have an interesting life, and I don't mind being included. What do you want?"

"Do you know where to find Colly?"

"He's where he always was, with those grandparents. They won't let go of him. So yes, I can find him."

"Can you take him a message from me?"

"From you Max Starling? Or you the policeman? Or you Bartolomeo? Or is it from you the escaped, not-dead, kidnap victim?"

Max hadn't thought of that. "Does he know I'm not dead?"

"He's smart. He knows things weren't the way they seemed, but he doesn't know exactly what went on. He's too busy these days to think much about it, with his new job."

"I can't imagine washing dishes and sweeping floors is all that interesting for him."

"He's not doing that. He's learning how to keep the books. The owner—that Bendiff guy?—he talked to Colly before he hired him and I guess—well—anybody who talks to Colly has to see how smart he is."

Max decided. "You can tell him it's a message from his prisoner, and then he can be sure I'm alive."

"He'll be glad to know for sure. So, what's the message?"

"Tell him he should take the ferry up to Summer on a weekday afternoon, and wait on the plaza until—it'll be sometime around half past four—he sees a young woman, alone. She's usually dressed in dark colors, she wears a hat, she sits by herself at a café and has coffee and reads the newspaper until the five o'clock ferry comes in. Her name is Nissa, and if he asks her, she's someone he can talk to about books, and other things, too. She's well educated and—if he's interested—she also knows about paintings, and art. She's expecting him," Max told Tomi. "She'll know who he is."

"Colly certainly wants to learn and to go on," Tomi said. "I'll tell you, he might just figure out a way to become a lawyer. He'd be a good one, too. He'd keep people from taking advantage of the law for their own purposes, I bet. He's ambitious, which I'm not. What about you, Eyes? Are you ambitious?"

Max shrugged. "I have no desire to be a judge, or mayor, or rich," he said. "But I do want to be . . . independent. To do what I want. I expect that's pretty normal." Was it also normal to talk to somebody like this? About this kind of thing? In this way? As if you were just and only yourself?

"I'm ambitious to be useful," Tomi told him. They stood shoulder to shoulder, looking out over the water. "To make the city a better place for everyone to live in, not just the lucky ones with good jobs and big houses or old families, I mean. Plumbing, for example," Tomi said, and his face lit up with enthusiasm. "What if nobody had to use outhouses? What if every house had its own bathroom? You'd have to put in pipes, under the streets probably, to carry all that wastewater away—and if everybody had water, hot and cold, running into their houses . . . If things are clean, and all the water comes from clean sources, and people are clean, then the chance of outbreaks of things like typhoid and polio goes way down. Everybody knows that but nobody takes the necessary steps."

"You want to be a plumber?" Max asked.

Tomi hadn't thought that far. "I want to be someone in a position to make things better," he said. "City engineer? Or mayor, fireman, policeman . . . I want to make things better, that's all."

"Or a teacher," Max offered.

"I don't want a boring life," Tomi argued.

"But any life can be un-boring, can't it?" Max asked. He wasn't sure, now that he'd asked it, if he knew the answer to that question.

"Or any life can be boring," Tomi said, as if he was listening to a new idea.

They were both quiet for a minute. The lake water rippled gently. Then Max got back to work. "You'll tell Colly?"

"Sure. Right away. So I guess, all in all, you could say it was a good thing they decided to kidnap you," Tomi Brandt said. "As long as I was there to rescue you, that is."

Seeing the expression on Max's face, Tomi just laughed. "Relax, Eyes, it was a joke."

"Not at the time it wasn't," Max admitted. "You really did rescue me."

"Maybe, but you get credit for all the rest of it," Tomi assured him. "I don't know what it is you're up to and"—he held up a hand—"there's no need for you to tell me."

Max didn't know what exactly the mischief dancing about from Tomi's eyes to his mouth and back meant, but he knew it was mischief. If he hadn't been so sure that he could trust the boy, he'd have been worried.

That afternoon, Max wrote to Carlo Coyne to reassure him—as he had the young man's father two weeks earlier—that there was no danger stalking the person for whom he had so much concern. Mister Max was confident that in not too long a time, Nissa would confide in Carlo, and that he, Carlo, would then understand everything. He enclosed his final bill, sealed the envelope, and put it into the mail. That last job having come to an end, Max turned his full attention to his newest, most serious, most urgent, and most troubling problem: Andesia, and how to get himself there, and what self to be, once arrived, and—this most likely to be the most difficult—how to come into the presence of the King and Queen of that land in order to figure out what could prove impossibly difficult, a plan for their rescue.

He and Grammie had agreed to meet in Max's kitchen on Sunday afternoon, and Max wanted to be as ready as he could be with as many possibilities as he could think of. He took out the little notebook and considered what he had already listed. Then he added *Journalist, Butler, Valet, Footman, Import/Export Salesman,* and, although it was not at all likely, *Tourist.* None of his ideas seemed good enough. He hoped Grammie had managed to think of some better ones. When they had settled themselves across from one another at the kitchen table and exchanged lists, however, what Max noticed first was that all of Grammie's suggestions required two people.

He looked up at her.

She was looking at him.

He did not say what he was thinking, and he suspected that she, also, was holding her tongue. Instead, he studied her list some more, and waited.

Finally, Grammie spoke. "It would take you at least a year of study to learn enough to be able to pass yourself off as a geologist. You know that, don't you? I don't think we have a year."

Max couldn't object.

"So I'll just cross that off, shall I? And a banker presents the same difficulty, except you'd have to learn economic theory as well as banking practices. Agreed?"

Max agreed and then he pointed out to her that while she might be qualified for the position, he could not be part of a pair of teachers, for the same reason.

Grammie couldn't argue. She announced, "I won't have you acting a mountaineer, which takes years and years of practice, and even then it's deadly dangerous. Besides, anybody would see how untrained you are. I wonder, too, about this collector of folk tales. Because," she explained, and Max had to admit that as a librarian she would know, "the people who do that are scholars. They know every kind of story from all over the world, and while you are familiar with fairy tales and sort of with the Greek gods, that's all you know. Also, these collectors—anthropologists is what they are—talk about stories in a particular way. I might just be believable as an anthropologist, maybe for a day, because I've read a lot, but then what reason would there be for you to have tagged along? As for butler, or any one of the menservants . . . the trouble is, Max—and it's not your fault, there's nothing you can do about it—you don't have a beard. Not any kind of beard and all of these are grown men, who would have beards growing."

"Nobody's noticed that before," Max pointed out.

"Maybe," Grammie allowed. "But Andesia is going to be different. You'll be on view for longer, and you'll be stared at, as strangers are. It's not like here where you appear and then disappear as soon as possible."

"We don't have any puppets and we don't know how to work them, if we did, besides not having a puppet stage, so I don't think puppeteers is going to work, either," Max said, with his own forefinger now on *her* list. "I could always be a tourist," he added.

"On your own? Nobody would believe it."

"They might," Max grumbled. He knew what she wanted and planned: Grammie wanted and planned to go along, and interfere, or—worse—run the show.

"I suppose we could both go as tourists," she said now. "On an around-the-world tour, which would explain our showing up in a remote place like Andesia."

"Aren't you a little old for a trip around the world?" Max asked, by then quite annoyed with his grandmother.

"Or maybe—this is better—I could be a rich, eccentric old woman who wants to visit every country in South America or—even better—who wants to see all the great mountain ranges of the world before I die. That wouldn't be a total lie. I *would* like to see the Himalayas and the Andes, the Rockies, the Alps. There are some wonderful single peaks, too—Mount Fuji, Mount Kilimanjaro. We'll have to spend your father's fortune, or a fair amount of it, for me to be convincingly rich," she warned.

Grammie's stubborn insistence on being in charge was getting in the way of solving this problem. "You're forgetting about me," Max grumbled.

"No I'm not. You can be my grandson—which you are, after all—who is traveling with me. Or a paid companion, if you're worried about your independence," Grammie snapped. She was getting impatient with him.

"I could be a refugee," Max said, "hoping to escape from somewhere there's civil war, or from an oppressive regime. It wouldn't matter then how old I was, and that I was alone. They couldn't turn me away," Max said.

"Maybe not. Or maybe they could. They're a government, after all, and governments aren't like individual people. They don't care about being good, or kind, or about what their neighbors will say. Refugees might well just be thrown in jail, as a possible danger to the country," Grammie argued. "They certainly wouldn't let us talk to the King. No, being refugees won't take us where we need to go."

"Where are you going?" asked Ari, coming in through the dining room. Then, because he was quick to notice things, he said, "Are you quarreling? Would you like me to leave?"

Grammie looked at Max, and Max looked at Grammie. They both knew they'd used up all their ideas and they both had to admit, to themselves at least, that they hadn't had a good enough one.

"Or maybe I could help?" Ari suggested, still standing in the doorway. "I don't know what it is you're talking about," he began, smoothing things over the way he could by not using the word *arguing* or even *disagreeing,* "but I do know that sometimes a new point of view—"

"I *always* have a new point of view," came Pia's voice. She jostled Ari into the kitchen. "What's going on? What are you two doing and why do you have— Are you *fighting*? Are they fighting, Ari? But what do they have to fight about? Does anyone else want a cookie? I can't stay long, my mother has invited guests for tea, but there are things my father said he had to see to at *B's,* although if you ask me he just wanted to get out of the house for an hour. Of course, nobody asks me. He says I can ask a guest to the opening night, he said a friend but I don't— So, Max, do you want to come with me?"

"No!" Max cried. The last thing he wanted to do was go out in public, where people might recognize him as the Solutioneer or as Max Starling. Being recognized as either would ruin everything.

"You don't have to be awful about it," Pia said. He'd have thought she'd be angry, but it wasn't anger he saw on her face.

"It's not what you think," Max said.

"How do you know what I think? You have no idea, no idea at all, Mister Max, whoever you are, smart as you think you are. I didn't want to take a guest, anyway."

"I'm sorry to hear that," Max said, as smooth as Ari, "because I was just wondering if it wouldn't be fun for you to have Nissa be your guest." As soon as Max made the suggestion he knew what a good idea it was.

"My mother would hate that," Pia answered sulkily.

"Nissa might make a . . ." he hesitated, to choose the right word, "an interesting . . ." probably not a friend, because Nissa was a grown-up, "cousin kind of person. I bet. I've talked with her and she knows a lot about the world."

"My mother would *really* hate it," Pia said, but now she was smiling. She sat down at the table, and before they thought to stop her, she pulled the papers over in front of herself. "What's this?" she asked. "Unless . . . Ari, would you be my guest?"

"I'm sorry, Pia, I'll be out in the kitchen. In case they need an extra hand. It takes a few days for a restaurant to settle into a routine, and if Gabrielle needs me, I want to be there." He, too, sat down at the table—but he didn't take possession of the pieces of paper.

"I know that, and I know my father wants everything running right for when the royal family comes. The Mayor's asked him to lead the welcoming parade from the train station all the way to The Lakeview. Our car, I mean, but that's also my father, but I'm not going with them. I'm going to watch from our gates and see everybody. What's this list, Mrs. Nives? What are you two getting up to? We have an old puppet theater in the nursery. I used to love puppets and I'm good at working them. I could help out." She looked from Max to Grammie to Ari, then once again around at each of them. Unable to stop herself from asking, she demanded, "What? What is it? What do all of you know that I don't? I can tell there's something."

Max studied Pia's face, and thought.

"You think I just talk," she told him, "but if you think again you'll notice that I've never told anyone that I work with you, or about the way you wear costumes or who you are or—or anything," she said. "I haven't and you know it."

"He's Max Starling." They all looked up at the back door, taken by surprise.

It was only Tomi Brandt, who leaned against the frame of the open door and grinned down into Max's face to ask, "Surprised to see me, Eyes?"

Ari said, in an unexcited voice, "I think we're all surprised to see you. But why *do* you call him Eyes?"

"Max Starling of the Starling Theater?" Pia asked, and glared at Max.

Tomi answered Ari. "It's what we called him at school. Which he left in April, to go on tour with his parents, or that's what he said. Because of his weird eyes," he explained.

"Your parents are the actors?" Pia demanded. "You went to school with Tomi?"

"What are you doing here?" Max demanded.

"Can he be trusted?" demanded Grammie.

Only Ari was unperturbed. He got up to fetch a fifth chair from the dining room. "Have a seat," he told Tomi, who did. "Be patient," he advised Pia, who nodded. "This is up to Max," he told them all. Then he turned to Max, and smiled in a calm and friendly fashion. "It's up to you, Max. Don't you agree, Mrs. Nives?"

"I guess," Grammie admitted reluctantly. "I do see your point." She looked across the table at Max, and waited.

Max had no idea how to make the choice between denying his secret, for the sake of the rescue of his parents, or telling these people the whole truth, for the sake of finding the solution he couldn't find for himself for *how* to rescue them. It was not an easy choice, but he knew it had to be made and he knew it was his job to make it. He thought. They waited.

Secrecy was the armor his independence wore. However, like any armor, secrecy not only protected but also slowed him down and weighed him down, and if he fell to the ground he'd have trouble getting up, he knew, and if he fell into water he would drown, with the weight of secrecy to take him right to the bottom. But could he be useful to his parents without his secret? And what about the risk to the Solutioneer if even more people knew more about him? Then, what about his independence, would he lose that if he told?

How could he know, unless he tried it? And, he wondered, the questions following one another like the steps in the proof of a Euclidean theorem, was he truly independent if he needed to wear this armor?

Imagining himself without it, stripped of its protection, Max felt uneasy, and small, and in danger—as if he were once again locked in a small room facing a knife-wielding enemy and his parents also in danger half a world away. He felt panic enter his brain. But Max knew from recent experience what he had to do about panic, and how to do it. He stepped back, as far as he could get from his own feelings, to look at the choice only in relation to how it might help him help his parents. Because that was the difficult problem at the center of things, the really important thing, the only important thing. That was the problem that absolutely had to be solved.

Max knew he would have to be in Andesia to solve it, but he also had to admit that he and Grammie could not seem to come up with a workable plan. So on the one hand there was his secret identity, whether as Max Starling, abandoned boy, or as the Solutioneer made no difference, and on the other hand there was the trouble his parents were in and the need to get them out of it.

Really, looked at like that, he had no choice.

So Max told everybody the whole truth about himself, beginning at the invitation from the fake Maharajah of Kashmir and omitting almost nothing. He did keep those buttons a secret, because what use would it serve if everyone, especially Grammie, who was already worried enough, knew about them? Also, he didn't reveal the amount and location of his father's fortune, admitting only that they had the coins to finance any enterprise. He concluded by explaining the purpose of the lists he and Grammie had been quarreling over when Ari interrupted them.

When Max finished his story, there was a short silence as his listeners fitted the unknown pieces of information together with the ones they'd already guessed or been given. "You aren't so old at all," Pia eventually pointed out, sounding resentful, but Tomi was amused. "If I'd come by sooner, I'd have seen your sign."

Ari, who had been listening closely and who had not only lost his own parents in South America but also knew something about suddenly becoming a person other than the one you started out being that day, just pulled the papers over in front of him, to consider what Max and Grammie had already thought of. He had just one question. "Is there anyone else, anyone at all, who knows or suspects?"

"Joachim knows; he's the only one. I take painting lessons with him."

"My mother has one of his pictures," Pia announced, "but it's just some flower."

"Can you trust him?" Ari asked.

Max almost laughed. "Yes, and besides, he doesn't know exactly what's happened to them. He knows that I'm living alone, that's all. He's the one who warned me about what could happen if anyone official found out about me, but, really, you have to understand, Joachim's an artist. He only pays attention to painting. He probably doesn't even remember what he knows."

Ari had decided. "Then let's put our minds to this. But Max has to have the final say. Are we agreed?" He glanced at Grammie and one look at her face made him speak sternly, "You won't agree to that, Mrs. Nives?"

Grammie shook her head vigorously. "No, no, that's not it, I was . . . What it is, is, I never saw you like this before, in a diplomatic mode. I think I'm finally understanding you. You really are the Baron Barthold."

"Not yet," Ari said. "Not without Gabrielle and even then

not for years I hope. But yes, I probably have to be, sooner or later. I can't escape the title. But that's not what matters right now." And he passed the sheets of paper to Tomi and Pia. "See what you think."

It was no surprise that Pia was the first to make a suggestion. "We could be a band of fortune-telling gypsies. Write it down, Max, you should write down everything and you already know I can be a good fortune-teller. Or we could be a theatrical troupe."

Max wrote down both ideas, but he pointed out, "Someone there knows my parents are really actors and that person also knows that I exist. A theatrical troupe would rouse suspicions."

"We *could* say we wanted to open a school, in Apapa," Grammie offered.

"What about a whole family of refugees, not just one person?" Pia asked.

"Why do you keep suggesting things that require a lot of people?" Max asked, although he thought he could guess.

Grammie ignored the interruption. "Ari and I already know how to teach, and Max could offer art and drama classes."

"But I could never pass myself off as a teacher," Tomi objected.

"Athletics," Grammie answered, without hesitation, as if it had already been decided that Tomi would travel with them.

As far as Max knew, nothing had been decided and, besides, wasn't it supposed to be up to him?

Grammie told him, "There's no sense in trying to think freely if you don't include everything."

"A group of philanthropists?" Ari suggested. "A group of wealthy people who want the native people to have better lives. Who build schools and make sure there is clean water. Who encourage them to produce items they can sell outside of their own country, but things they can make in their own homes. They raise llamas, don't they? In the mountains. Or is it alpacas? They produce wool."

"Can anybody here weave?" Pia asked. "Because I can't. I can't even knit."

"There's shearing and carding and spinning and dyeing, too," Grammie added. "We'd have to learn all that and we just don't have the time."

"How about a scientific expedition?" Ari asked, adding, "Maybe mapping the mountains?"

"Cartographers," Grammie named them. "Does anyone know anything about surveying?"

Nobody did, but Max added it to the list, anyway. Grammie was right. Ideas produced ideas, like scattered apple seeds grew apple trees that produced apples that had in their cores more seeds to scatter.

Tomi spoke up. "It sounds to me like we should be a group of mercenaries, come to fight for whoever pays us the most money, because unless we actually go into battle nobody will know what we do or don't know about it." He turned to Grammie. "You could be the camp cook and you"—he turned to Pia—"could be the drummer boy, and I could be the expert in starting fires and putting them out, Ari would be the captain of course, and Max could be an ordinary soldier. Mercenaries don't need much by way of costumes."

They didn't say anything about this, although Max dutifully wrote it down, including every suggested role.

Ari's next idea, like his first two, was of a kind that would benefit a small nation and its citizens. "Could we be a scientific expedition from one of the international societies? To catalog flora and fauna, and also to learn how they farmed and suggest improvements in methods of cultivation. We could study their bridges, and how they build houses, while we take notes about plants and wildlife. Probably, they have things to teach us, as well."

Max waited for Grammie to point out to Ari, as she had so quickly to him, that they would have to spend at least a year studying these various subjects before they could hope to pass themselves off as scientists, but Grammie was just staring at Ari. She didn't say a word.

"I think gypsies is the best idea," Pia announced. "You don't have to know anything special and you can look ragtag, and I can learn tarot cards in about ten minutes, I bet, or at least within—"

Grammie interrupted. She started to speak, slowly, as if the idea was just taking shape in her mind, like egg whites slowly taking shape in the frying pan. "If," she said.

"I was *talk*ing," Pia complained. "I was saying—"

"A diplomatic mission," Grammie went on. "If there was a diplomatic mission from King Teodor to the King of

Andesia . . ." Her speech resumed its normal rate. "Diplomacy is a guaranteed introduction into the court, and, Ari? You'd be the head of it, like an ambassador, and besides a secretary of some kind, your diplomatic party could be as large or small as we wanted. And, Max?" She turned her attention to her grandson, who was about to remind her that they were *his* parents, he should be the ambassador, it was *his* decision. "You don't want the leading role. You want to play a minor part, so you'll be free to wander, to be too unimportant for anyone to pay much attention to, but with a known identity so you're not mysterious and maybe dangerous. You could talk to whoever you want to talk to and nobody would notice if you were young and beardless because . . . because an ambassador's private secretary, like the cabin boy on a ship, is often a young relative, a cousin, a nephew. It would be perfect, if Ari will do it, if Ari asks the King—"

Grammie suddenly stopped speaking. It was the look on Ari's face. "What?" she asked. "What's the matter?"

Ari held his hands up, palms outward, to say, "It's not possible."

Grammie sighed. "It would be a lot to ask, I guess. I can understand that you don't feel you can leave Gabrielle again, especially now. So it looks like our best bet is the rich old lady and her grandson, Max," she said.

"It's not that, Mrs. Nives," Ari said. He brushed his red hair back and leaned toward her, across the table. His handsome face was troubled. "That's not it; it's not that I don't want to help. It's because . . . the royal family shuns the

Barons Barthold. They refuse to have anything to do with the family." He could see in their faces that some explanation was needed. "The past Barons have been not only cruel, and rapacious, and insatiably greedy, they've been lawless, too, when they could get away with it. Sometimes, everybody knew they had committed crimes but they were too powerful to be brought to justice, or too rich, or they bribed judges, or—the Barons Barthold have been famously corrupt. The royal house can't legally take away the title or the lands, because they've never been proved traitors. But Teodor *can* refuse to have anything to do with us, and he does. I don't blame him," Ari concluded.

"Your great-aunt isn't a criminal," Max objected. "She's not cruel, either; she's just . . . She's just not at all nice, is all."

"Her father was vicious, however, and his father before him, and *his* father before *him*," Ari pointed out. "If you think about it from the King's point of view, this is the only way he can make it clear to all the other powerful and well-born people, who like being privileged, that you don't get off scot-free even if you can get away with things."

"But your great-aunt didn't do—"

"Think about it, Max," Ari said. "She hasn't returned the Cellini Spoon, has she? It's been weeks since you found it for her and she knows that it belongs to Teodor, or at least to the Royal Museum. She knows it's stolen goods."

Max was silenced.

"I'm sorry," Ari said, and Max believed him. "If you send me to the King to ask for diplomatic credentials to present to a foreign government? Even if he'd receive me, which he wouldn't, he'd never believe me. The plan would fail before it even began."

"What if my father were to promise the King that you're not like the rest of them?" Pia asked.

Nobody wanted to say it, so it was Grammie who had to. "Your father is a fine man, and remarkably successful, but he's not someone the King would grant an interview to. Except for the Bartholds, nobody else around the lake is . . . significant enough to have a claim to the King's attention, not while he's on his family holiday. He might have to entertain other heads of state while he's here, and he'll be surrounded by his most intimate courtiers, but nobody else gets near him."

Grammie sighed again, and Pia said, "That makes gypsies the best," but Tomi objected, "Soldiers can always find work."

"I know something about science," Grammie told Max, as if they were alone in the room. "We could go as amateur botanists. I'd gather specimens and you'd paint them. If I were a wealthy, eccentric old woman, it might work. Nobody is surprised by anything old women take it into their heads to do," she pointed out.

Max nodded, maybe agreeing with Pia, maybe with Tomi, maybe with Grammie, but it was just something to do to keep people distracted while, inside of his head—as if he were the director of a Starling Theatrical Company production—the drama began. The proud, handsome, redheaded Ambassador, shining in a red jacket and glittering with medals, an elegant, aristocratic man, so important a personage that he traveled not only with a personal secretary and a bodyguard, but also his own cook/housekeeper to arrange his every comfort. Such a man would command attention whenever he came on the scene. All eyes would be on him, wondering if he was to be feared, to be flattered, to be trusted, wondering what his secret mission might be, mistrusting the interest a king in a distant country might have in their small nation. While this Ambassador was strutting about in the spotlight at the center of the stage, being charming and ominous, his secretary would be in the shadows, unnoticed. Grammie was absolutely right about that. The secretary could go anywhere, could be doing anything, talking to anyone. This unimportant person would have a freedom the major players in larger roles could not hope for. This insignificant person might actually be able to do something.

But the Ambassador had to be genuine. He couldn't be a costume, a pretense, an act. He needed the King's seal on his papers, the letters of introduction, the state credentials. And if Ari couldn't ask for these . . .

What about Max? Why couldn't Max explain everything to King Teodor, or even, maybe, could he manufacture some urgent reason for the King to send a diplomatic mission to Andesia? But how would Max find his way into the King's presence?

Well, wasn't he the Solutioneer?

"Max?" Grammie asked. "Why aren't you saying anything? Don't you agree?"

"Maybe," Max said. "Maybe I do, if I have to. But before that, there's something I want to try . . ."

"What?" asked Pia. "What do you want me to do? I can help, can't I?"

"We don't have much time," Grammie warned him. "It'll take weeks to get there, remember, and we don't know just what's going on, what that Balcor has planned. We don't have any time at all."

"I know," Max said, and he did. But this sense of urgency, the need to hurry, to be doing something it didn't matter what, didn't make for good planning. He hoped to keep urgency in its place, which was in the background, causing as little disturbance as possible. "I know."

Grammie sighed a third time, in frustration. Then she looked at him more carefully. After all, she was the person here who knew him longest and best. She could tell when he was hatching some plan. "All right," she agreed reluctantly. "I'll wait."

"How can you give up so easily?" demanded Pia. "And I *know* gypsies make a better disguise than eccentric old ladies."

Max defended his grandmother. "How can *you* be so stubborn?" he asked Pia, before explaining to her, "I'm thinking." He explained it to Tomi and Ari, too, because none of them knew him as well as Grammie did. "I'm solutioneering. That's my job and I'm good at it." He rose from the table and announced, "I'm going to paint."

"Now?" they objected.

"And think," he said. He had to think of something, and

fast. He didn't want to still be in Queensbridge when the next gold button arrived. "Alone," he told them, because that was the way he worked best, at the start of a job. "Can we talk about this later? In a day or so?" he asked. He *was* sure that the worst way to try to rescue his parents would be to do it on his own, and he knew he could trust these people, sitting around his kitchen table and looking up at him.

They all watched him, waiting. Grammie had been with Mister Max all along, Pia had glommed on to him almost as soon as he'd laid eyes on her, Ari had recently become an active ally, and Tomi had been on his tail for weeks: Max accepted that he was no longer acting alone. Together, he thought, they might just be able to do it. Together, they'd already shown they could make the plan and execute it, write the play and perform it.

But first Max had to think. "Let's meet up again tomorrow afternoon," he said.

"Where are you going?" Pia protested.

"To get my beret," Max said. "And my paints," he added, grinning at their various expressions. "And easel," he laughed. With or without his secrets, he was still the Solutioneer.

And the Solutioneer had a problem to solve. Two problems, really, because there were two kings. And he would need the assistance of one—King Teodor, due to arrive shortly in Queensbridge—to have any hope of saving the other—King William, and his dear Queen, impatiently awaiting rescue in Andesia.

Join Mister Max on his next adventure in solutioneering!

Turn the page for a sneak peek.

9

The Arrival

Max had been at sea for three weeks when he could finally put his feet down on the soil of South America.

He might be standing on dry land, but it seemed to Max that the ground under his feet was still rocking. He walked uneasily along the dock to the customs shed, where Ari and Mr. Bendiff were presenting credentials and answering questions about the members of their traveling party. Max's attention was turned inland, eyes looking toward Caracas, although he couldn't possibly see it for the low hills and thick woods. That didn't matter. He knew that Grammie, who stood quietly beside him, was also picturing the map they'd spent so much time looking at, a nearly heart-shaped mass of land that tapered down to a narrow point, and the long spine of mountains running from the north to the south of it, on which a tiny worm of a country perched. In that country, huddled together for warmth and comfort, two minuscule figures, half the size of ants, were waiting. He tried not to urge them all to hurry, hurry, get into the coach waiting to take them into Caracas, stop wasting time.

On arrival in Caracas, the party went first to the Hotel Magnifica. They planned to take two days to arrange passage to Andesia and ready themselves for a long journey under harsh conditions, to write letters home and walk down city streets, looking in shop windows, eavesdropping on conversations, stopping to eat local foods.

Those plans changed immediately.

Max, in his role as Alexander Ireton, heard the news first, because he happened to be in the writing room setting out stationery and pens for Ari while the doorman gossiped outside a window opened to let in the morning air. Max heard it and his hands stopped moving and he fell out of character entirely, concentrating on the Spanish words. It was the name of Andesia that caught his ear and not many words later—struggling to understand—he heard *los reyes,* which he thought meant "the king and queen." He heard more words but couldn't string them together: *tiro*, "shot"; *cocinera* "cook"; *anarquista*, which he guessed had to mean "anarchist," one of those people who opposed any sort of government at all, any order imposed on society.

Max stumbled back into character and into the reception area, where the rest of the party was waiting for the desk clerk to give them their room keys. It was Alexander Ireton who came quietly up to his employer to say, "I think something has happened, sir. In Andesia. I overheard a conversation which I only partly understood. . . ." But he couldn't go on and he glanced desperately at his grandmother.

"Oh, M—" she started to say before his quick head shake stopped her.

"M-my goodness." Mr. Bendiff took charge. He sent Colly to find a newspaper. "In our own language, for preference." But Colly could bring them only a Spanish edition, which Grammie translated, in the privacy of the suite Ari had been given.

As soon as the door closed behind them, Max asked, "Did the palace cook shoot them?"

"Give me a chance to find the article," she snapped. When she had, on the back page where news from such an unimportant place is reported, her translation was not smooth, or complete—"a word I don't know," she often interrupted herself to say—but the bare facts were clear. There had been an explosion in the palace kitchen in Apapa; a serving woman had been killed and the cook wounded. The article reported that a large confection had appeared in the kitchen that morning, set out on a silver tray. Nobody knew where it came from, but it was obviously intended for the royal table. A bomb had been hidden within the many layers of a cake that had been frosted with chocolate and decorated around the edges with wildflowers. The cook had no reason to question its presence, or so she said. The great houses often sent gifts of food to the King and Queen. This cake was larger and more elaborate than most, the cook allowed, but why should that make her suspicious?

"They must have mistimed the explosion," Mr. Bendiff said.

"Who are *they*?" Max asked miserably.

"There's something else here," Grammie said.

At the end of the article, the writer mentioned an incident that took place a few months earlier, a shot that had been fired as the newly crowned royal couple was coming out of the cathedral. "That's the photograph we saw," Grammie reminded Max, who didn't need reminding. He went to the window and looked down onto a busy street, where ordinary carriages filled with ordinary people wandered up and down, and women carried parasols against the strong sun.

"The police blamed anarchists for the shot. They never caught anybody. And the newspaper says this explosion in the kitchen happened almost two weeks ago. The reporter got the story from one of the soldiers in the occupying army. One of Balcor's soldiers," Grammie concluded.

"Is this Balcor one of those military strongmen?" Mr. Bendiff asked.

"Was Balcor behind the bomb?" Colly wondered.

"We don't know anything, do we?" Grammie observed.

It was Tomi who said what they were all thinking. "We'd better get there as fast as we can."

They spent two days and one long, wet night on the open deck of the packet that took them along the coast and up into Lake Maracaibo, where the houses stood on stilts, out in the water. Then followed two long days and longer nights jouncing in a coach from Maracaibo to Cúcuta. After a night in a rough country inn, where the entire party slept on cots set out in one room, they joined the wagon train on its regular biweekly run between Cúcuta and Apapa. There followed four days of walking a well-traveled wagon track from damp dawns until gray evenings with only a brief midday rest, moving at the pace of mules on rough ascending roadways. After the first morning, Ari insisted that Grammie ride on the tailgate of the wagon that was carrying their luggage.

A squadron of soldiers accompanied the wagons, at the front and rear, but the wagon train boss was a loud, stocky Andesian named Stefano, who spent much of the journey cursing at the muleteers and porters when anything went wrong. They all wore loose trousers, rough shirts, and heavy boots, but the soldiers carried rifles on their backs, and their chests were crossed with bands of ammunition, while the Andesians, even Stefano, wore woven ponchos against the rain and wide-brimmed chupallas against the sun.

The soldiers didn't mix with the Andesians or the strangers, the Andesians didn't mix with the soldiers or the strangers, and so the rescue party learned little during the long trek—except more than they cared to know about the insect and animal life of the landscapes through which they moved, the lowland tropical forests and the barren uplands. They all slept with their boots on.

They had not understood how close they were to their

destination, and nobody had warned them that this was the day of arrival, so when the wagon train rounded a long curve of ridge and the valley opened out before them as suddenly as if they were emerging from a long tunnel, every member of the rescue party inhaled sharply, but whether for the unexpectedness of the scene or its beauty, none of them could have said. The valley that lay before them was surrounded by jagged mountains, their crests still white with snow. The lower slopes of the mountains were bright with white and yellow flowers, and occasional one-room earth-colored houses were scattered on the foothills, where movement could be seen, some of it human, some animal. The strong midday sun washed over the whole narrow valley, at the heart of which a small city had grown up on both sides of a fast-flowing mountain river.

Max stared down at the city where his parents had been held for almost five months. His heart beat fast and he did not dare look at his grandmother.

On the side of the river beneath the three peaks, the small houses crowded around an open space so perfectly square it had to be a piazza. There was one long, low, brown-roofed building among the houses, and he couldn't see any real streets, just twisting alleys. A single bridge crossed the river. On that western shore, the buildings were fewer and larger, three with gardens behind high walls, one a big stone building with a short square tower at its side, and, built at a distance from the others, a long, whitewashed one-story building with next to it a wide dirt rectangle, the edges as clear as if it had been cut out of the grass with a sword's blade.

"Do you think the one with the tower is the royal palace?" Max asked Ari.

"Where's your hat, Alexander?" Ari answered, reminding Max of the role he was supposed to be playing. "This occasion requires hats."

Max dusted off the detested bowler and decided, "The white building is probably the barracks. How many soldiers are stationed in Andesia?" he asked.

Ari settled a plumed tricorn on his red hair and answered, "We'll find out. Enough to protect us, I'm sure."

Not too many to fight our way out through, Max hoped.

Going slowly, the wagon train followed the road down steep hillsides scattered with low adobe buildings, some set among terraces that were plowed and ready for planting, others standing solitary in grassy pastures where wildflowers grew thick. They passed herds of woolly-coated animals that grazed close to some of those houses, but they saw no one. No one came out even as far as a doorway to greet their caravan, soldiers marching smartly at its front and rear, or even to stare curiously at the foreigners.

From closer up, three mangy blotches on the mountainsides could be identified. "Must be the mines," Mr. Bendiff said. "See those railroad tracks leading into the mountain?"

Ari pointed out three narrow dirt roads winding down to meet theirs not far ahead. "They must bring the ore down in carts, to be stored." When he looked, Max could identify a low building surrounded by soldiers at the point where the three tracks intersected with the roadway.

In fact, the caravan stopped there, leaving off two of the wagons, their empty beds covered tightly by tarpaulins, and all of the soldiers, who took with them a small locked chest. Stefano's own two covered wagons were the only ones to make the final slow descent, through darkening air, into the city.

Night fell fast and hard in this high valley. By the time Stefano's goods had been unloaded and their suitcases piled into a handcart, his single lantern was the only light to guide the party along winding dirt alleys lined with small adobe houses to a stone bridge, its railings no higher than a man's knees. The only sounds were their footsteps and the creak of cart wheels and the rush of water. The entire city lay in dark silence.

The embassy was too busy being sure of their footing to find anything to say to one another, during these final steps of the journey, and too tired, and especially too eager to, at last, arrive. When they came up to it, they sensed rather than saw the dense shape. Behind them, the three jagged peaks blocked most of the star-studded sky.

Stefano dropped the luggage and walked off, without a word of farewell, pushing the cart ahead of him. As his footsteps faded away, the party banded closer together, facing a mass that seemed to loom in front of them, and above them. Nobody had anything to say. The surrounding silence grew deeper as the darkness thickened.

Then a door was thrown open and a tall, silhouetted figure stood in the blinding burst of light.

Nobody moved. Nobody spoke.

The light from the doorway also revealed two armed soldiers stationed in the shadows at each side of the entry. The silhouette called, "Come! Come forward! Envoy of the King, Teodor, welcome!"

They looked quickly at one another, like actors about to step onto the stage and begin the play, and Ari moved into the light, resplendent in a red military jacket, a short row of medals at his breast, gold epaulets on his shoulders, gold trim at the sleeves and hem of the jacket itself as well as gold stripes down the sides of his black trousers. He carried his plumed hat under his arm. A sword hung at his side, and he did not smile or extend his hand. Instead, he clicked the heels of his shining boots smartly together. "Andrew Robert Von Bauer Cozart, heir of the Barons Barthold," he announced stiffly, and bowed. "To whom do I present myself?"

The man was taller than Ari and attired with equal formality in a black suit that fitted him close around the chest, with silver buttons down the front of the short jacket and silver trim at the military collar, the sleeves, and the flared hem of his trousers. His sword's scabbard gleamed silver. He was a long-nosed man, with no spare flesh on him and a restless cleverness on his face. "I am Juan Carlos Carrera y Carrera," he announced. His dark hair shone and his thick, dark mustache glistened. "I am your welcome here, into the royal guesthouse. You must enter. It will be warm, there is food." He stood back and swept an arm, to usher Ari in.

Max had a sudden melodramatic impulse to shout at Ari *Don't do it!*

Ari stepped into the house, but stopped just inside the entry to wave Mr. Bendiff forward and introduce him as "a man adept in the field of business, whom King Teodor has named to this embassy."

Mr. Bendiff, his homburg in his left hand and a wide smile on his face, reached out his right hand to shake the Andesian's. "Señor, it is a pleasure."

"Señor," echoed Juan Carlos Carrera y Carrera with a smile and a bow. "Delighted, welcome, enter, enter."

Oily. Max could almost hear his father's voice pronouncing the words *An oily feller, that'un.*

"My secretary," Ari announced.

A properly-suited Alexander Ireton received a brief nod of the head and a slight gesture of the hand from the Andesian as he stepped eagerly into the light, to see . . .

He didn't *expect* to see his parents waiting. Not really. He did know better. But still, he looked all around, down to the staircase at the back of the entryway and into the two rooms he could see, both lit by oil lamps and chandeliers, and both empty of people. One was a long sitting room, furnished with a sofa and chairs, desk and bookcase, where nobody waited. The other seemed to be a small dining room, where a round table offered loaves of bread and thick wedges of cheese, as well as a roast of some kind, ready to be sliced. Tall silver goblets and long-necked silver ewers were also set out, and no royal couple stood at the table, ready to laugh at the surprised look on their son's face.

CYNTHIA VOIGT is the author of many books for young readers. Accolades for her work include a Newbery Medal for *Dicey's Song* (Book 2 in the Tillerman cycle), a Newbery Honor for *A Solitary Blue* (Book 3 in the Tillerman cycle), and the Margaret A. Edwards Award for Outstanding Literature for Young Adults. She is also the author of *Homecoming* (Book 1 in the Tillerman cycle), the Kingdom series, the Bad Girls series, and *Young Fredle*, among others.

You can visit her at cynthiavoigt.com.